PUSHKIN
VERTIGO
ORIGINALS

PRAISE FOR
THE STOCKHOLM TRILOGY

'A dark, atmospheric, powerful thriller, the best debut novel I've
read in years'
Lynda La Plante

'Atmospheric Scandi retro, but Chandleresque to its core'
The Sunday Times Crime Club

'Punches you in the face like one of Kvist's knockout blows'
Crime Scene

'A real tour de force… a fascinating race through 1930s Stockholm'
Kate Rhodes, author of *Crossbones Yard*

'A fabulously classy twist on pulp fiction'   *Elle Thinks*

'A tough thriller that packs a punch'   *Daily Star on Sunday*

'Blending noir with gritty violence, *Clinch* is a visceral, compulsive
thriller'   *Col's Criminal Library*

'This is noir writing at its best'   *The Bookbinder's Daughter*

'As original as it is remarkable'   *Borås Tidning*

'Scandinavian Crime meets Film Noir, the crime novel of the year'
Alexander Bard

Born in 1974, Martin Holmén studied history at university, and now teaches at a Stockholm secondary school. *Down for the Count* is the second instalment in *The Stockholm Trilogy*, which began with *Clinch*. *Slugger* will also be published by Pushkin Vertigo.

MARTIN HOLMÉN

DOWN FOR THE COUNT

A HARRY KVIST THRILLER
THE STOCKHOLM TRILOGY

PUSHKIN VERTIGO

BAINTE DEN STOC

WITHDRAWN FROM DÚN LAOGHAIRE RATHDOWN
COUNTY LIBRARY STOCK

Pushkin Vertigo
71-75 Shelton Street
London, WC2H 9JQ

Original text © Martin Holmén 2016
Translation © Henning Koch 2017

First published as *Nere för räkning* by
Albert Bonniers Förlag, Stockholm, Sweden

Published in the English language by arrangement
with Bonnier Rights, Stockholm, Sweden

First published by Pushkin Vertigo in 2017

1 3 5 7 9 8 6 4 2

ISBN 978 1 782272 18 2

All rights reserved. No part of this publication may be reproduced,
stored in a retrieval system or transmitted in any form or by
any means electronic, mechanical, photocopying, recording or
otherwise, without prior permission in writing from Pushkin Press

Text designed and typeset by Tetragon, London
Printed and bound by CPI Group (UK) Ltd, Croydon CRO 4YY

www.pushkinpress.com

For Sandra

WEDNESDAY 20 NOVEMBER

Our time is up.

A sound of knocking vibrates between the graffiti-covered stone walls. The cowslip-blond youth, resting his head on my hairy chest, flinches. Every fibre of his body's musculature tenses up. His nails dig into my ribs.

We're lying naked on the fold-down metal bed on the longer side of the cell. I push my head forward, hushing him, my boxer's nose buried deep in his tangled locks. He smells of sweat, sex and ingrained dirt.

'We still have a few minutes.'

His cloying, salty taste sticks to the roof of my mouth. I clear my throat, then caress his hair and kiss his neck. It's blotched with scratched flea bites. I lie back again. The wood shavings in the pillow crunch as I turn my head.

On the floor beside the bunk is a pile of three books. At the bottom the New Testament, in the middle the Psalms and at the top a thin pamphlet entitled *In My Lone Hour*. A wall-louse laboriously clambers up the book spines. In the holding cell next to ours, a fellow prisoner slowly whistles 'Death of a Drinking Girl', although it's forbidden.

'Doughboy.'

He hardens against my thigh as I squeeze him in my arms, even though we've only just finished.

'I hope you haven't played a trick on me now. For some it's one thing while you're in here and something else on the outside.'

Doughboy shakes his head and makes a little sob. Again, I press my nose into his hair. Oh, that boy! That fragrance of his is so honest.

There's more thumping on the door. Harder, this time. It's Wednesday, the twentieth of November 1935, a year and a half to the day since I entered through the heavy front gates.

I shift Doughboy's head and climb out of the sheets. He sits on the edge of the bed, covering his groin with his hands and hanging his head: a wilting cowslip on a wiry stem. Two violet bruises shine on his prison-pale body. Around his nipples, a few blond hairs spread outward like rays of light.

I pull up the rough grey trousers, the shirt and the vest with the blue and grey stripes. Doughboy shrugs his bony shoulders: 'We'll see each other again in a week. Time will go by quickly. Even quicker for you on the outside.'

'You remember what I've told you?'

'I should come directly to you on Roslagsgatan. Over a funeral parlour.'

'Do you remember the house number?'

'Forty-three.'

I nod. Beard stubble rasps under my fist as I rub my chin.

'The screws will want you for the Home Guard but don't listen to that. Come straight to me. I have gas and wood stoves, an ice cupboard too. Lundin, the bloke I'm renting it off, is not niggardly about turning up the heating, and anyone in the house will tell you that. It's not big, but at least it's bigger than this cell and it'll do for the both of us.'

'You've said that a thousand times.'

I do up the wooden buttons of my uniform jacket. Doughboy looks up as the lock rattles and the door opens. Jönsson stands there; he's an evil-eyed day-shift screw with a black full-length

8

beard divided into two forks, hanging over his chest. He's not tall but his girth almost fills the doorway from side to side. The emblem on his uniform cap glitters in the frail morning light.

'Damn it, Kvist! Never before have I had to yank someone out of their cell when they're being released.'

'I paid for a full half-hour.'

'You've overshot that bastard half-hour by a mile. Move it! The director's waiting.'

I fumble with my clothes. Kneeling while putting on my prison-issue shoes, I rest my fist on the bed.

Doughboy quickly runs his hands over the scars on the back of my hand. My gaze runs into his eyes of pale blue. The same colour as my own.

'If you're released at the same time as others, don't throw your lot in with them, they're only after your money. Just make sure you come home to me in Sibirien, and I'll make sure you're well taken care of. You remember the house number now?'

'Forty-three.'

'Maybe I'd better meet you here instead.'

'No need. I'll find it.'

'No, it's probably better. Let's leave it like that. I'll wait for you outside the gates at lunchtime in seven days' time. Twelve o'clock. I'll bring the suit.'

'I can manage without it.'

I stand up. Doughboy stares intensely at the wall behind me, as if he's found something new and interesting among the usual graffiti. The screw takes a few steps into the cell and grasps my arm. I twist out of his grip, then nod at him. He turns around and walks out onto the top gallery.

'A promise is a promise and I've promised you a suit, have I not? In exactly a week. Twelve o'clock outside the gates. Time will pass quickly, you'll see.'

I run my hand through Doughboy's mop of hair, and a second later I'm following Jönsson through the door, away from my love and out onto the suicide gallery. A wave of giddiness hits me; I put my right hand on the railing. It's about six, or eight, metres down to the hard concrete floor. Despite all the hours spent up in the rigging during my years at sea, I have never got used to heights, even after all the woodpeckers' eggs I had as a child. If it hadn't been for them I'm not sure what would have become of me; probably I wouldn't even be able to stand on a chair.

The yellow door slams between me and Doughboy, and Jönsson rattles his keys. There's a clicking sound as the bolt shoots into the lock.

We start moving along the row of cell doors, with me leading the way. Behind each and every one of them sits a scrap of humanity, steeped in loneliness, too weak or proud to fit into the machinery of society.

At every step the screw thumps his baton against his thigh. The keys rattle on his ring. A weary November sunlight only just penetrates the large skylight above us. It's spitting rain.

'Grey inside, and grey outside too,' I mutter.

Our steps echo desolately on the spiral stairs leading down to ground level. There's a smell of root mash, tarred rope and leather. Jönsson's big belly is rumbling. I hurry my steps and we walk into the large round central hall, all while the taste of the youth slowly withers in my gob.

'Bloody lucky you were banged up, Kvist, otherwise you'd probably have been accused of murder about a month ago.'

The screw laughs. I don't understand what he's driving at. I shuffle on.

We emerge into the light rain and walk down the imposing manorial steps, skirting the prison buildings, built from stone the dirty yellow of a lion's mane, past the old wool-making house, the kitchens and the sickbay, towards the main guard post. I put my hands in my trouser pockets and start whistling an old Ernst Rolf tune.

The air is loaded with a scent of hops. In the distance I hear the sounds of the city, more intense than usual, like a demonstration at Gärdet on Workers' Day, the first of May, or outside a football ground on the evening of a match.

A rush of wind drives the raindrops under the brim of my cap, and I look down. The wet gravel mutes the sound of our steps. Jönsson overtakes me; his broad arse seems about to burst out of his uniform trousers. He's breathing heavily.

A guard in the inside courtyard follows us with his eyes. He purses his mouth when I give him a sunny smile, and turns his back on us. Since our little altercation last winter he rarely smiles back. He still has a few teeth missing at the front. It cost me a week in dark solitary. For a moment I toy with a thought: if I give the fatty in front of me a workout, it might put back my release by a week, and then I'll get out at the same time as Doughboy.

We press on through another gate and reach the outermost area, where the screws are armed with revolvers and rifles. The heavy reception door creaks when Jönsson opens it. I lift my cap and smooth down my hair before I put it back on. The swine have left it to grow for three months, without the regulatory cut. It will take another year at least to tame it and get my usual hairstyle back. Damned way to treat a grown man!

11

I follow Jönsson into the reception to meet the director, a middle-aged bloke with a handlebar moustache. He's wearing a uniform. As we walk in, he's waiting next to his desk with his hands clasped across his back. He gestures at his helmet.

On the dark-panelled walls hang rows of portraits of his predecessors, also the rules and by-laws that have held sway over my life between half past five in the morning and ten at night for the last year and a half. My clothes and personal effects have been placed on a bench. The director sits at his desk and clears his throat.

'Prisoner 420, Harry Kvist, I presume?'

His voice is hoarse, as if after a night of schnapps-drinking and singing. The floorboards creak as Jönsson shifts his weight to the other leg.

'Yes, that's him all right.'

The director's tongue emerges at the left corner of his mouth. He continues leafing through the papers in front of him on the desk.

'Do you not have the common sense to take off your cap when you're talking to me?'

'Not today.'

The director recoils and continues looking through the papers.

'This is Kvist's third internment. For intimidation, this time. And a serious assault involving an alcoholic-beverages delivery man and his son.'

'Just get the papers in order.'

The director looks up, I see his eyes grow intense: 'What can you mean?'

'Just that I've heard the lecture before.'

The director leans back in his chair, the armrests made of cherry wood or mahogany, and puts his hands together on his belly. He looks amused now. Again his tongue flicks over his lips.

'Six times in this term we had to put you in solitary and dark confinement; on a couple of occasions there was even talk of having you transferred to an institution for the mentally ill.'

'As I said, get on with it!'

'Kvist, you should show some humility.'

'You can't throw me in the cellars now, or threaten me with more beatings, so just bloody well get this over with and let me get out of here!'

The gruff, schnapps-tinged voice of the director is silenced. Behind me, Jönsson coughs gently. There's a gleam in the director's eye.

'Well, at least you've behaved yourself these last six months. As I understand it, this may be ascribed in some way to a certain Gusten Lindwall, serving a six-month sentence for bread-thieving?'

I shut my mouth. The director rises and walks round the desk. He hands the screw a fountain pen and a form.

'Jönsson will have to conclude this. I need time to get changed for the inauguration.'

'Yes, sir!'

Jönsson takes over. The director picks up a blue envelope from his desk and gives it to me.

'Just short of a hundred kronor, that's what you've earned. I suppose we'll be seeing each other soon, I just hope it won't be too soon. A queer like you, Kvist, has a detrimental influence on the other prisoners.'

Involuntarily, I clench my fists. A vein in my forehead starts to throb.

'For a year and a half I've slaved for your profit, that much is true.'

The director smiles brightly and gives Jönsson a nod before he leaves the warders' office through an adjoining door.

'Right then,' says Jönsson, walking up to the table with his form. 'You can get undressed.'

I do as I'm told while the screw goes through my clothes and belongings, ticking them off on the form and loudly pronouncing: 'Outdoor clothes: a black three-piece suit in light wool, labelled Herzog, a white shirt, a grey necktie with silver stripes, braces, singlet and elasticated underpants. A pair of shoes labelled J.J. Brandt of size 41, also a black hat with a narrow brim, labelled Paul U. Bergström, size 57. It's all there.'

'It seems so, yes.'

'That wasn't a question. Other loose items: under the hatband, a razor blade. A notebook and address book, an aniline pen. A Viking pocket watch with a gold chain, two cigars of the brand Meteor in a cigar case of wine-red leather embossed with the name of L. Steiner, a penknife, a comb, a bunch of keys, a box of matches, and a wallet containing six kronor and seventy öre, various receipts, and a photograph of a young girl. Sign here at the bottom of the page.'

I would be stark naked were it not for the prison-issue underpants. My skin is covered in goosebumps. Jönsson's face is heavily flushed after all his reading. He catches his breath. I take the pen he holds out, and draw my scrawl at the bottom of the form.

I put on my own clothes while Jönsson watches. The trousers have become a few sizes too large, but anything is more elegant than the prison uniform. I fish out one of the dry Meteors from the cigar case and drill a hole in the end with the nib of the fountain pen. I may be as poor as a church mouse, but at least I have a cigar case that used to belong to a millionaire. My belongings drop into my pockets with a rattling sound.

'If you hurry up you'll make it in time for the inauguration.'

I look up. 'What inauguration?'

'West Bridge. The official opening's today.'

I grunt. I'd thought it was getting close. For one and a half years I had seen them toiling on it a stone's throw from my day-cell window. Morning to evening I had listened to the monotonous singing of the pole cranes, the spattering of the rivet-punchers and the faint rattling of the cement mixers. In the autumn evenings I had caught sight of the spark-fleas of the welders above the thick granite walls of the prison. Now she spans Riddarfjärden, hundreds of metres of her. In two mighty leaps she joins the two poorest parts of the city.

I pick up my hat from the table. To hell with humility: 'Kvisten doesn't take off his hat for anyone.'

'What was that? Stop mumbling, man!'

'Nothing.'

I push the hat down on my head. Jönsson gestures at the adjoining door, and I press down the handle and step outside into freedom – which greets me with a gust of ice-cold easterly wind that claws at my eyeballs.

A little girl aged about five squats a few metres from the door, wiping her fingers in the wet grass along the side of the ditch. She stands up when she sees me coming out.

I turn up my collar and strike a match. The first draw on the cigar smoke makes my body tremble with well-being. I flick the match into the nearest puddle.

The girl is wearing an eighties-style cardigan with puffed-up arms and a beret. Across her forehead are a pair of black lines, as if she's wiped herself with soiled fingers. In one hand she holds a rag doll with a missing eye. She breaks off a couple of sprigs from a bush, still with foliage on them. I insert the cigar into my mouth, button up my jacket and fold up my collar. When I went inside it was early summer. Not now.

15

The girl takes a few steps towards me. She has folded her woollen socks over the tops of her boots. As she peers curiously at me, I have a sudden notion that the child looks like my own daughter, Ida, even though she must be more than fifteen years old by now.

'Are you here to meet the King?'

'He's not here to meet me, that's for bloody sure.'

'You swore.'

'I did.'

I exhale a heavy lead-grey cloud of smoke and look up at the sky. The light rain is mixed with the odd puzzled streak of sleet. The tobacco smoke whirls through my brain. I squat down, one hand on the ground, drawing air into my lungs. The girl is next to me in two seconds flat.

'Are you all right?'

There's a sharp pain in my chest: 'I feel fine. Better than in a very long time.'

'Have you been in prison?'

I nod.

'But I was released today.'

'Why were you in the prison?'

'Someone wanted to hurt me.'

'There were no flowers.'

'Beg your pardon?'

I stand up, put the cigar back into my mouth, scrape at a couple of flea bites on my chest.

'For the King. I picked some leaves.'

I smile. There's a snapping sound as I pull back the elasticated band of my wallet.

With one eye half-closed I peer into the coin compartment, find a five-öre piece and flick it over with my thumb and finger. It bounces against her chest and lands in front of her feet. She picks it up and curtsies, before she suddenly charges off as if someone had set fire to her bloomers.

I drop my wallet into my inside pocket and shove my fists into my trouser pockets. The taste of the youth has blended now with the dry smoke of the cigar, reduced to a hardly noticeable saltiness. I speed up in the same direction as the girl, leaving Långholmen's correctional institution behind me. As I jog across the Bridge of Sighs, my footsteps thud hollowly as if I'm jumping around a boxing ring just before a bout.

On the rocky outcrops of Långholmen, a great jumble of Söder residents are crowding together on that harsh November day. They are wearing black overcoats and raincoats. From up here you can see the entire length of the new-built bridge, stretching across the water. A small white-keeled steamboat, puffing along, passes under one of the two mighty spans and sounds its whistle.

The bridge is black with people and umbrellas. In one of the middle lanes there's a stationary tram carriage. I pull my jacket tighter around myself and put my hands into my armpits.

'How damned cold can it get?' I mutter to myself and gob on the rock, trying out a couple of half-hearted uppercuts just to work up a bit of body warmth.

A sturdy, red-nosed old lady in a shawl keeps snuffling next to me. On the other side of the water, coal smoke has swathed Kungsholmen in a haze. It has the same yellowish colour as milk gone sour. Above the little wind-tormented wooden hovels on Kungsklippan, the tall chimney of the Separator, the turrets of City Hall and the church spires, the sky is suspended like a wet woollen blanket hung up to dry. The cargo boats, loaded with firewood, lie moored close together along the wooden jetties.

A sudden gust of wind makes the black-dressed crowd from Söder huddle together like a group of penguins. A stoker with his hat worn at a jaunty angle, a pound of contraband in his hand, swears loudly about the fine gentlefolk down there on the bridge.

'My brother actually helped build the bloody thing,' he splutters, throwing out his arm.

'Hot sausages, come and get your hot sausages!' yells a hot dog man with a box hanging on his stomach.

The people talk in dinning voices, as people tend to do when they have no secrets to guard. I close my eyes for a moment. It takes you a minute to reset your frequencies after eighteen months inside.

Behind us, the bells of Högalid Church strike a half-peal. The old woman blows her nose between her thumb and her finger, flicking the snot off her hand. I set my pocket watch and wind it.

'Eye-glasses for sale, cheap eye-glasses!'

The gruff voice sounds familiar. I push back my hat with my finger and let my eyes wander over the crowd on the crest of the rocky slope. Almost at once I see a face that I recognise: old man Ström from my home haunts in Sibirien.

The junk dealer from Roslagsgatan is a hefty bloke, a head taller than most others around him. His eyes are close-set, and he has a bushy blond beard shot through with long grey hairs, covered in a sprinkling of raindrops. He's wearing work trousers of a heavy fabric, with a thick moss-green waistcoat under his jacket. Telescopes stick out of his jacket pockets like baguettes, and around his neck he has three binoculars. I make a gesture towards the brim of my hat.

Ström's face lights up when he sees me.

'Kvisten,' says Ström, shaking my hand. 'It's been a while. Where's your coat?'

'Left it at home.'

'When were you released?'

Ström ejects a substantial load of tobacco juice over the rocks, and sniffs.

'Just now.'

A murmur runs through the crowd when a cortège of black cars approaches the bridge from the Kungsholmen side.

'Here come the bigwigs. We'll have a drink on Roslagsgatan later, shall we? They're having a November knees-up tonight in number 41. Borrow an eye-glass for a minute.'

Ström hands me a small brass tube, we exchange nods and then he pushes his way into the press of people.

I extend the telescope to its full length and hold it up to my eye. In the middle of the span, a choir of schoolboys starts wailing, led by a wildly gesturing conductor. Maybe he's trying to keep warm? He's wearing coat-tails, after all. The wind tosses fragments of the 'King's Song' to those of us who are standing on the rock.

Yet more murmuring erupts when the cortège of cars stops by a royal rain shelter made of a deep-blue fabric with three crowns. The car doors open. People charge forward with umbrellas.

First comes Prince Carl, closely followed by Princess Sibylla in a grey fur coat. A gasp runs through the spectators when she momentarily loses her balance and has to support herself on the Prince's arm. She quickly recovers her poise and waves off a fat bloke who was rushing to help her.

'There he comes, the beanpole!' the snuffling woman yells in a high-pitched voice. King Gustaf V gets out of a black Cadillac. He's tall and thin, and the man holding his umbrella has to stretch as high as he can to clear his regal top hat.

I've never seen him before, and yet through the telescope he's suddenly right up close. I can make out the small, silly white moustache, the deep furrows around his mouth and the gleam of his oval spectacles. He's wearing an overcoat with a substantial fur collar and a pair of heavy-duty galoshes.

A light fog rising from the water starts enveloping the festivities in a grey wash. I take the tube away from my eye for a moment to scratch the flea bites on my throat.

The festively dressed men on the bridge remove their top hats and bow as the King takes to his royal seat under the rain cover. The boys finish their song and are rewarded with applause.

A formally attired corpulent bloke goes up to the microphone set up on the little podium, and gives it a tap. He holds his cylindrical hat under his arm. A young conscript in a light-blue uniform and long white leather gloves puts his full lips to a trumpet's mouthpiece. His chest heaves and there's a danger his uniform will split when he gives it all for King and country.

'That's it, my lad, keep your back straight.'

I lick my lips. The fat man at the microphone starts talking once the fanfare has stopped, but it's impossible to hear a thing from down here on the rocks.

The King points at the speaker and says something, causing everyone on the dais to smile from ear to ear. The King also bares his teeth in a broad smile. Someone walks up to the fat man and presses his hat onto his head. He turns around and throws out his arms. I'll be damned if I know what's going on. For a few seconds there is confusion on the podium. Four blokes in black poplin overcoats, flanking the guests of honour, step forward briskly and encircle the King, like tithe cottages around a manor house. I study two of them through the telescope. The bloke on the left is a wiry, sinuous man with a hooked nose, and thin, bloodless lips. The bloke next to him is older: a tall, broad type with a white bushy moustache. He has a flat boxer's nose and a pale thick scar running through one of his eyebrows.

'Some villains have to break stone in Långholmen's quarry, others guard royalty. That's how the world works.'

I retract the telescope with a snapping sound and put it in my jacket pocket. I get out my remaining cigar and shield the frail flame of the match with my jacket collar as I'm lighting it.

In the meantime things have cooled down on the podium. The King stands up to speak, and the fat man stops talking. Immediately another man traipses forward to raise the microphone by a foot or so. A mumble runs through the crowd, perched up here on the rock.

The lanky figure totters forward with one hand on the brim of his hat. For a moment it looks as if the gusting winds are going to knock him down, but he leans into the wind and overcomes the problem.

I draw deeply on my cigar. The King gets out a little slip of paper and holds it up. He says a few words into the microphone, and people break into such enthusiastic applause that it can be heard all the way to where we're standing. Someone calls out for four cheers.

The Söder crowd on the rock do not at first realise what's in the offing and they only fall in with the last few cheers.

I turn around and catch sight of the little girl from the prison doors. She is standing swept up in a woman's long skirts and apron, a few metres away on the rock. The girl waves at me and I wave back. She forms her lips into a ring, like a pale rose. Her whistle can be clearly heard despite the gusting wind. I nod in appreciation and smile at her; she smiles back and disappears under the woman's skirts again. She really does look like my Ida.

The cortège of motor cars moves off down Långholmsgatan on the Söder side. A couple of coppers in uniform, sabres dangling by their sides, remove the barriers. From both sides, people spill onto the bridge like dark storm waves.

I fling my arms out and slap myself a couple of times to try to work up some warmth, and, in the process, almost hit someone standing close behind me.

'Watch what you're doing!'

I take the cigar out of my mouth and turn around. Ström is standing there, smiling at me. A couple of eye-glasses poorer, and a couple of kronor richer. I give him back the telescope. He gestures at the moss-covered rocks, which look slippery in the rain. Ström leads the way and I try to keep my balance behind him.

'Does our good friend Lundin know you're coming home? He had to bury some poor bastard and couldn't make it today.'

'I don't know. Either way I have keys to the undertaker's so I can pick up Dixie.'

'Dixie?'

'That film star's mutt.'

'The miniature schnauzer?'

'I inherited her.'

'You know Wallin, from round our way?'

'The asylum nurse.'

'He had one just like it last year. There was something wrong with its eye. It jumped out if one of the gang boys kicked it hard enough up its arse.'

'I know.'

'Just hung there, dangling on the end of the optical nerve. You can be sure those lads spent night and day running after that poor dog.'

'Well, at least there's nothing wrong with Dixie's eyes.'

'People said Wallin used to take that dog out with a soup spoon in his pocket, so he could put its eye back in if he had to.'

'I'll be damned if I believe that. His hand was probably trembling too bad for one thing. What with the schnapps.'

'An unfaithful friend. Unlike the bloody dog.'

Ström slows down; I put my cigar in my mouth and stretch out my arms to keep my balance.

'We can take the number 4 across the bridge and all the way to Odengatan,' Ström continues.

'I just have to swing by Lindkvist's betting shop first.'

'Are you putting your prison pay on a match?'

'I might even have to go a few rounds myself to get my hands on some dosh.'

Ström checks the lie of the land, blows his nose with one hand while pointing at a fissure in the rock with the other. He inserts the tip of his shoe into it and springs across to a little foothold half a metre away. I jump and land heavily behind him.

'And then? What do you do on your first day of freedom?'

'The barber. Try to get my damned con's hairstyle into order.'

'Nyström's place?'

I nod.

'And then I'll drop off my lousy clothes at Beda's laundry.'

Ström stops on a ledge in front of me. We have another few metres to go before we hit a gravel path running through the gloom cast by the mighty bridge span overhead. The freshly painted white pillars reflect in the waters of Riddarfjärden.

Ström sniffs: 'Sailor-Beda?'

'She hasn't gone west, has she?'

Ström wipes his nose with the back of his hand.

'You missed her by a couple of months.'

My heart skips a beat. A feeling of loss sends a tremor through my body.

'Cancer? She had a growth on her eye.'

'It was Petrus, her full-grown idiot of a son.'

'What the hell are you saying?'

'While she was in bed he sneaked up and beat her to death with a stone from her own mangle. A damned bloodbath, I've heard. Can you imagine?'

Ström sloshes his tobacco juice around in his mouth. His lips make a sound rather like when a bricklayer slaps a good dollop of mortar on a brick.

I shake my head: 'No.'

'What do you mean?'

Ström claws at his beard again.

'I can't see that. Like hell he did.'

Anger starts pulsating through my limbs. I clench my fists so hard that the dry cigar between my fingers is pulverised.

Ström turns his back on me, adding over his shoulder: 'Petrus was quite a simpleton, wasn't he?'

The vein in my forehead throbs. A flash cuts through my skull. I draw my foot back and gather steam; then, as hard as I can, give Ström a broadside in the arse. The old jumble dealer is flung over the drop and slides down the rock. His body tears a dark brown wound in the green moss, the broken strap of one of his eye-glasses trailing his body a couple of metres below, as he rolls a few more turns onto the gravel path and ends up on his belly. He writhes about and starts whining.

A white motorboat thumps along under the bridge. For a moment, my heart beats in perfect time with the pulsing of the motor. A gull cackles harshly. I keep my eyes on it as it dives towards the surface of the water: 'Like hell.'

WEDNESDAY 20 NOVEMBER

I'm still in a bad mood when half an hour later I walk into the Toad, the betting shop in Klara. The place smells of horse harnesses and tack-boxes. Along one of the long walls, two drivers with swaddled legs peruse the large blackboard, on which the odds are written in chalk. One nudges the other with his elbow when I come in. They peer over at me. I don't know if they recognise me or if I just look like an old lag.

Behind the wooden counter at the far end of the room sits an old man with white wisps of hair around his ears. He's wearing black armbands over a white shirt, and half-frame spectacles. He plasters a smile across his face. I tip my hat at him. His name is Lindkvist; he seems to have aged more than the years that have gone by since I last saw him.

The cashier is busy with a posh-looking bloke in a topcoat and gaiters. The receipt makes a thwacking sound as he skewers it on a five-inch nail that's been hammered up from beneath the desk. The customer makes a farewell gesture and walks out. One of the drivers leans forward and whispers something into the ear of the other. The lid of the counter slams. The old man quickly limps up to me and offers me his hand. I engulf it in my own, with a good shake.

'Kvisten!' beams Lindkvist. 'I thought you'd take me up on my proposal, but I never thought it would take you years to make your decision!'

He aims a punch with his right hand and taps me gently on the shoulder. I let him get on with it.

'His Majesty's pleasure.'

'Oh, is that it? But now you're out? And in need of funds?'

'Mm…'

'In fine shape, it seems to me?'

'It's the pitch-black solitary confinement cells in Långholmen. They pour the rye porridge into a hog trough leading into the cell. You have to fight the rats for it. Does wonders for your figure.'

'Fancy that. When will you be ready for a fight?'

'I want to get a haircut and a couple of drams, so… tonight?'

The old man laughs. The drivers have finished their discussion. One of them comes up to the counter.

'Still undefeated?'

Lindkvist smiles ingratiatingly.

'He's never even taken a count. He was already hard to beat as a child.'

'Three matches with a week between each? The first with two opponents?'

'A hundred per match. Half up front.'

I claw at my throat.

'I have to pitch you against decent younger blokes, or no one will bet against you.'

'They probably won't remember.'

'They'll remember all right. We're putting on a match a week until Christmas. Advent matches. The legendary Harry Kvist makes a magnificent comeback.'

Lindkvist slaps his hands together in the air and looks up as if he's seeing the words written on a banner right in front of him.

'No gloves. Keep fighting until one man hits the floor.'

A memory flashes across my mind: a Christmas gala at Cirkus in 1922. I don't remember the name of my opponent. I was at the peak of my career and I utterly destroyed him before he was

26

knocked out, and had to be carried out feet first. A year later my life had gone to pieces and I was standing, hat in hand, begging for soup from the Salvation Army.

I pick up my notebook and flick through it until I find a blank page. I spit on my aniline pen and write down the dates.

'Until the other bloke is on the floor.'

'Is that something we could influence?'

I shake my head.

'Once I tried a rigged bout, and look how it ended.'

I hold up my left hand. Where the last finger should be there's a stub with a red-streaked knot of skin. Räpan, the old smuggler king on Söder, removed it with a pair of pliers and a mallet when I broke an agreement some ten years ago.

Old man Lindkvist sucks in air between his lips.

'How do I get hold of you?'

'I live above Lundin's, the undertaker in Sibirien. You can telephone me there.'

I write down the number, Vasastan 4160, on a page in my notebook, tear it out and hand it to him. The old man folds the slip of paper and tucks into one of the breast pockets of his shirt. He produces a cigar from the other.

I accept the cigar and bite off the end. Lindkvist offers me a light and I puff it to life. I look around the shop.

'You used to have an assistant. A red-haired lad?'

'I had to get rid of him. He couldn't be trusted.'

'I don't suppose you need a new one, do you? I know someone who might suit.'

'Not at present.'

'Who have you got taking care of debts?'

'The National Socialists. The Reaper, Rickardsson and his gang. Ploman's blokes.'

27

'Nazis?'

'That's what people call them.'

'How much do they charge?'

'Twenty.'

'I charge fifteen.'

'I'm not going to argue with the Reaper for the sake of a five per cent discount. To hell with that.'

'I see.'

The old man nods.

'The legend, Harry Kvist, a magnificent comeback,' he repeats.

I grin. An unctuous smile spreads across Lindkvist's face again, and we shake hands. When I release his hand he takes aim again with another right-hand punch at my shoulder. I quickly dart forward, roll under his arm and come close to his furrowed face. A quick left jab and the old man would be stuck to the wall like a damp patch. He smells of sweat and tobacco. We grin at each other.

I'm back.

In the foyer at the undertaker's there's a bottle of Kron on the desk. My favourite brand. There's a note in front of the bottle:

> *Brother, welcome back to freedom. This litre of spirits is a welcoming gift, no need to pay for it. The bloody dog awaits you up the stairs. See you at the residents' party at number 41.*

I twist off the bottle top and take a couple of big mouthfuls. Still shivering with pleasure I walk through the office and flat, emerging into the stairwell. As I move along I have time to take another mouthful. Damn, how I've missed this.

A dank smell hits me as the front door glides open. Dixie's claws scratch against the cork mat. She whines excitedly. I crouch in the dark hall, stabilise myself with one hand against the wall and hold out the other to her. She licks it.

'You could also do with a visit to the barber's, dearie.'

Dixie hasn't had a trim for nigh on two years, and she really isn't much more than a fuzzy ball of black fur. As she makes a few joyful spins, I notice that she's limping. She yaps and lies with her belly facing up, playing dead.

My knees click as I straighten up. I hit the round, black Bakelite light switch and peer at the buzzing lamp. Awkwardly, Dixie spins around, and gets back on all fours. I hang my jacket on one of the brass hooks, toss my hat onto the hat shelf and, passing the big full-length mirror in the hall, almost stumble over Dixie, who's buzzing around my legs. I go into the narrow kitchen. For a while I look at the thick layer of dust which has settled over the little drop-leaf table and its two chairs.

The double window facing onto the courtyard is so covered in soot that you can hardly see through it, and the rag rugs from Ström's jumble shop are coated with dog hair.

'This place needs a clean before Doughboy moves in.'

I have another few gulps of the Kron, then put the bottle down on the draining board and go up to the window, unhooking the latch and opening it by pushing with my wrist.

There's a cat meowing in the yard and Dixie laboriously scales one of the chairs to make her way onto the table. She points her cropped ears and gazes out fixedly at the November evening. Down in the courtyard you can make out the dark protuberance of the potato shed and the row of latrines. No one uses them any more, not since Lundin installed water closets in the stairwell.

I root through the top kitchen drawer for gas tokens but don't find any. I come across an unfamiliar object and pick it up. It's a cigar trimmer. I stare at it. Where the hell did that come from? I have no memory of ever having bought one.

The vodka is starting to spin in my head. With a sigh, I pick up a couple of clumps of wood from the basket beside the cooker. I pile them up with an eighteen-month-old issue of *Social-Demokraten* and light the fire with a phosphor stick. The wrought-iron hatch chimes dully and hollowly as I close it.

I fill the small copper saucepan with water and put it on the ring. Dixie yelps and I pick her up from the table and put her down. She limps ahead of me into the main room, disappears into the hall and takes her post by the front door.

'Calm yourself, doggie. Just a minute…'

The prison smell has lodged in my clothes. I leave the kitchen, take off my shirt and singlet, and throw them on the big oak desk. Dixie whines desolately. I find yet one more dry cigar in the desk drawer, stick it in my mouth and place myself in front of the mirror with my palms pressed to the wall. The tattoo of a full-rigged ship on my chest breaks through the hair as if it's cutting through dark storm swells.

The hard labour of Långholmen and its spartan diet has near enough returned me to my old physical shape. The flesh around my upper arms, shoulders and chest is firm and clearly defined. My skin has a prison pallor, but my trunk is almost flat. I run the flat of my hand across my broad nose and scarred face.

'…magnificent comeback. Harry Kvist…'

I totter slightly as I walk out of the hall, passing the large, square ceramic wood-burner with its blue-relief pattern, and open the dressing-room door. The light comes on automatically. The smell of mothballs and gun oil fills me as I step inside. I put the cigar in my mouth, bring down a shoebox from a shelf and give it a slight shake. The heaviness and a rattling sound indicate that the Husqvarna and the shells are still inside. With a smile I recall being given the pistol by a doting commanding officer during my military service, as thanks for some pleasant moments we shared.

I put the box back on the shelf and slide my hand over the clothes on the hangers. I have six decent suits hanging there, arranged in dark to light colours; also more than a dozen shirts. I choose a broad silver-coloured tie to match a dark-grey pinstripe shirt with a fixed collar.

I close the door behind me. On the way to the window I pass the sleeping alcove with the wide wrought-iron bedstead. Bedded with proper feather and down bolsters. I briefly spare a thought for Doughboy in his hard prison bunk. That boy. Beautiful in a way that almost awakens a desire to bruise him. I close my eyes to see him more clearly. He fills my senses with a subtle, but powerful joy.

'Seven days. If there's one thing Kvisten knows about, it's how to wait – he's hardly ever done anything else.'

I stand by the window, putting on my shirt. Roslagsgatan lies steeped in darkness, almost deserted. A stray dog hobbles southward past Bruntell's general store, but it stops for a moment and sniffs the air before heading off in the other direction. A bloke in a felt hat and hunched shoulders is zigzagging along in a northerly direction. I think it may be Wallin, the psychiatric nurse. I have the hiccups, and I belch sourly. I've been off it for a long time and the spirits've already made a mess of my head.

Down the hill on Ingemarsgatan comes Nisse's Eva, the baker's wife, hurrying along with a tray of smooth buns. The party is in the offing.

I slide on my tie and knot it with a certain amount of trouble. The street dog limps through the semi-circle of light spilling onto the pavement from Beda's laundry. I remember how Beda used to pat me on the cheek when I came to pick up my suits. The way the skin of her hand used to be chapped and the nails cracked after too many years in the washtubs. I shake my head.

That old girl was damn well made of dynamite. She walked her own road, didn't care about gossip or slander, always kind to each and every person she met.

I bite off the tip of my Meteor. The match scrapes against the strip and, for a moment, I can see the reflection of my scarred mug in the window. I puff some life into the cigar and kill the flame with a jet of grey-black smoke. I have another pull at it. Out of the corner of my eye, I sense a shadow speeding across the floor of the laundry down below.

I clench my fists, raise my eyes and gaze into the darkness. My lungs are smarting from the heavy cigar smoke. The shadow does not reappear.

I exhale, I shiver, I stumble.

'A cup of java, that's right. Should clear the head and see off the ghouls.'

Back in the kitchen, the water is boiling on the stove. I put aside the pile of letters, take the saucepan off the ring and throw in a couple of generous scoops of ground coffee. After it has brewed for a bit, I find a cup and pour the coffee into it with a tot of schnapps, then I go back to the window.

I stick the cigar in my mouth and start going through the letters. None from America. I grunt.

One of the envelopes has no postage stamp and lacks a full address.

I see the words 'To Kvisten' pencilled on it in wonky letters. I hold up the letter against the remaining daylight and grunt again.

Again I see the shadow moving about inside the laundry.

I take a few big gulps of java, break the seal of the envelope and open the folded paper. The words stick in my mouth as I read out loud:

The 1st of September

Dear Mistr. Kvisten.

The thing is in the autum you prommised to take care of my Petrus. Its all goin to be over with me one of this days but theres no way of agetting away from a prommise. Not that I wold think such a thing off Kvisten. I have seen to it theres a monthly bob or too for Petrus so Kvisten wont have to fork out for him but if he cold make shure sommetimes that no one takes avantage of him it wold be good. Hes kind harted and does what hes told if he understands you.

As ever

Beda Johansson

'Brother, how the hell can you turn up at a party with such an objectionable hairstyle?'

Undertaker Lundin beams at me, displaying his tobacco-stained fangs. He's a tall, lanky bloke of about seventy. Always dressed in a black three-piece suit and a high top hat. A couple of grains of snuff stick to his bushy white moustache. His hand-shake is firm and hearty.

'Nyström didn't have a lot to work with.'

I smile, pulling my hand through my hair. Lundin nods, still beaming. I put a fresh Meteor from widow Lind's cigar shop in

33

my mouth, and adjust my tie. I am wearing a pinstripe chocolate-brown suit. It's about a size too generous about the waist now, but the jacket sticks to the outline of my shoulders like tar to a hull, and coming home today on the tram I read that waistcoats are no longer worn in America, so I left mine behind. Looking around the premises I start wondering if I've done the right thing. You shouldn't ever believe all the rot you read in the newspapers.

The meeting house of the tenants' association in the yard next door measures about five by seven metres. The walls are plastered and whitewashed but tobacco smoke has turned them yellow after years of meetings and parties, although there's a pleasant enough smell in there of food and liquid soap. A couple of the trade union blokes have draped their red banners over one of the walls.

Along one of the short walls the old girls of the quarter have laid out a spread on a trestle table with a long white runner. My gob starts salivating when I let my eyes wander over the goodies. The dishes are overflowing with herring salads, ribs, jellied pig's trotters with beetroot, grilled potatoes, parsnips and carrots, no less than six kinds of brawn, and pils from the München Brewery. In large zinc vats under the table, I catch the glimmer of schnapps bottles, enough for ten ration books. Maybe Lundin, the local schnapps baron, has contributed something to the tally. With a touch of luxury, they've been put on ice.

A haphazard collection of plates from several families have been piled up at the far end by the wall. There's a silver jug; nickel silver, of course, but still. Everyone on our block seems to be here for the big party of the autumn, and it's already getting crowded. Bruntell, the general-store owner from the other side of the street, has positioned his Kodak so that he can preserve the table for posterity. He's put on weight around his waist since last time I saw him, and got himself a ludicrous little postage-stamp moustache. Ström, the jumble dealer, drags another zinc vat of ice across the floor, and peers warily in my direction, even though I have already apologised for kicking his arse this afternoon. Wallin runs his hand down his asylum staff uniform and shifts his weight to his other leg. He's guarding the schnapps glasses, lined up at one end of the table.

Nilsson, the sheet-metal worker from number 5, paces the floor from side to side with his hat in his hands, as confused as a tenant farmer in a water closet. The Good Templar, Wetterström, and his wife are hanging up colourful lanterns. They are both wearing Sunday best and Wetterström has a water-combed side parting.

Probably it's Johnsson from the Oden-Bazaar down on the corner who's supplied the lanterns. Johnsson peers cautiously in my direction. A few years ago I was compelled to give him a proper beating to set him straight. He was never quite himself after that. He limps now. He went cock-eyed too. There's another click when Bruntell takes a photograph. Lundin gets out his accounts book, looks up the letter K and runs his snuff-yellow finger down the page. He hums.

'One thousand, nine hundred and twenty-seven kronor and fifty öre.'

A droplet of sweat frees itself from under Lundin's brim and runs down his furrowed cheek like a tear, then gets caught in his moustache. His left hand is shaking so badly that he drops his accounts book. He grabs his fist with his other hand and holds on tight.

'As much as that?'

I pick up his accounts book for him.

'Rent, radio licence bills, dog food and porter.'

'Porter?'

'She wanted porter for breakfast.'

'You've been giving Dixie beer for breakfast?'

'You can work some of it off. I've got myself a motor, but I'm still short of a pall-bearer. My hand won't quite do what it's supposed to do.'

'Why's that?'

'My health's a bit iffy these days. I get a prickling sensation in my legs and it's hard getting out of bed in the mornings. Dragging stiffs down a lot of stairs is out of the question.'

'Porter? Why porter?'

'It's bracing.'

'It'll abort a foetus.'

'Only if heated up.'

The door opens and a trio arrives with a violin, an accordion and an American banjo. The man with the violin nods in my direction. I have no memory of having seen him before, but as I really don't have much of a memory about anything at this time, I nod back. Eckman, the managing director of the cement company, tinkles a glass and shuffles into the middle of the room. His hair is oiled, his lips are thick. It must have been five or six years since he left number 41 to move into a house in Djursholm, but he's still invited every spring and autumn to the house party.

'*Meine Damen und Herren,*' the managing director begins, with a jovial laugh.

The murmur of voices immediately dies down, only for the door to be thrown open and a pair of heels to come clattering over the wooden floor. A young bottle-blonde woman makes her way inside. A few of the old girls give her the evil eye. The blokes in the quarter call her the Jewel; the old girls call her the Mannequin. She has a small child hanging on her arm and a rough-hewn dark-haired man in tow. He looks like Gunnar Turesson, who I fought in '21. A short, squat Western Geat, a fairly decent slugger but he liked to fight dirty. He tried to rip my eyes out with his glove straps during the clinch. Strong enough to tear a telephone directory in two, they used to say. I decked him in the third round. The swine only woke up a month later, and he never came back after that. A part of me envied him. I'd rather have ended my boxing career like that.

The Jewel blushes and smiles assuagingly, while keeping her eyes on the floor. The buzz of voices starts up again. Her bloke removes his cap.

Managing Director Eckman clears his throat: 'As I was saying, *meine Damen und Herren…*'

'When did the minx have a child?'

I gesture towards the Jewel. Lundin caresses his luxuriant moustache and leans towards me. The wrinkles around his eyes deepen as he squints to get a better look.

'After a lot of faffing about they got married. The daughter came along pretty quickly after that, weak from the very start. Of course the hags stood around at Bruntell's counting the days but, as I understand, it all added up.'

'There you are, then.'

'She'll be studying fashion, apparently. Quite different from how it used to be when she was driven home by gentlemen in taxicabs every other night. Her bed linen filthy after two days, that's what people said.'

'Bloody gossip-mongers.'

'Bruntell's wife claims she saw her hanging up nappies to dry in the attic a few weeks earlier than the official date, but you know what she's like.'

There's a burst of applause. The managing director makes a shallow bow and gestures at the *smörgåsbord*. A rising din of voices follows.

I hook onto Lundin's sleeve and set course for the overflowing serving dishes. He limps along behind me. People get out of our way as we plough forward. With a decent haul of food each, and glasses of cold schnapps in our hands, we find a couple of chairs by the door. I get stuck in, with the plate on my knees, tearing the flesh off the greasy ribs with my teeth and unloading dollops of potato into my mouth. The warmth of the schnapps sluices through my upper body, sending shivers of pleasure down my spine. In a corner, three girls are eating standing up. Now and then they look over in our direction and titter. Two of them are blonde and look a lot alike. They're all dolled up, wearing brightly coloured dresses. A boy with the Secondary Grammar School badge on his cap is waiting on them, mixing grogs of pure vodka and sugared soda.

'Just two people missing here.'

'So you know about it, brother?'

'Ström told me.'

Lundin puts down his plate between his feet and waves his finger at a little boy in shorts. He gets out a five-öre piece from the mirrored slot in his snuffbox, and points at the vats of schnapps bottles. The boy darts off between our neighbours and comes back before long with a litre of Kron.

There's a snapping sound as Lundin breaks the seal. He fills our glasses to the rim and we knock back the shots. At regular intervals the door beside us opens, bringing a whiff of the row of the shit-houses in the courtyard. More people turn up. The women have taken off their aprons for a change, and altered their dresses. The blokes are wearing their Sunday trousers. Their little lads are wearing sailor suits; the girls have pink or red bows in their liquid-soap-washed hair.

In due course, as the glasses are emptied, the voices get louder. It's getting properly crowded, people are standing or sitting in double lines along the walls, but around us there's still room to swing a cat: one of the few advantages of a bad reputation and a prison haircut. Lundin refills our glasses and clears his throat.

'Sometimes it was difficult to know which of them was most addled, Petrus or Beda.'

'Neither one of them had a completely clear head.'

'She was a compulsive liar. Everything was a fairy tale to her. You remember her stories, my brother? Those kings and barons and other members of the gentry who visited her at night? How they praised her fine laundry and well-formed feet?'

'She wasn't out of her mind, though. And neither is Petrus, just a touch simple.'

'A bit? With that skull? A typical criminal physiognomy.'

'That's irrelevant.'

I stumble over my words. The alcohol courses through my veins. I've been off it, I used to be able to handle ten shots and more.

'They say he sneaked up on her while she lay sleeping. Crushed her skull with a heavy iron.'

I shrug. Lundin looks at me. He has a bit of amber-coloured jelly in his moustache, from the pig's trotters.

'How do you know that?'

'That was what they said.'

'Did you bury her?'

'Someone else was called in for that, thank God.'

The accordionist can't hold himself back any longer. Not everyone has stopped eating, but the first notes of a waltz start ringing out. I study the way his fingers wander across the keys. It's been a long time since I heard music.

Lundin hands me yet another filled glass and we knock it back.

I raise my voice: 'Petrus may be a bit retarded but he's no murderer.'

'You should have seen her towards the end.' Lundin shakes his head slowly. 'Cancer everywhere, bed-bound the whole time. Her skin completely yellow. You could see the skull under her skin. I suppose he didn't know any better, that damned youth. I think he got that way from too much pleasuring himself.'

'What happened to him?'

'Långholmen, I suppose?'

I shake my head. The violinist gets his instrument out from the case and falls in with the waltz. A couple of blokes stamp out the rhythm until the floorboards start complaining. Wetterström and his wife are the first on the floor, and before long two other couples are keeping them company in a whirling dance. Wallin rises out of his chair and howls at the ceiling, like an excitable hound. The schnapps has pressed itself out of the pores of his skin, making his face chafed and red. He's a big drinker: from time to time he boozes until he sees little men. Another bloke seizes hold of his epaulettes and tugs him back into his seat.

'She made me promise…'

'What's that?' Lundin cups his hand behind his ear. 'Promise what?'

I shake my head. There's a tightness across my chest. A dozen years ago it all went to hell and my boxing career came to a sudden end. I moved to Roslagsgatan and Lundin and Beda were the only people who welcomed me. Lundin, because no one else dared live above an undertaker's shop. Beda, because she didn't know any better. Or maybe she knew better than most. Her coarse hand against my cheek and her soft words still live on in my memory: 'Kvisten can't do nowt about who he is. The heart's not some old nag you can harness any way you like.'

I shiver with unease and look up. The dance has already turned wild, there's shouting and commotion, and a scramble for the three young women soaring across the floor so their colourful skirts billow out around their slender waists. Their legs are exposed right up to their knees. The old men pretend they're looking in another direction. Nilsson from floor five knocks the filth out of his harmonica and holds it up to his lips.

Lundin brays into my ear: 'Promise what?'

'Nothing.'

I put the plate on the floor and push it under the chair with my foot. I take out a Meteor, bite off the end, blow off the tobacco fragments from my lips with a spurt of spittle. I loosen my tie and run my finger around the inside of the collar.

'He who makes no promise makes no sin.'

The music stops abruptly after Lundin's godly words. There's cheering and applause. Now the banjo player has also joined in, and someone stamps out the beat of yet another melody. The widow of the Lapp, a gnarled old woman with small eyes dark as pieces of coal, legs it out of the door in her reindeer moccasins, her apron loaded with stolen deposit bottles.

One of the young women, the brunette, separates from her girlfriends and places herself in front of Lundin with her back towards us. She has arranged her dark hair over one shoulder. On the nape of her neck sits the clasp of a golden chain. On the other side of the room, the other two blonde girls stand tittering and whispering among themselves. A couple of blokes have to turn around sheepishly after drumming up the courage to ask them for a spin.

'As I mentioned earlier, you can work off some of the debt.'

Lundin has raised his voice to make himself heard over the music.

'I've also set up a couple of matches with Lindkvist at the Toad. And Wernersson may have a couple of jobs for me.'

'He's been on the telephone.'

I grunt. Wernersson's Velocipedes is my main employer. I reclaim bicycles that have been bought on credit, when payments aren't made. There's a welter of impoverished sods who put their hopes on an expensive delivery bicycle, thanks be to the Lord. Every recovered unit can net me in the region of forty kronor, if I'm really lucky.

'Once I get my advertisement in the daily newspaper, the wheels should start running smoothly again, as ever.'

'A toast to that!'

We clink our glasses and drink our shots. Lundin has the hiccups, his long, rangy body is jerking, and his face is a deep scarlet.

The girl in front of us turns around and smiles. She has slanted white teeth at the front. Her red-painted lips are full, and her plucked eyebrows accentuated with scorched cork. She leans towards me. I pull my hand over my close-cropped skull and try to arrange what little hair I have left.

'I hear Kvisten is a real swell at dancing. That right?'

For a few seconds I stare into my empty schnapps glass before I look into her green eyes, shiny from booze and tobacco smoke.

'That's right.'

The emptiness in my head chases away the music for a moment, neutralises the cheerful cries, Lundin's hiccuping, the sound of the dancers' heels against the floor, the ringing of glasses and the slamming of cutlery and crockery.

'But the bloody dog. I have to walk the dog before it gets dark.'

The sounds of the party come back, full force. The girl purses her red lips.

'Course you do,' she hisses, tossing her dark hair as she turns around. She elbows her way across the dance floor.

Her girlfriends laugh soundlessly, their mouths like black holes. I clench my jaw but do not say anything.

She'll be called all sorts of names for what she'll do tonight in her drunken state. I have another shot and put the glass down on the floor. I lean forward, my elbows on my thighs. The music stops but restarts before the applause has ebbed away. Another foxtrot. Slower, this time. I regain my breath and give Lundin a poke on the knee.

He jerks to attention as if I've just woken him up. I stare down at my hands, my fingers crooked with fractures, the scarred knuckles flattened. I've spent half my life trying to retrain myself to twist my fist at the moment of impact, using the bony ridge instead, but my muscle memory wants to do it another way. You are who you are: sometimes it hurts, nothing can be done about it.

'I'm thinking of taking a lodger. To halve my rent costs.'

I caress myself soundlessly over my well-shaven chin. The barber, Nyström, and his soap-girl, did a thorough job this afternoon. Lundin stops hiccuping.

'Anyone particular in mind?'

I nod at the floor.

'Doughboy. A lad. Met him inside. He'll be out in a week and I want to help him get back on his feet.'

There's a glugging sound as Lundin pours another glass. Cigarette smoke hangs heavily in the air. The smell of food has been replaced by a reek of tobacco, aquavit and sweat.

'There'll be talk.'

'There already is.'

Lundin hums. I notice that I've been holding my breath for a while. I exhale. The brunette has said yes to the grammar school boy. She's laughing as they glide past. His hand slowly slides down her back. He risks getting a proper slap any moment now.

'Do what you like. You do anyway.'

Lundin picks up his snuffbox and, with a certain amount of difficulty, kneads together a solid plug and shoves it under his lip. I fidget with my jacket. In the inside pocket is my letter from Beda.

'Who's taken over the laundry?'

'Beda's? No one, as far as I know. It's been empty since it was put on the market.'

I stand up and have to support myself against the back of my chair when I lose my balance. I put my hat on, hang my overcoat over my arm and pick up the half-full bottle of Kron from the floor.

'So soon?'

I nod.

'Too many people. Not used to it. And it's time for Dixie's walk.'

Lundin gives me a nod and raises his snuff-brown fingers towards the brim of his hat. I do the same and turn towards the exit.

'Brother!'

I turn around again.

'Don't go back inside for a while, not this time.'

Grinning indifferently, Lundin's head drops onto his chest. I laugh out loud. The Jewel pushes her stocky little bloke out of my way as I stumble out into the cold November night, bottle in hand.

In the asphalted courtyard I can make out the yellow-painted latrine huts and the outhouses in the dark. I press the palm of my hand against the smooth pointing of the house wall and sway slightly as I feel my way to the door leading out of the courtyard, some three or four metres away. It's cleared up. The stars seem to be dancing a quadrille across the night sky and I take deep breaths to purge my mind. The clean evening air mixes with the smell of refuse and excrement. I accidentally kick an empty bottle which clatters across the yard. A door slams somewhere.

The dark stairwell between the street and the courtyard smells faintly of coal fumes and turpentine. Drunkenly I pant, reaching for the wall. Slowly, my eyes grow accustomed to the darkness. Somewhere ahead of me there's a scraping sound, and I look up. A damned night light in this entrance would not have done any harm.

'As dark as a tomb.'

I take a few breathless steps and tumble into a soft body. Someone sighs deeply. I bounce back a full metre across the marble floor before I regain my balance.

'Watch out, will you!'

My voice is hoarse from the schnapps. I squint, trying to focus. The features of a large man slowly emerge from the gloom of the stairwell: pronounced eyebrows, a rough-hewn nose riddled with gaping pores, full lips and broad, strong shoulders that completely fill his coat. It's Rickardsson, the gangster who lives up by Roslagstull. Working with the Scythe Man, the ugly fuck is part of Ploman's inner circle and controls a large share of the vodka trade in Vasastan. Lundin pays the swine ten per cent every month so he can pursue his own business in peace. Every time we bump into each other in the street he sizes me up as if he's challenging me.

'I'd say Kvisten's had a drop too much.'

'None of your damned rat poison, you can be sure of that.'

I hiss the words out of the corner of my mouth, like a cobbler with his gob full of tacks. I take a small step towards him, grinning as if we're in opposite corners of the ring.

The whites of his eyes seem almost yellow in the darkness. He holds up his left palm. I catch sight of a wedding band on his finger. With his other hand he quickly opens the single button of his coat and folds open his overcoat and jacket. He's not wearing a waistcoat either. From his waistband, the butt of a revolver sticks up like the head of a hammer from a carpenter's belt. He puts one hand on it.

'Let's take it easy now, boy. Shall I help you home instead?'

For an instant, an image of Doughboy and his flea-bitten neck flashes before me. I stop, still grinning.

'Has Rickardsson got so old that he needs a crutch for support?'

'No trouble now. Take a bit of fresh air. Maybe I can take you for a stroll round the park.'

Rickardsson gives me a wide berth as he leaves. His expensive rhinoceros-hide boots ring out on the floor as he backs away into the courtyard. He has folded up his trouser legs so that the heels can be seen better. I grunt and show him my back as I continue on my way. Damned weakling to rely on his shooter like that.

The door creaks. An Ardennes mare harnessed to a gig clatters by on Roslagsgatan. The driver sits there all black and stiff, the reins in one hand and the whip in the other. The whiplashes show up as pale streaks across the horse's glistening, sweaty hindquarters. One of the grey-painted ambulances of the Epidemic Hospital drives slowly northwards. I bumble along in the same direction. The light is still falling across the pavement from Beda's old laundry. I put my cigar in my mouth and quicken my step.

I'm left standing for a moment outside Lundin's undertakers. His sign squeaks unpleasantly in the faint breeze. I look up at the dark façade and get the feeling that the entire house is about to fall down on me. I gasp and stumble backwards into the road.

'It's been a good while since... Kvisten had a taste of the strong stuff.'

I sway to and fro, staring up at the clear, starry sky. It reminds me of the darkness of the packed crowd during a fight, pierced by hundreds of glowing cigarette ends and wide-open eyes.

'Harry Kvisten Kvist... in a... magnificent comeback.'

I laugh and close my eyes. I hold up my arms into the air, spilling booze from the open bottle over my shirt front, while I jog clumsily on the spot.

For an instant I am there again: the darkness calls my name.

Dixie's claws sound against the cork mat as I take her lead down from the hook next to the mirror. It's time for a walk.

The faint tones of yet another waltz make their way into the street from the tenants' shindig in number 41. The cold tears at my vodka-drenched shirt breast. I hear the far-off sound of laughter and chatter.

'The schnapps in there must be flowing like butter in the Sahara.'

The cold November evening startles me out of my stupor. It's blowing so hard that the cigar in my mouth burns at twice its normal rate. For a long while I stand on the other side of the street, keeping my eyes on the laundry. There's no sign of that mysterious shadow.

Dixie whines and pulls, but I drag her along. We walk towards the Veterinary Institute and take a detour over the Johannes School's yard. Dixie starts panting and her limping gets worse.

I put my hand in my pocket and finger the letter from Beda. I don't have much of a sense of recall at the moment, but I remember my promise to the washerwoman, and words are there to be honoured. I have failed to keep a promise I made to someone I cared about one too many times already. Never again.

I hold the letter up in the light cast by a street lamp, and stare at the date. If old man Ström was right, Beda only wrote it a few weeks before she died. We cross to the opposite pavement before I drag Dixie back south again.

Up in Vanadislunden St Stefan's Church strikes nine times. From the train station towards Albano, a freight train lets out a shriek. The air smells of burning spruce.

We are almost home now. Across the deserted street, Lundin's shop sign is banging in the wind. Suddenly the pale light, falling over the pavement outside the laundry, is turned off. A bell tinkles, a door creaks and slams. I stop; my heart misses a beat.

Only a few metres in front of me, a figure with an upturned coat collar is hunched over the lock. He has a walking stick hooked over his lower arm. The silver hilt glitters in the dark.

'Bleeding lock!'

The man curses, tugging at the key. His voice is deep. He's still not seen me. Soundlessly I tie Dixie's lead around a drainpipe. There's a click as the lock clicks into place. The man in front of me sighs and tries to pull the key out. I glance around once, making sure I'm alone. Quickly I take off my tie and fold it up in my coat pocket before I charge at him. I move quicker than I have for years.

I twist the man round with a hand at his collar before I thump him into the laundry door. Dixie barks. The drainpipe rattles when she tugs at the lead. The man roars and pumps his arms up and down. Somehow he manages to whack me just under my eye with the silver hilt of his stick. The pain surges through my head like a piercing wolf-whistle.

My fingers quickly work their way up to his throat. His yelling comes to an abrupt end when I give him a squeeze and at the same time twist a left hook into his liver. It's not an especially hard punch. My knuckles connect with his bottom rib. I let him go and the fucker goes down on all fours.

His hat rolls off and ends up in the gutter. His pocket watch falls out of his waistcoat and dangles under him like a pendulum. He gasps and coughs. Viscous threads of phlegm trail out of his mouth, like the tentacles of a jellyfish. I put my foot on his neck and press his face into the pavement. He still has too little air in him to yell. He starts fumbling with something, then holds out a black wallet.

I take my foot off the man's neck. I turn towards the laundry and try to get the lock open. It gets caught and I have to fiddle with it for a moment before it releases. The man on the pavement thinks he can crawl off. He's turned his arse towards me. I take aim and drive home my boot between his legs. Only now does he protest. He falls onto his side and yells, with his hands on his crotch and his legs drawn up into a foetal position. I hastily look around before grabbing him by the shoulder of his fur-trimmed overcoat, then drag him inside backwards. On the way in I hit the light switch.

The laundry looks the same as the last time I was here: a large square room five or six metres wide. Across it runs a counter of dark wood. There's a sharp smell of starch and ammonia. For an instant I feel the vodka wanting to come back up. In a corner lies Petrus's broom with the worn bristles pointing at us.

I drag the man a bit further and he rolls onto his side. His dark hair is greying at the temples and thinning on the crown of his head. A straight nose cleaves his grimacing face. He's well dressed but under his waistcoat his cravat's come undone and his watch-chain curls over the floor. I stand on the pocket watch and snap off the chain with my hand.

'And your name is?'

'Don't hit me!'

His voice is shrill, desperate. A walkover.

'I'll beat you to death if you don't tell me your name.'

In my stupor I stumble over my words. I smack my lips clumsily to soften up my mouth.

'Kullberg. John Kullberg.'

'And what are you doing here?'

'I've purchased the shop. With the intention of opening a delivery firm.'

'And when did you buy it?'

'Yesterday.'

I bend down and grasp his collar. He raises his hands to protect his face. I pull him up onto his feet and dust him down. He's wearing a thick tweed suit and galoshes on his feet. He whines and bends down to pick up his pocket watch.

'Where do you keep the keys to the bedroom downstairs?'

I point to a door behind the counter.

'These are business premises and according to the health and safety authorities cannot be used as a dwelling.'

'Either bloody way they slept down there, the two of them. Do you know a murder was committed here?'

The man twists and turns and fingers his broken watch.

'I was told that people around here didn't know about it.'

'Every snotty-nosed kid knows. Well? The keys?'

'It's probably open.'

'Get out.'

'But who'll lock the front door?'

'There's nothing here to steal.'

'What about homeless people?'

'Wait outside, then, for Christ's sake!'

The man twists again, still shaking. I wait until he's gone, then I open the counter. A swelling thumps to life under my eye. Bruised by a bloody old codger. Wouldn't have happened if I'd been sober. Harry Kvist in another amazing comeback.

The back door glides open without a sound. Another door behind it leads to the shed in the courtyard, where the boiling pots and mangles are kept. I go down the dark staircase and enter the small cellar room.

I light a match and find the light switch. The lamp doesn't work. The stench of piss and mould finds its way into my misshapen nose. The match head burns my fingertips, I shake it out and light another. The shorter wall of the little room is covered in tarred pipes. Behind one of the welds is a large, black wet patch on the cement wall.

Along both of the longer sides are narrow cast-iron beds. Again I blow out my match. A cellar rat darts over my feet. I flinch and drop the box of matches. It hits the floor somewhere in front of me. A surging sound comes from one of the pipes.

'Damn it.'

Through the door above comes a faint light.

I wait a while but my eyes don't adjust to the dark. My knees click as I go down on all fours. I fumble over the coarse concrete floor. In the end I find the matchbox. As I get up I kick something. A bucket falls over with a clattering sound. The sharp smell of month-old piss assaults my nostrils. Again my stomach turns but I'm not someone who wastes vodka unnecessarily. I light another match and breathe through my mouth.

Between the beds lies a zinc bucket which has been used as a chamber pot. The bed linen is disordered. I check one of the mattresses. It's lumpy to the touch, stuffed with rags and other cast-offs, but there's no blood on it. I hold up the sheets in the flickering glow of the flame. They're completely white. I toss them back and throw aside the match. It hisses and goes out on the floor.

Yet another match, forming a shivering ball of light. I lean over the other bed. On the pillow are a couple of scattered, rust-red drops, and that's all I find. I stare at them. Possibly Beda died here, but no skull was ever crushed in this bed. I've worked over a couple of blokes in my day, and I know what a damned nasty mess results when you make a proper job of it. I curse as the flame burns the tips of my fingers again.

My steps echo as I go up the narrow stairs. In the shop the sudden light blinds me, like when you're released after several days in a dark solitary cell. Little Doughboy appears in my head, and I slow my steps. The greying bloke is standing outside with his broken pocket watch in his hand. I let him wait a few minutes more.

The cash register has been emptied of money. In a cardboard box on a shelf underneath is a pad of carbon paper. Squinting so I can focus my eyes, I look through a dozen receipts at the top. There seem to be several different handwriting styles. I know Beda's handwriting and she has not written these. The topmost receipt is dated the seventeenth of September. Ström, the junk dealer, apparently handed in a shirt and overcoat. The slanted pencilled letters seem to be leaning against each other on the grey-hued paper. I copy everything into my notebook and lift the hatch in the counter with a thump. I open the door. A northerly wind raging down the street hits me square in the face. It stinks of winter. I turn to Kullberg, who's working on reacquiring his dignity by firmly clenching his jaw. I go back and talk to him.

'Who sold you this property?'

'Miss Johansson.'

'Who?'

'She inherited it from her mother.'

'Inherited?'

'And I certainly didn't think that I'd be assaulted the first time I came to look it over.'

'You looked like a burglar.'

I pull the elastic strap off my wallet.

'But you said yourself that there was nothing here to steal,' he complained.

I hand over two five-krona bills: 'So you can have your pocket watch repaired.'

'I've a good mind to call the police about you!'

The wrinkles around his mouth deepen when the measly old bloke purses his lips, but he takes the money. The vein in my forehead starts to throb. I feel like putting my feet on the bastard's neck again. This time I'll make sure that he puts his teeth against the edge of the pavement. I clench my fists: 'Listen: not a soul saw what happened here. It was a mistake, the whole thing. Get lost now!'

I get out another five-krona bill and tuck it into the breast pocket of his overcoat: 'Welcome to Sibirien.'

THURSDAY 21 NOVEMBER

'Six days left. Six miserable days.'

With an aching head, I mutter to myself as I help Lundin lug out a black, pre-manufactured coffin from the little workshop inside the funeral parlour. It's an early November morning: ice crystals on the windows and a pair of thick woollen socks in my boots. I'm wearing a black suit and white shirt with a black silk cravat, and I also have a very nice blue shiner under my left eye.

Lundin has lent me a bowler hat that's a size too small for me. He unbolts the front door of the funeral parlour and hunches over as he backs out into the street.

The hearse is a black-painted Chevrolet ambulance. It has three side windows and double doors at the back. They creak when Lundin puts his knee under the coffin and opens them with one hand. I push the coffin in. There's a dull thudding sound as Lundin tries to slap some life into his old legs. He's been working on them since morning coffee.

'Damned hangover I have this morning.'

Lundin's breath is steaming. I nod, pushing back the tight bowler hat with my finger. I crack my finger joints and smack my lips, my mouth as dry as if I've been serving half a crew of sailors through the night. Again I think about Doughboy, the taste of him burns on my palate.

'And now?'

'You go up to Nisse's Eva and pick up the pastries and the cake.

I'll stow the other stuff. The sheets, the bands, the runners, the porcelain and the pastries have to fit inside the coffin.'

'Where's the body?'

'By St Eriksplan. The caretaker is called Ola Petterson. Let's get moving so we don't get caught in that.'

I follow the direction of Lundin's gnarled, snuff-yellow finger, raising my eyes to the black-grey clouds building up overhead. I grunt and Lundin limps off. I cross Roslagsgatan and pant my way up the hill towards the bakery in Ingemarsgatan. Cold air tears at my throat. Eighteen months have made me forget how badly a proper hangover can floor a bloke.

Under the sign of the golden bun outside the bakery lies a knee-high, tousled crossbreed of some kind, trembling with cold. The bitch has a suppurating wound across her nose. She whines and shakily gets to her feet when I hold out my hand. I show her I don't have any food. While I'm scratching behind her ear, I peer in through the shop window. There's a pleasant smell of freshly baked bread.

On one side of the brown wooden counter, on the black and white floor, is a jumble of tables and chairs. On the counter are slanted copper troughs of biscuits and rows of pastries. A variety of loaves stick out their noses from the shelves behind the counter, like the tips of shells in an ammunition store.

I straighten up. Just as I'm about to go in through the door, emblazoned with the words PASTRIES, A VARIETY OF TARTS, NAME-DAY CAKES, a little girl comes darting along. She's wearing dirty woollen tights and, just like the little maid I met outside Långholmen Prison, she's folded her wool socks over the top of her worn boots. Her scarf, knitted from all kinds of cast-offs and snippets, flaps by colourfully as she slinks in just ahead of me. I grunt and catch the door just before it closes.

'Five öre's worth of pastry crumbs, please!'

The little girl raises herself onto her toes, exposing her worn soles, and holds up her coin over the countertop. Apart from Nisse's Eva we are the only people in there.

Nisse's Eva has just the sort of chubbiness that a cheerful baker's wife should have, and her cheeks are red. There's a little flour speckled over the sleeves of her black dress. She looks at me with big green eyes.

'Can you wait a moment, Kvisten?'

'I should think so.'

It's hot in there. I take off my bowler and run my hand over my short hair. Nisse's Eva scrapes the crumbs out of some empty baking trays, filling a newspaper cone and handing it to the girl, who receives it with a curtsy. The baker's wife turns to me, mopping the sweat on her brow with the arm of her dress.

'How can I help you, Kvisten? Looking very gloomy today.'

'Lundin's order.'

'Is that so. Did you bring payment?'

'I assumed it would be billed.'

'Lundin already has twenty cakes in our books! You'll have to tell him, Kvisten, he has to come in and pay up without delay.'

'I will.'

Eva disappears through a door behind the counter, returning before long and lining up the order in front of me. The cake is decorated with the initials of the dead man, a master mechanic. The pastries are wrapped in black silk paper with tasselled ends, and decorated with crucifixes and pictures of the Redeemer. I nod, and Eva packs it all into cartons. Outside, the rain starts falling against the window.

'Maybe you haven't seen our new electrified cash register, since you've been gone so long?'

'Have to be another time. In a hurry.'

'But it's right here. A Patterson. From America. It won't cost you anything to have a look.'

The baker's wife pushes over the cartons and gestures towards the machine at the other end of the counter.

'Another time.'

Nisse's Eva pulls a sour face, I take the cartons under my arm, the doorbell tinkles, I'm back in the street. The rain is now interspersed with large, wet snowflakes melting against the cobblestones. The street cur has abandoned the bakery and is lying in the middle of the right-hand lane of the road. Possibly she was on her way to seeking shelter somewhere, but gave up halfway. I whistle for her, her head moves sluggishly. For a fraction of a second her brown eyes meet mine, then she dismisses me. I hunch my head between my shoulders and continue down the hill.

Lundin meets me at the car with a brass candelabrum in each hand. Carefully I put the bakery cartons in the wooden casket, leave the carrying straps on top and close the lid. Lundin closes the doors.

'Nisse's Eva wants to be paid.'

'They're taking it in vodka.'

'Shall I bring it up to them?'

'I'll do it.'

'I have to make a call.'

'Long distance?'

'Police station.'

'Please do. I'll add it to the bill.'

I dig out the cigar case from my inside pocket, open the lid, fiddle with a Meteor, bite off the end and get it going. The black windowpanes of the laundry are staring at me from the other side

57

of the street. They're trying to tell me something, I'll be damned if I know what. My breast fills with sorrow.

The foyer of the undertaker's consists of a desk, a couple of dusty plants as tall as a man and a telephone mounted on the wall. When the cool voice of the telephonist answers, I ask for the police station, and then, when I get to the next operator, the smuggling unit: 'This is Chief Constable Hessler, how can I help you?'

'Open your mouth wide and swallow when you're told.'

For a moment there's a silence, apart from the faint voices from crossed lines.

'H-Harry…?'

'Have you met someone else, Hessler? I'll get jealous if you have!'

Lundin shuffles out of the refrigerated mortuary with a couple of vodka bottles in his arms. The ration book allows for extra supplies of booze at funerals, and he often takes a part of his payment in vodka, which he sells on. He keeps the bottles in a child's coffin in there. I think he does it on purpose, to stop me helping myself. He disappears outside. Over the door is a wall hanging embroidered with the words 'All Things in Their Place'.

'You mustn't call me here,' whispers the chief constable.

'What about at home, then?'

'Damn it, Harry!'

'I need your help.'

'I didn't even know you'd been released. I don't think I can—'

'That's what you said the last time, and in two seconds you were on your knees in my living room. Listen to me: on the eighteenth of September there was a murder in Roslagsgatan. The victim: Beda Johansson. The alleged perpetrator is her son, Petrus Johansson.'

'That's a completely different unit. I don't know what they're working on down there.'

'Where's he banged up? I was going to send him a postcard.'

'A postcard?'

'Put a call through to Lundin this afternoon. Vasa 7160.'

I hang up. Hessler responds best when you keep him on a tight leash. Lundin opens the door and calls out to me that I have to get in the car and drive. I press my bowler down over my head, fold my overcoat over my arm and walk out. It's stopped raining. The hearse coughs like an old man with TB.

I steer the heavy crate down Odengatan, past the library, and smarten up the pace on the incline by Vasa Church. At the yellow-striped pedestrian crossing, I stop for a nanny pushing a pram with a woven basket. She's wearing a starched hood of white fabric over her head, and under the almost full-length cape there's a hint of a grey uniform. I speed up again, muttering to myself: 'Only Ström saw them removing Beda's body, although it was in full daylight.'

I pick up more speed.

'People weren't around, because they were at work. Damn it, my bloody hand is killing me.'

'And then there's the letter.'

I get out Beda's letter from my pocket and let it flutter in the wind. I've already read it out to Lundin, over morning coffee.

'Couldn't it have been the jumble dealer who did it?' Lundin asks indifferently.

I sense him watching me out of the corner of his eye. I remove the cigar from my mouth. Behind us, the bells of Vasa strike ten times. The Plaza is showing a film called *Do Not Desert Me*. The undertaker tries to get rid of the pain in his left hand by flicking it up and down.

'What do you mean?'

59

Under one of Vasa Park's bare trees, a gang of ragged fellows are standing about in a tight cluster, trying to warm themselves up. Homeless, thirsting for compassion, work and vodka. Lundin keeps his eyes on them as we pass. He opens and closes his hand a few times. His accounts book lies in his lap.

'It may very well have been Ström who was paying up every month to secure Petrus's future: Beda did mention something to that effect in her letter. You've heard the rumours. Maybe he'd had enough of shelling out for the boy.'

'All the talk about that damned bloke eating rinds and crusts for breakfast while keeping ten thousand in banknotes and silver under a floorboard in his junk shop?'

'You know what I'm getting at.'

'People like to prattle, it's all a lot of blasted nonsense – that much is true at least.'

'Will you at least admit that they look similar. Blond, tall. The same sloping forehead.'

From Sigtunagatan, two horses pulling a wagon clatter into the traffic. I brake abruptly. Lundin puts a hand against the dashboard. The load is thoroughly lashed with coarse rope, without a tarpaulin, and so tall that it almost reaches up to the overhead tram cables. I crane my neck, put my foot down and overtake.

'There's one or two other tall blond blokes in this country. Wasn't the father supposed to be a sailor? Why else was she called Sailor-Beda?'

'Worth looking into. Ask someone to check the Parish Registry for the father's name.'

Lundin takes out a pen and makes a note in his accounts book. I say: 'There's a sister. Maybe she did it? What's the street number again?'

'I never heard anything about any sister. Park there on the other side of the square, by the haberdasher's.'

'How much money have I worked off so far?'

Lundin checks his gold watch, opens the book, spits on his pen and writes up the figures: 'One krona sixty.'

I change down and try to make sense of the house numbers, but soon give up. Behind me, the number 2 tram rings its bell by the stop. The sound reminds me of the porridge bell at the poorhouse. A bastard of a childhood I had.

Lundin and I are sitting at his kitchen table drinking afternoon coffee when the door of the funeral parlour tinkles. In my head, I can still hear the mourners' out-of-tune rendition of 'I Go towards Death Wherever I Go'. I'm leaning my kitchen chair back against the green wallpaper with the yellow floral pattern. Lundin spills some snuff over the tablecloth. There's a sighing of pipes as someone uses the shared water closet on the stair landing.

Lundin winces slightly as he pushes back the chair and stands up. He thumps his fists a couple of times against his legs, and then chops his left hand up and down in the air. As soon as he's disappeared into the front of the shop, I take the bottle of Kron and pour another tot into my coffee cup. I spin the contents around, then knock back the warmth.

'Yes, he's here all right,' I hear Lundin say. The floorboards creak as he limps back.

In front of Lundin's desk waits a woman of short stature, her hands clasping a handbag made of imitation crocodile skin. Under the beret, her full red head of hair frames a square-hewn face with a broad, mannish chin more or less like that Italian on the balcony, whose name I've forgotten – although, come to think of it, I'm not sure he has quite so full a bosom. It's rising up and plunging down in time with her breathing.

The firmly tightened belt of her coat makes her hips swell. Her skin is pale and waxy, but her cheeks are flushed as if she pinched them before coming inside. I'd say she's a good way past forty.

'Mr Kvist?'

She has a deep voice, which seems to emanate from the bottom of her sturdy body.

'In person.'

I try a smile: 'And who do I have the honour of meeting?'

Her bottle-green eyes narrow into a squint, and she takes one hand off her handbag to push a lock of red hair behind her left ear.

'Miss Johansson. Elin Johansson.'

'And how can I help, Miss Johansson?'

'It would be enough if you kept your nose out of my affairs.'

She spits the words from her unpainted lips, and raises one of her bright-red eyebrows defiantly.

The flush spreads over her face. I straighten up and insert my thumbs into my waistcoat.

'What do you mean?'

'I can understand that might be difficult, bearing in mind the width of the nose in question, but I'd be grateful.'

There's a dash of ridicule in her green eyes.

'What the hell are you saying to me?'

'Cursing and fighting, that's all you blokes are good for.'

I take my thumbs out of my waistcoat and form my hands into fists. The woman stares intently at me. There are not many who can hold my gaze for more than a few seconds.

'I don't quite understand…'

'Hardly surprising.'

'Are you calling me stupid?'

'You said it yourself.'

'I've been all around the world and I've seen a thing or two.'

'Such as?'

She's certainly mouthy, that damned woman. I rock back and forth on my feet and think it over.

'For example, did you know that there's a sort of edible rubber in America now? They give it all sorts of sweet flavours. You put a piece in your mouth and chew it without swallowing, and the taste stays in your mouth for at least ten minutes but it gives you no satisfaction at all. Did you know that?'

'Every other ragamuffin is chewing gum these days.'

'I'll be damned.'

'My turn: did you know that I have a purchaser of the laundry opposite, who wants to renege on the agreement because a certain violent type, also drunk, and according to people in these parts almost certainly you, assaulted this said purchaser last night?'

That damned delivery man with his broken pocket watch. Didn't I toss him fifteen kronor so he'd forget about the whole thing? I forget things all the time, completely free of charge.

'Kullberg is telling an untruth.'

'And yet you know his name? And you have a bruised eye to back his story up?'

Elin takes a step forward in the little foyer, and leans over the desk. There's a faint waft of pickled herring.

My heart rate picks up, and at last my brain engages: 'Johansson? A relative of Beda and Petrus? Are you the daughter?'

'I managed without her when she was alive, and I'll manage just as well without her now she's dead. But I'm warning you, my dear sir, I work at Standards corner and I can be here in five minutes. From now on you'll leave Mr Kullberg well alone.'

'Beda was…?'

She interrupts: 'You've gone too far.'

I recoil when the shrill tone of the telephone cuts into our exchange. I stare at my visitor. She has those eyes in common with Beda.

'I should like to have a word with you.'

'And I'd like you to leave me and my buyer in peace.'

Miss Johansson's mannish chin is set firm. She nods firmly. Behind me the telephone is ringing again, and I hear Lundin's tottering steps approaching.

The woman turns towards the door in the same moment that Lundin answers. I raise my voice: 'Listen to me, damn it, I just want to talk to you for a moment.'

Awkwardly I reach out towards her back.

'Keep your dirty paws off me. Goodbye.'

She hisses her farewell across her shoulder, as if she had just seen a black cat crossing her path. The doorbell tinkles. Through the soot-stained windows of the funeral parlour, I see her lolloping off briskly in a southerly direction. Before I know it, her red hair and sturdy posterior disappear down Roslagsgatan.

'I'll be damned.'

I root around in my pockets for a cigar as I walk towards the door. I grasp the handle.

'Constable Hessler wants to talk to you.'

I turn around. Lundin is holding the receiver of the wall-mounted telephone. I peer out into the now-empty street. Dusk has already started falling. I make a grunting sound, then take the telephone.

'It's me.' Hessler sounds out of breath.

'I know that.'

'I'm calling about Petrus Johansson.'

'And there I was thinking you wanted to invite me for supper at the Grand Hotel.'

'Damn it, Harry, I'm trying to do you a favour.'

'Well?'

'He's a maniac.'

'Right?'

'He's been placed in a lunatic asylum. Lindström, the senior physician at Konradsberg, signed the order.'

I pick up the notepad from my pocket and dab the end of my pen against my tongue.

Hessler reads out loud: '"Johansson suffers from imbecility and homosexuality. Further, the patient displays various traits of hysteria, largely on the basis of hereditary factors." Do you have any idea what that means?'

For a moment I'm overwhelmed, standing there with the notepad pressed against the wall.

'Anything else?'

'That's the thing…' Hessler clears his throat at the other end of the line. 'There's nothing else in the investigation file. No proper examination of the crime scene, no pathologist's report, no documents from the court. Apart from the senior physician and Johansson, there are no names mentioned at all. As far as the justice system is concerned, Johansson only exists as a couple of lines written on a pre-printed form.'

'You're as pale as a damned shroud.'

I've just hung up, and Lundin stands there, stooped, rubbing his bloodless, twig-like legs while watching me. I put my notepad in my pocket and pick up Dixie's lead. She wags her tail with delight.

'Something smells rotten here and for once it's not one of your blasted corpses.'

'What are you driving at, my brother? This is a businesslike operation, I follow the health regulations rigorously.'

'Did you know they're keeping Petrus locked up in Konradsberg?'

'Not a day too soon. Lunatics should be kept in asylums.'

'And the filth never even investigated the murder?'

'What was there to investigate? A witless whoreson kills his own blessed mother. Happens all the time in America, Bruntell with the Kodak told me.'

'What the hell would a shopkeeper know about that?'

I head for the door with Dixie.

'I need a hand with a couple of coffins; tomorrow morning you have to pick up a boy at the stiff-house.'

'Tomorrow I'm all yours.'

'Sounds like a good line for a movie. I actually also need your help today.'

The door closes behind me. It's got even colder. I pull out my Viking watch from my pocket. It's five to three. Not much daylight left. Outside Beda's old laundry a couple of girls are playing hopscotch. In the doorway to the right stands a young woman without a hat, wrapped in a grey coat with shoulder pads. She is watching them, holding a lit filter cigarette between her thin fingers.

There aren't many cars or carts in evidence, and Dixie and I can calmly cross Roslagsgatan while I bite the end off a cigar. I cup my hands around my eyes and try to peer inside the darkened laundry. Bearing in mind the shortcomings of the police investigation, I wouldn't mind taking another look.

I miss the constant mist outside when the hot steam of the laundry tubs hits the cold air in winter, and then also the old woman herself with her toothless smile and her warm heart. She always had a friendly word on offer, even for someone as queer as me.

'Standing there smoking for everyone to see? And nothing on your head either!'

I turn around. A young man is holding the young woman in the grey coat by the elbow. He's a short bloke, wearing brown plus fours. There's an empty pack of Bridge cigarettes between them on the pavement. There's a slapping sound as he hits her face with the bony back of his hand, and the woman's nose springs a leak. A scarlet droplet flies through the cold November air and lands in one of the chalked hopscotch squares.

The rhythmic jumping of the girls stops abruptly. Dixie puts her head on one side. The woman draws breath. Blood drips onto the grey lapels of the coat, melting into the fabric. The man raises his hand again. One of the girls hides behind a friend.

'That's enough.'

The young man stops himself; his eyes meet mine. I strike a match and light my cigar. The woman flushes, covering her nose. The man opens the door so fiercely that the handle crashes into the wall, and then pulls her into the stairwell. I take another deep puff, and cough. He should have used the flat part of his hand if he had to hit her. It reduces the risk of mess.

The normal sounds of the girls' play start to come to life again. One of the girls squats in front of Dixie and cocks her head too. Another one looks first at me, then at the pack of cigarettes on the pavement. I nod at her.

The bells of Stefan Church up in Vanadislunden and Johannes Church strike six times in unison as I walk two blocks down Roslagsgatan. Dusk is falling quickly now.

The door leading into old man Ström's shop needs no greasing: it glides open without a sound. A light bulb in the ceiling spills a white luminescence across a floor stained with street dirt and rat droppings. It smells of small beer, dust and poverty. I call out a couple of times before the bearded face of the jumble dealer peers at me from behind a batch of wooden crates and rag rugs.

'What're you after, Kvisten?'

Ström is holding a unica box of banknotes and coins in his hands. The jumble shop is a mess of piles and stacks of all kinds of rubbish. There's no cash till in the proper sense of the word, apart from the one he's holding.

'Good to see that the house pixie's at home.'

I take a puff and blow a jet of smoke at the ceiling.

Ström looks timidly at me, but summons up some courage: 'Don't yell. I'm hung-over today from the party. Didn't open until eleven.'

He smacks his lips and swills the tobacco juice around in his mouth. As far as I've heard, the jumble dealer sleeps on the floor at the back of his shop wrapped in a couple of layers of newsprint and rags.

'Is that so.'

'Why are you out and about, then?'

'On my way to Nyström to see if he trims dogs.'

Ström sniffs loudly.

'I heard that the little one has to have a drink of porter every morning.'

'You were the last to see Petrus?'

Ström puts down the unica box on a pile of wooden crates, pulls out a handkerchief and blows his nose with a trumpeting sound. When he's done he folds it and tucks it into his trouser lining. Outside, the number 6 rattles past. Somewhere in the house above us a woman can be heard; I can't tell if she's laughing or crying.

'I handed in my coat to be washed before winter set in.'

I get out my notepad and turn a few pages. Dixie growls at the back of her throat and tugs on her leash. Something is moving behind a box filled with nails that Ström has straightened. Probably a rat.

'To Petrus? On the 17th?'

'Petrus was taking care of everything at the end. Customers and the washing. After closing for the day he'd bring home a food box from the Restaurant NORMA, or tinned soup.'

'Did he manage all that?'

'He was slow, but it seemed to go all right.'

'And there was nothing unusual about that day?'

Ström closes his eyes: 'I also handed in a shirt with lingonberry stains on it. There're bloody loads of lingonberries this year. I don't usually take shirts to the laundry.'

'I mean unusual about Petrus?'

'No, he was giggling away, working hard. He signed to me that I should write my own receipt. Couldn't do it himself, couldn't read either. Everything was the same as it always was.'

For a moment I reflect on what Lundin said this morning. About the tall jumble dealer in front of me possibly being Petrus's father. I had to admit there were certain similarities.

'You said he killed her with an iron.'

'A stone.'

'What do you mean?'

'He killed her with a stone from her old mangle.'

'Before you said it was an iron.'

Ström raises a beer bottle to his lips, takes a couple of gulps, then lowers the bottle into a vat of soapy water where he washes and sorts his empties. After sucking the last few drops out his moustache, he goes on: 'It was a stone.'

'How do you know?'

'The police told me. I went back the day after to pick up my clothes.'

'What did the copper look like?'

'Nothing special. Like any old bloke. Skinny.'

'No uniform?'

'Not when I saw him.'

'So how do you know he was a policeman?'

'What else would he be?'

'Did you see when she was brought out, or when they took Petrus away?'

'From a distance. I heard someone yell out, and I stuck my nose out of the door. I saw them putting Petrus in the car.'

'At what time?'

'Around half one, maybe.'

'Do you know if anyone else saw?'

'No, there was a couple standing outside Lundin's, but they weren't from around here, I don't think. I went over to Bruntell's to ask if anyone knew what was going on, but no one had heard about it. What are you fishing for?'

'Nothing.' I lick my aniline pen and make a couple of notes in my book, in purple.

'Are you playing detectives, Kvisten?'

Ström peers at me. I feel like a copper, standing there with notebook in hand. Only the sodding brass is missing. I shiver with distaste, then, with a nod, pull Dixie towards the exit. Ström holds the door open for me: 'If you're buying porter for the mutt, I could do with one myself.'

I turn around. He's an arselicker if ever I saw one, old man Ström. I clench my fists.

'If you haven't spilled the whole truth to me, I'll be back to kick your arse again. And this time I'll drag you up on the roof first.'

His grin fails. White-faced, the jumble dealer backs into his shop and closes the door.

While Nyström reluctantly works Dixie over with a cut-throat razor and scissors, I cross the street to the cigar shop. The widow Lind has been replenishing my supply of Meteors for over ten years. Almost for as long there's been a black molly cat sitting on the first step. As always I get her purring by tickling behind her ear. I think she recognises me. The little bell over the door tinkles warmly as I step into the gloom of the little shop.

I'm enveloped by the smell of fresh tobacco. In one corner, a fire is blazing in a square ceramic burner, soot marks running across the ceiling at the top by the joist. A metallic-green winter fly shimmers in the half-light, buzzes over the glass counter, on which a brass cigar cutter lies next to piles of newspapers and stacks of postcards, continues along the side wall with its enamelled plates of beaming, curvaceous blondes and perky young men advertising Gillette razors, or various magazine covers and cigar brands.

On the wall behind the little glass counter, the shelves are almost empty, but five sturdy knots of tobacco trail down from hooks in the ceiling. Under the glass are lighters, pipe cleaners, tobacco pouches and penknives, all in separate compartments with handwritten price tags. On the cash till the proprietress has taped up a sign: SHOP FOR SALE, BUSINESS CLOSING DOWN.

The widow Lind comes out of the back room of the shop. She's a short, square woman with substantial hips and a heavy bust. Numerous fair-coloured bristles sprout from her chin. She wipes her hands on her striped apron and gives me a broad smile. A couple of top teeth are missing. I touch the brim of my hat. Without even asking she digs out a box of a hundred cigars.

71

I count out seven kronor and put the coins on the counter. It feels good to be home.

'Closing down, are we?'

I gesture at the till, take the box of Meteors and tuck it under my arm. The old woman's smile fades.

'I've done my bit. My pains are getting worse… parsley water and rose hips don't help me no more. Or aspirin powder neither.'

'Sorry to hear it.'

The doorbell goes, saving me from the outpouring that usually follows whenever the question of the widow's aches and pains comes up. Instead, a foetid smell settles over the little room. A bearded vagrant walks in, hat in hand. The soles of his shoes are fixed with metal wire. He bows slightly.

'God bless you, Missus Lind.'

His yellow teeth glow in the midst of his beard when he smiles. The widow nods half-heartedly, keeping her eyes on the cigar cutter on the counter.

The vagrant snatches up a cigar stump from the ashtray and stuffs his corncob pipe with the tobacco. The fly starts buzzing through the air again.

'God bless you, missus,' the vagrant repeats, retreating into the street.

Clucking thoughtfully, the widow Lind straightens the piles of newspaper in front of her and wipes the dust from the cash till.

'This is a good shop I'm selling. Kvisten should think about taking it on himself. So he won't need to run about harryin' impoverished poor things from mornin' to night.'

I push up my hat with my finger and raise my eyebrows.

'How much you asking?'

'Twelve hundred. The stock's not been fully inventoried yet, but there should be goods there for a good few hundred.'

'Is the stock included in the price?'

'Naturally.'

'Turnover?'

'About two hundred a day. A little less at the start of the week, but the nearest cigar shop is a long way down Sveavägen.'

'There's one next to the Metropol.'

'That closed about a year ago. Not for you to know. You've been away, haven't you.'

The doorbell goes again, Nilsson, the sheet-metal worker who lives in my apartment building, comes in. His trousers are shiny with dirt and stiff as a pair of drainpipes. We greet one another and he buys five grams of lip snuff. I spit on my pen and scrawl down the figures in my notepad.

'Will you shift at all on the price?'

'It's already a good proposition, and there's many who's interested. You can rely on the regular clients. I'd recommend it, naturally.'

'Can I think about it?'

'There's a man by the name of Wång, a sea captain with a family, who's favourably inclined. I gave him a week to sort out the financials, but Kvisten can have until Wednesday morning. If you are quicker than Wång, the shop is all yours to do what you will with. Kvist's been loyal to me through all the years. And surely it's time for a new start.'

That's the same day Doughboy's released. I tighten my tie with my free hand and push out my chest. I look around. A blond, blue-eyed youth stares down at me from one of the advertising signs. He's wearing a bow-tie and a knitted tennis jumper, holding a filter cigarette between his fingers. There's no dirt under this lad's fingernails.

'Two hundred kronor per day, did you say?'

73

'Towards the end of the week.'

I make a quick calculation and stay there a moment, a ridiculous grin on my face. Fourteen hundred a week and a new tie every Saturday.

I've worked myself to the bone in all the ports of the world, I've been a fire watchman, I've been a so-called sandwich man while waiting to be enlisted in San Francisco, and I've thumped countless people in the gob for money, but I've never been a till rat. I give the widow a sparkling smile and touch my hat before turning around.

Still with a big grin plastered over my face I step outside into Roslagsgatan. It has grown colder; darkness has fallen entirely. Paraffin lamps have been lit in the windows above Nyström's salon, and the ceiling light is on. An image of Doughboy in one of those knitted tennis jumpers flashes through my mind as I walk down the street. He could mind the cash register and deal with the customers while I sat in the back doing the accounts, solving crosswords and sharing the odd porter with Dixie. Unfortunately I have no idea at all how to lay my hands on twelve hundred kronor in the next six days.

'God bless you, Mister Kvist,' I mumble to myself to see how it feels, then I push the door handle of Nyström's barber shop. Dixie's claws are scrabbling among the clumps of hair on the floor. I go inside and squat next to her. Her characteristic beard and long eyebrows are in full view once again. Pleased, she licks my hand.

'Already back for a second cut? Want to give the stubble a bit of a polish?'

Nyström, tall and gaunt with his bushy eyebrows and a cigarette always stuck in his weak mouth, smiles, sending his ash plummeting over his white barber's coat. Involuntarily I clench my fists. He's got a nerve to be poking fun at my prison haircut. There was a time when people practically stood to attention and held their breath when I opened the door. But I just grunt by way of an answer, take Dixie's lead and straighten up.

'What do I owe you for clipping the dog, plus a jar of Fandango?'

I pay up without a word and leave with Dixie. The number 6 tram ploughs through the dark afternoon in a sea of green sparks from the power lines. I thread the leash around my wrist and button up my overcoat. Together, we stroll back towards the flat. As we amble along I think about the piece of skirt who came storming into Lundin's office earlier today.

'Elin Johansson.'

I quicken my steps until Dixie's leash is pulled tight behind me. In the decade that I knew Beda she never once mentioned her daughter. Only now has it come to light that she works at Standards, just a few blocks to the south.

'I wonder how the hell things were between them.'

A harried-looking co-minister, his fingertips stained blue with ink, shows me the way to August Gabrielsson's diocesan home, in the shadow of the Katarina Church's mighty dome opposite a beer café known as the Stone Angel at the east end of Högbergsgatan.

'The rector is always up before the crowing of the cock, and usually he'll take a nap before supper, but he should have woken by now. You said you are old friends?'

The co-minister glances at me for the fifth time. I kill my Meteor with the heel of my boot and quicken my pace.

'Been a long time since we saw each other.'

'He still has the calling.'

'We met during his time as a naval chaplain.'

The additional information that Gabrielsson once saved my young life in Buenos Aires at a time when I was almost going under on account of my self-denial, I keep to myself. Since then he's helped me in times of need on a number of occasions. I must owe him a couple of hundred but what the hell. If I only manage to bag the tobacco shop, I can pay him back.

'I see, I see. Here it is.'

Someone has carved a large swastika into the wooden door. The knocker gives off a hard, jagged sound. The steps come closer. The co-minister removes his hat. I leave mine where it is. The maid is wearing a dark-blue dress with a white pinafore. She holds a large key in one hand. She curtsies slightly and throws me a furtive glance.

'Good evening, little Karin. Say, has the rector woken up? He has a visitor, an old friend.'

'Certainly he's awake. If the gentleman could wait in the hall, I'll go and see. What was the name?'

'Kvist.'

'Come inside, Mr Kvist.'

The spacious hall is lined with brown wallpaper. Running along the back wall is a storage crate for firewood. There's a good cooking smell, probably game, maybe a casserole. I remove my coat and hat and hang them up. At the same time as the bell in the steeple strikes the quarter-hour, I pull the comb through my damned Långholmen stubble. My bloody hair won't lie down on my scalp, even after I've slathered it with half a handful of Fandango.

'The rector will see you in the drawing room.'

The maid gestures towards the first door on the left. I nod by way of thanks and take a deep breath before pushing the door open. I'm attached to Gabrielsson but he has a tendency to engage in boring topics of conversation. I walk through the passage into the drawing room.

An irate electric whining from upstairs fills the whole room and even drowns out the ticking of the white Mora grandfather clock in the corner. The room is sparsely lit. The walls are lined with plentifully stocked bookcases. In front of the windows facing onto Högbergsgatan are two settees, each placed on a large rug. The angry whining stops abruptly.

'Would you be kind enough to turn on the light, Harry, so I can have a good look at you?'

I can hardly make out the person lying in the sofa at the far end of the room, but there's no mistaking the soft timbre of his voice. I fumble over the wall until I find the Bakelite switch. The electrified chandelier hanging from the ceiling wakes up with a click.

The room measures at least five by six metres. In the middle, by another door, is a small altar for engaged couples who wish to tie the knot in private but still have a religious ceremony. It's covered in green fabric.

'Thank you, Harry.'

With a tired sigh, Gabrielsson grips the back of the sofa with his large hand, and pulls himself up. The settee, rather than the old sod himself, moans as he swings his black trouser legs over the side and gets up on his feet. He's a beanpole of a bloke, his hair almost as white as his dog-collar.

His handshake is firm. He glances at my miserable hair but he has the sense to withhold comment, gesturing at a big floral-patterned armchair. I take a seat. It's too hard. The whining from upstairs resumes. Gabrielsson raises his voice: 'That's Aunt Gerda. She's been given an electrified sewing machine.'

'Sounds like a mosquito on a motorised bicycle.'

77

'What can I do for you?'

'A good friend of mine has ended up in Konradsberg after his mother's passing away in September. I have to find out who the father is, or if he has any other living relatives.'

'Someone in my congregation?'

'No, he was the proprietor of the Roslag Laundry round my way, in Sibirien. Petrus Johansson.'

'Date of birth?'

'The mother's name was Beda. She died on the eighteenth of September. Her boy is about the same age as myself. Deaf and dumb to boot. I promised her I'd look after him.'

Gabrielsson notices the gravity in my voice.

'Should be enough. Let me go and make a telephone call. Would you like a cup of coffee?'

'Thanks, I already had one.'

Gabrielsson nods and the sofa creaks again when he stands up. He stops: 'You're a reliable man, Harry. If you have ever failed in your promises it's on account of forces over which you had no control. I know you.'

I scrutinise the rug while the rector leaves the room with long strides. The whining sound from above stutters, then stops. I look around the room. No ashtrays.

Gabrielsson is back before long. He moves in an agile, alert manner, as if considerably younger than his actual age.

'Please do sit down. They'll ring back in a moment.'

'My thanks to you, Rector.'

'Helping you keep your promises is thanks enough, Harry.'

Gabrielsson sits on the sofa opposite. He crosses his legs.

'Stay for dinner. The housekeeper is making a delicious elk stew.'

'There was a fine smell in the hall.'

'Excellent!' Gabrielsson smiles and puts his hands together in his lap. 'Now tell me, it's been such a long time since we last saw one another! Are you keeping busy?'

'I have a mind to start my own business. A cigar shop further down the street's for sale. There's also talk of, what's it called, a comeback.'

'That's good. You know what I've always said…'

'A noble sport, a sport for gentlemen.'

'You have a good memory for a pugilist.'

'I don't know about that.'

'But you're still in the same line of work, I mean outside the ring?'

With a gracious smile he nods at my black eye. I shrug. Blackfrocks always have to stick their noses in, and you can't snarl at them either and tell them to shut their mouths.

'I saw the swastika on the door.'

Gabrielsson sighs and slides forward in the armchair.

'We're living in confused times. In one of their recent publications the Swedish National Socialist Party called me a lackey of the Jews.'

'Nothing but a bunch of girl scouts.'

'Quite the opposite.' Gabrielsson shakes his head with dismay. 'National Socialism is a spiritual plague, and the infection is sweeping across Sweden. Have you heard what they are preaching?'

'The only one I know has a bad stutter.'

'You see, it really is a contagion, of both a spiritual and a corporeal kind. My evangelical brethren in Germany have started referring to one's race as something just as indelible as sin.'

Gabrielsson gesticulates with his hands, quivering with rage.

'They're harmless.'

79

'Were you aware of the fact, Kvist, that they go after homosexuals?'

'Over there and over here as well.'

From the upper floor the sewing machine splutters to life again, angrier than ever. The sound stops abruptly, and then the aunt stamps on the floor. Both Gabrielsson and I look up at the ceiling for a moment. His cheeks are as red as winter apples. He catches his breath.

'When the day comes I know you will choose the right side. And that day will come, mark my words.' Gabrielsson twists his old hands in his lap. 'But there we are. Let us forget politics and go back to you. Do you have any contact with your family? Was it in North Dakota they were living, your wife and daughter?'

'Grand Forks. I sent them some money a few Christmases ago.'

'Is that all?'

'How should I know?'

'What do you mean?'

A telephone trills at the back of the house. Someone picks it up on the third ring. We hear steps approaching, and there's a knock on the door. Gabrielsson keeps his eyes on me as he leaves the room. I root about for a checked handkerchief and mop my forehead. My stomach is rumbling.

'I asked Hildur to set the table for one more person,' he says when he comes back a minute later. He's holding a sheet of paper in one hand, and in the other a pair of round spectacles with a thick frame.

'Many thanks.'

Another creak of the sofa as Gabrielsson sits down.

'Right, let's have a look.'

I get out my notebook and dab the aniline pen against my tongue. Gabrielsson puts on his spectacles and reads: 'Petrus

Valter Johansson, born on the twenty-sixth of August, 1902, at Södra Children's Hospital, son of Beda Johansson, father unknown. The closest relative is an uncle who emigrated in 1898, and a half-sister named Elin.'

'That damned woman I met.'

'Be careful with your words, Harry.'

'Surely the years you spent as a naval chaplain have hardened you somewhat. No one else?'

I make notes.

'Not as far as one can see. Has been resident in Roslagsgatan from 1903. In 1915 he was admitted to the Asplunden Institute for the Deaf, Mute and Blind.'

'What's that?'

'The school behind the Garrison Hospital.'

'Sounds expensive, doesn't it?'

'I assume he was admitted on a non-fee-paying basis, probably at the cost of the royal household or by use of the school's own charitable funds. He only remained at the school for two years. After that he was sent back home.'

'Is it not clarified there who paid his fees?'

'Maybe the school could help you with that.'

'I'll have to pay them a visit.'

Wearily I tap my pen against my notebook. The trail is twenty years old. Not much of a trail.

'This seems important to you.'

'I made a promise.'

I hear the grandfather clock in the corner tense its muscles, only for its ringing to be lost in the outpouring of Katarina's bells. We wait for her to finish. Gabrielsson takes off his spectacles and sits back in his armchair.

'How old is your daughter?'

I hold my breath. I knew he'd come back to it and start poking about. On the way here I was worrying about my debt, but this is even worse. I look down at my battered fists in my lap and silently count my knuckles.

'Surely you must know, Rector – you officiated at the christening.'

'Age withers, memory fails.'

'She was fifteen in September.'

'So she must have been confirmed by now.'

'I don't know how they do it over there.'

My heart is thumping as loud as that church bell just now. My knuckles turn white, the scars on them turn crimson as if I'm drunk.

'Send her a line. Explain why you have not been in contact.'

I mumble, unsure of whether he can hear: 'I'm sure people also gossip over there on the other side of the Atlantic. She knows well enough where her old man is.'

I rummage about in my pockets. Whenever I'm with the rector I always seem to shrink into a shamefaced confirmation candidate. It puts me in a bad mood.

'I'm afraid I've forgotten my cigars and have to be on my way home. The widow who owns the cigar shop closes at six.'

'And dinner?'

'Another time.'

Gabrielsson turns around and looks at the Mora clock.

'Promise to come back. We can talk about old reminiscences.'

'From Buenos Aires?'

Gabrielsson's breathing seems to fail. He looks away. I save him: 'Next week, if that would suit?'

My knees click as I stand up. Gabrielsson follows my example. We go into the hall. I put on my coat.

'I want to thank you, Rector. You were a great help.'

'The first time we met you weren't much more than a midshipman. How long ago is that now?'

'Must be twenty years.'

'Must there still be a bottle on the table for us to put aside the formalities?' he says, then sighs when I answer with a grin:

'Rector, surely you must know where that can lead. But if you buy a jug for next week, we'll see.'

His self-assurance deserts him, then he recovers. 'It was just the once. Harry,' he whispers, reaching out and squeezing my arms. The old man's strength surprises me. Something glimmers in his eyes. For a few moments I just stand there, before I turn around and leave. There's a Meteor between my lips even before the heavy front door has had time to close. I bite off the end and spit out the tobacco flakes on the pavement. A match scrapes; my fingers tremble as I draw life into the cigar.

Light falls across the paving stones from the beer café, the Stone Angel, on the other side of the street. Along Högbergsgatan a brown autumn leaf is whisked along in the wind, as weightless as a lie. I turn up my collar. Keeping my cigar in my mouth, I pull the strap off my wallet and check its contents.

I need a proper dinner. I need a couple of drinks.

I need a bloody plan.

It ends up being more than a couple of drinks, and by the time I tumble out of the tram at the end of the line in Sibirien, it's past ten. I take out a quarter of contraband which has been tapped into a beer bottle. There's a plopping sound as I pull out the cork. The vodka glow swills around in my belly like burning cinders.

There's a light rain. I shuffle down Roslagsgatan. Darkened by moisture she cuts a furrow through the northern districts of the city. The streetlights are reflected in the cobblestones. A couple of black shadowy figures move along, hugging the house walls to avoid the rain and wind. The number 6 tram rattles back into the city, empty as a church on a hot summer's day.

A figure comes out of the shadows and walks into my field of vision. It's Wallin, a drinker. He walks up to me. When his daughter drowned herself in the sea about ten years ago, he started drinking openly, without any care, and they say he can smell vodka at a hundred paces. Life and death shook him up too hard. It can happen to the best of us.

The brim of his hat is dripping with rain, and translucent droplets are clinging to the worn fabric over the shoulders of his coat.

'Fancy a drop?' I say, offering him the bottle.

'Oh yes, certainly.'

Wallin snatches the bottle and takes a gulp. The vodka seeps from the corners of his mouth. He wipes his beard stubble with the sleeve of his coat.

'Damned weather we're having.'

Wallin passes back the bottle. He offers me his snuff tin but I shake my head.

'November.'

From an inner courtyard somewhere a dog starts howling, as if it's being beaten. On the other side of the street, Rickardsson passes with his collar turned up, on his usual evening walk.

He doesn't look in our direction. Wallin and I stand there drinking until the bottle is empty: 'Thanks for that, Kvisten.'

'Sometimes it's good to have a bit of company.'

Wallin keeps his balance, heading north. Only when I hear his door slam behind him do I remember that he works at Konradsberg Asylum. I should have asked him if he's seen Petrus.

I get out my notebook and scrawl down his name in sloping letters before continuing homeward. Halfway there the vodka slams into my skull like a fierce right-handed punch. My field of vision narrows, and before long it's as if I'm looking at the world through a porthole. I stumble, grunt to myself and lean against a house wall.

Screwing up one eye, I peer at Beda's old laundry in the brick building opposite my own. I look around. Roslagsgatan is as clean as a saucepan before Friday payday. A cat meows somewhere.

'Maybe Kvisten should have himself another little look.'

I'm slurring. I struggle up to my flat, find an old Fenix lantern, fill it up with paraffin and then go back outside. Like an old lamplighter I amble across the street in a tremulous circle of light. I press down on the door handle a couple of times, then lower the wick of the lantern and put it down on the pavement. I back off a bit and look around again.

No one's about.

'Harry Kvisten Kvist in a magnificent comeback,' I mutter, then take a deep breath, and hurtle towards the door, bracing myself with my shoulder. I hit it full force. The pain makes me close my eyes. There's a crashing sound as the wooden door frame splinters around the locking bolt, and before I know it I'm lying on the dusty floor of the laundry.

I crawl back on all fours and snatch up the lantern. The door closes with a slam. I sit with my back against it, knees drawn up to my chin, listening in the dark.

The laundry still has an ingrained smell of starch and lye. I let a minute or so go by before I get out a Meteor from my red-leather cigar case. I turn up the flame in the lantern, open the cover and light the cigar. I close my eyes, puffing away. After a few minutes I stand up and brush myself down, all the while swaying back and forth.

'Let's see, then.'

Petrus's old broom still lies there, flung in a corner. I lean it up against the wall, open the hatch in the counter and go through. When I hold up the lantern, the bars over the window form a faint striped pattern against the wall.

I follow the counter to the right until I reach a door. I open it and go through into the heart of the laundry. The smell of lye and soda gets even sharper.

In the middle of the room are four cement basins in a line, for soaking. They measure about a square metre each. Next to them are two large zinc vats on wheels. On a shelf along one of the walls are cartons of various chemicals, a couple of washboards and some old pressing irons.

I examine the irons carefully, turning them this way and that, but I find nothing unusual there. Nor do I see any sign of a stone mangle anywhere.

'Both Ström and Lundin were mistaken about that. Maybe that copper fed Ström a tall story.'

My voice echoes hollowly between the walls. I stumble through the premises, shining my lantern at both walls and floor.

'Nothing here except rat shit.'

My inebriation churns inside. I sigh heavily and gob on the floor. She wouldn't have liked that, Beda.

All of a sudden I recall an incident about a dozen years ago when I first moved here to Roslagsgatan: everything had gone to hell and I suppose in those days I was staring into the bottom of a bottle too often. Dead drunk, I had fallen asleep in a snowdrift and picked up a nasty lung fever. Every evening for two weeks, when everyone else had turned their back on me, Beda brought me some hot food and lit the ceramic stove before night set in. I don't know why. Maybe because I was bed-bound and had no choice but to listen to her nonsense.

I smear my gob with the sole of my shoe, walk out of the room and move closer to the cellar stairs. Keeping my handkerchief pressed to my nose, I descend to the sleeping area.

There's still a stink of old piss from the bucket I kicked over last night. I gag into the handkerchief and try to control my impulse to vomit.

My stomach calms down. For a few seconds I stare at the droplets of blood on the pillow before I lower my lantern and examine the floor. The zinc bucket rattles as I kick it under one of the beds. If this floor was ever covered in blood, it's all been cleaned up now.

I bend over one of the beds, then the other. I check the sheets and mattresses again but find nothing of interest.

The pipes sigh. I raise the lantern and look at the coarse cement wall. I reel as I take a step closer and put my hand against the wall. Something feels amiss; my heart leaps and skips a beat.

In the middle of the large damp patch around the pipes by the head end of the beds, I see a small hole in the porous concrete.

'I'll be damned.'

I put the lantern on the bed and open my penknife. The damaged wall does not put up much resistance. I cup my hand under the hole and flick out a small object with the tip of the knife.

A bullet.

FRIDAY 22 NOVEMBER

The sun still hasn't hauled itself up over the haughty brick façade of City Hall as I park Lundin's hearse on Norr Mälarstrand, but a couple of half-hearted rays are reflecting off the three golden crowns at the top of the tower.

In front of the yellow walls of Karolinska Institute, a street sweeper is slowly making his way along the pavement. The whispering sound of the broom against the paving stones is punctuated by the tread of his wooden-soled work boots. His blue eyes flash cheerfully under his cap when he catches sight of something outside the entrance to the morgue. He leans his broom against the cast-iron railing fence that surrounds the buildings, picks up a long cigarette butt and carefully inserts it into his trouser pocket to dry it out.

Shivering from my hangover, I light a fresh Meteor and stay at the steering wheel for a moment, smoking, my head thumping, missing Doughboy. He fills my life, he blocks out my miserable existence, and I can't think of anything else. Wherever I look I see that boy's eyes and I seem to have been swept up in an enchantment. Only once I know he really means those pretty words and solemn promises, smuggled to me by couriers on little bits of paper, will I be able to breathe easily again.

'Five days, that's nothing, get a hold of yourself, you silly bastard.'

My vodka-hoarse voice sounds pathetic. When blokes are crowded in with other blokes and their physical urges take charge, in prison or at sea or in a navvies' barracks, there's a certain way of seeing things; but this can change as quick as a flash once there are women in the frame. I've seen it more than once.

The heavy car door slams so hard that a homeless dog on the other side of the road scarpers with its tail between its legs. I cough to get some kind of lubrication into my bone-dry throat. I roll the gob around my mouth and finally let it fall between my black boots.

I drop the car keys into my trouser pocket and, at the same time, double-check that the bullet I dug out of Beda's wall last night is still there. I put on my leather gloves and stick the cigar in my mouth as protection against the smell.

I'm wearing a three-piece woollen suit with wide lapels and a white-collared shirt. I'm hoping that picking up the corpse this morning won't be too much of a messy affair.

The stiff-house is squeezed in between two hospital buildings down one of the wings. The entry telephone buzzes angrily. I have to pace about for a good few moments by the scarred green door before a bloke comes to open it.

'From Lundin's, you say? We have him in the locker. Please, come in, come in! Have you brought a cart with you?'

The man in front of me smiles, showing the snuff-blackened gaps in his teeth. He's wearing a grey caretaker's coat, stained with red. Gaunt, with long white hairs sprouting from his knotty fingers, and a chaotic pattern of thin veins covering his cheeks and nose.

'These days we're on four wheels,' I say, gesturing towards the hearse.

'And maybe a bit more horsepower?'

'Should be capable of carrying a load of your tenants to their graves, if push comes to shove.'

'But today you're only picking up one of them, is that right? Örjan Nilsson, fourteen years old, tram accident?'

'Correct,' I say, handing over the bundle of documents that Lundin gave me over morning coffee.

'Well come in, then,' says the caretaker and steps aside.

The smell of autumn is more noticeable indoors than on the outside. It reminds one of damp moss, old trees and rotting flowers. The caretaker rattles a bunch of keys, standing in front of a white-painted, peeling door with a sign on it, *Open Weekday Mornings 9–10*. He finds the right key. I breathe through my mouth. The door creaks.

'I hope you'll excuse us, sir. I can't remember ever having so many bodies here.'

I take a deep puff on my Meteor before clamping the cigar into my mouth once more, and taking a look around. The lockers are arranged down the long wall: rectangular doors with chrome handles, three up and ten across. The other side of the room is fully tiled in white.

From hooks hang various items of clothing and other belongings, bags and hats. Mostly old junk.

'In years gone by we were allowed to pile the corpses up along the house wall when it was below zero, but now they have to stay in here even when it gets overcrowded. We're under orders.'

The caretaker gestures at a double row of bunks running down the middle of the room. I have another puff, letting the smoke rinse every corner of my gob before expelling it from the corner of my mouth. I cough.

Those that have already been autopsied lie silent under their blood-stained sheets. Here and there, washed white skin can be seen sticking out from beneath the soft undulations of the material.

'They say he was run over by the number 5 on Karlbergsvägen. When they took him away they had to carry his brain along with them, swilling around in a bowl. No open coffin for him, you might say.'

I nod, letting my eyes skim over the dead. I recognise the swollen corpses of the drowned from my years at sea, shapeless piles of human flesh, green and black from decomposition, sometimes so far gone that it's difficult to see whether they were once men or women. Their hair is slicked back over their temples, always dark as if it never had time to dry properly. They spread their stench through the room. The combination of my hangover with the smell of corpses makes the hair on my arms stand up. I want to double up with nausea.

On the bunk to my right lies a suicide who was cut down from a rope, a purple necklace etched into her skin. On my left is an old woman, still dressed and in a foetal position as if she froze to death. I'm breathing shallowly, I start to gag.

The caretaker points at a locker in the middle of the room. Our steps echo desolately against the grey floor tiles. On the next bunk lie two naked men piled one on top of the other, as if someone had attempted a macabre joke. If so, then surely the caretaker's son would have to be the prime suspect. As far as I've heard, he stands outside the stiff-house in the evenings, selling craniums and other skeletal parts to superstitious old women, or exhibiting naked female body parts to his classmates for a backhander.

'No one said anything about a bowl.'

Revulsion is passing through my body like an icy northerly wind.

'What do you mean?'

'Lundin never mentioned anything about bringing my own bowl. Can I borrow one? For the brain?'

The caretaker smiles and puts his hands in his coat pockets, swaying back and forth on his feet.

'There's no need for a bowl. All the spill is sewed into the stomach once the doctor's done.'

I grunt with relief, and manage to take a couple of proper breaths.

'There's a fair amount of blood, isn't there? When someone gets their skull crushed?'

'You must know how people bleed from the head? I see you've been slugged once or twice yourself. A boxer, right? So, imagine the amount of fluid when the whole cranium collapses.'

'What about gunshot wounds? Do they bleed a lot?'

'Depends, but often not. Look here.'

We stop by a man of my own age. With a cleft palate under his blond moustache, he looks as if he's smiling slightly, as if he dared to grin at the face of the Grim Reaper in his last few tremulous seconds of life. Even in death, his young body looks hardened by physical labour; muscles are sharply chiselled into his pale pink flesh. His sex lollops halfway up his left thigh. I get warm about my ears. I grip hold of the bunk with my scarred hands, the nausea on the verge of overwhelming me. For some reason I feel a strong sense of identification with the dead man; possibly he's someone I've run into at some point.

'Do you know about Belzén in Birka, the smuggler further up the street? This is one of his boys. The police cut him down last night, down here on the quay.'

The hole in his almost square chest muscle is smaller than a shirt button. My little finger tingles.

'Sure, I know Belzén all right.'

I fumble through the memories inside my hung-over skull, but I don't get anywhere with the corpse in front of me. The caretaker nods thoughtfully.

'When the heart stops beating you don't get a lot of blood flowing out of a hole like that. More or less nothing. Not like having your head cave in on you, at least. Why do you ask?'

The caretaker rests his hand on the handle of one of the lockers, not far from the head of the dead man.

'It's good to know.'

'If I had a krona for every curious person I'd met, I'd be living in Solomon's palace by now. Anyway, here he is.'

The caretaker pushes the handle down; the bolt slides away without a sound, but the door screeches as it opens. With a whining sound the caretaker pulls out the gleaming stretcher, a slight bevelled edge all around it. The boy is swaddled in white, the sheet draped smoothly over the outline of his already rigid body.

'You want to reverse the car in?'

'No need. How much could he weigh?'

'I'll help you. You take the head end. You want a look?'

'I've seen corpses before.'

'Fourteen years old.'

'Still a bloody corpse.'

For a moment I think of Doughboy; the way he tastes. The dead boy was not many years younger. No, damn it, I don't want to see him. The old man laughs, a croaking sound. I grip the sheets with both my hands and close one eye when I get smoke in it. He doesn't weigh a lot, but he's ice cold and stiff in my arms.

The caretaker walks backwards and kicks the doors open with his wooden heel. The November sun has managed to drag itself over the top of City Hall, and now disperses its hazy light over the metropolis. The wind has picked up slightly. A few tired autumn leaves are rustling along the pavement. I fill my lungs with fresh, smarting air.

There's a thud when, with joint effort, we heave the boy's corpse into the back of the hearse.

Slowly I drive back to Sibirien with the fourteen-year-old boy and all the other junk rattling about there in the back. I go via St Erik Bridge and before long I'm passing the triangular square, Odenplan, in the middle of which stands Guido the Italian, with a bunch of balloons flying from his hand. In the sunlight, his dark, alert eyes look like globules of gleaming syrup. A couple of kids stand there, stooped over his suitcase, which is filled with firecrackers, poppers and bird whistles. My hangover has given me the hiccups; I swallow back a mouthful of sour bile and grimace, listening to the body in the back sliding across the floor as the number 15 tram screeches across the siding ahead of me and I step on the brake. The lad's head comes to rest against the driver's cabin with a slight thump. I fumble with a new cigar. Thinking about Gabrielsson, what he said about my daughter yesterday and how I should write her a letter and explain myself, I scoff out loud: 'Damned black-frocks, always sticking their noses in.'

I get the cigar going. Anyway the lass can probably hardly speak Swedish any more, and my English is not what it once was. I inhale deeply and blow a half-kilo plume of smoke into the driver's cabin. A pitch-black draught horse clatters to a stop next to the hearse, pulling large flatbed cart. The driver is standing on his board, pulling at the reins; the bit tightens, stretching the horse's mouth right back to its flat molars. She puts her ears back but obeys good-naturedly. Her body heat hangs like smoke over her back.

'Although Emma could probably translate for her at a pinch.'

I have another puff, then another. The almost empty tram passes and clangs its bell before the next stop. A telegram delivery boy, with his yellow free-tram pass between his teeth, disembarks with an agile leap while the tram is still moving, landing with both feet on the pavement before he runs off. The driver slaps the reins over the horse's back and I release the clutch.

I'm home in five minutes. I park outside the undertaker's, where Lundin is standing, polishing the shop window with an old sock and some turpentine. I wedge the cigar in my mouth and touch the brim of my hat.

Lundin smiles under his moustache: 'Briskly done. Whatever you lack in other departments, brother, at least you know how to dig in.'

'I do what I can.'

'Busy hands have no time for tomfoolery.'

'Oh really, how do you mean?'

'Well… You need help with the lad?'

'Hold the door open.'

Just as I open one of the back doors of the hearse, there's a high-pitched scream from the neighbouring house, some ten metres away. A yard cat puffs up its fur, the widow Lind on the other side of the pavement stops and removes a short cigar from her mouth, and a little girl with a greasy sandwich paper in her hand freezes to the spot.

The door of number 41 is thrown open and the Jewel comes streaming out into the street with nothing on her feet except her socks. Her hair is on end and her mascara's running down her cheeks. She throws her shawl on the dirty pavement, stretches up her arms at the sky, then doubles over for yet another piercing scream.

The door opens again, and behind her comes her square-shaped knot of a bloke. His eyes are bloodshot; he's in his shirt-sleeves. He scrabbles for the shawl and throws it over her as if catching a bird with a net. His rough arms envelop her waist. She stamps the ground and screams again. The bloke looks around and then picks her up and carries her back to the door. She wriggles in his arms.

Lundin removes his hat: 'Nothing for it but to knock up another white coffin.'

'Think so?'

'The child was frail from the very start.'

I inhale deeply and remember that time when Ida almost died from a cough when she was small. She had a close shave that time, and a few other times too, but the girl overcame it and struggled to her feet on the ninth count every time. I shudder with unease and push the memories back down into the darkness.

Lundin holds open the door to the undertaker's as I pick up the dead boy and haul him into the cool-room. By the time I come back, the funeral director has already poured coffee and a couple of morning drams in the kitchen at the back. He takes a sip of java and sucks the moisture out of his moustache.

'Our little ship's boy is buried tomorrow afternoon. North Chapel. Until then you're off duty, brother.'

I take the dram standing up to medicate against the hangover, swilling the glass in front of my second waistcoat button.

'I have a few things to get on with. Did you know that shrew who showed up yesterday was Beda's daughter? I'm inviting her for lunch.'

'Watch yourself with sparky women, remember how it went last time. That film star?'

'What the hell does that have to do with it?'

96

'Mine own familiar friend, in whom I trusted, which did eat of my bread, hath lifted up his heel against me.'

'That stupid old saw! What about us, we take our bloody breakfast together every day.'

'Unless you happen to be locked up.'

Lundin fills my glass with export-quality vodka and sits down on a kitchen chair with a grimace of pain. He gets out the accounts book from his pocket and slaps its binding a few times against his emaciated legs before thudding it on the table. With a snuff-dyed finger he finds my name under the letter 'K' and makes a couple of notes.

He hums to himself and looks up: 'Widow Lind's cigar shop is up for sale.'

'She mentioned as much.'

'How much?'

'Don't remember.'

I dig out my notebook from my inside pocket and give it to him. Somewhere in an apartment above, a couple of penetrating, off-key notes blast out from a brass instrument. It sounds like someone flung two wildcats into a bass tuba and left them to it.

'Are you listening?'

'What did you say?'

'I was wondering if these figures can be right. Twelve hundred including stock. Two hundred profit per day?'

'That's what the widow said.'

'The only figures you keep a careful eye on are the ones in your alcohol ration book.'

'It seems that people don't find me very convincing.'

'Perhaps they would if you stopped getting pickled all the time?'

'The numbers are right. I noted them down.'

'You don't have a nose for business, I always said that.'

I look up at the ceiling and knock back the second vodka. Lundin writes down a few numbers in his notebook and taps the end of his pen against the table, sweat glistening on his knotted brow.

'Twenty per cent of your profit until you've paid off your debt. And ten per cent from then on. So you don't have to rough up impoverished folk from dawn till dusk and end up back in a penal institution.'

My heart quickens. The horrible cacophony from upstairs finishes as abruptly as it started.

'It seems your neighbour, the occultist, bought himself a trumpet. When does the widow need the money by?'

'Wednesday morning.'

'No time today. How about you drive me to the bank on Monday and then we'll arrange the financing? I have to go in anyway, to sort out Rickardsson and his damned ten per cent cut.'

I stare at him as if I've seen a ghost. Without any expression on his face, he refills my glass for the third time in five minutes: 'Cheers to a decent business proposition! Now that you've come up in the world you have to stop drinking like a bloody fish.'

My head is reeling with all this news, and the schnapps too. I stumble up the flight of stairs to my flat, leaning heavily on the smooth-worn banister. Dixie spins around me, whining, but I push her off with my foot and hang up my coat and hat.

I stop in front of the hall mirror and stare at myself, mouth agape. The colour of my bruise ranges from dark purple to yellow. I get out a comb and try to arrange my stubble as best as I can. Then I clear my throat: 'Kvist, cigar shop proprietor. My friends call me Kvisten.'

I put away my comb and take out the bullet I dug out of Beda's wall last night instead. It's relatively undamaged, the shape and colour of an old blueberry. Possibly a 2.2. I hold it up so that it covers my right iris in the mirror. With a grin at my reflection I tuck it away in my trouser pocket. The cork mat creaks under my shoes as I go over to the oak desk and sit in the easy chair. When I pull out the big desk drawer it jams, and I have to rock it back and forth to get it open.

My scarred hands dive in and pull out a thick pile of letters, naval logbooks, testimonials and match summaries from *Boxing Monthly!* magazine, which I could never bring myself to throw away. There's also a bit of green cloth that I used to soak in sugar water and let Ida suck on – those were the Saturdays when I couldn't afford to give her anything better.

I find the three American letters that were posted almost twelve years ago. The last of them was posted from Arvilla, Grand Forks, North Dakota. My heart judders and my palms start to sweat. I don't have the strength to read it again; instead I just tear out a sheet of lined paper from my notebook and wet my pen against my tongue. I notice myself trembling with a sort of excitement as I scratch the words onto the paper:

> *Sibirien, Friday 22 November in the year 1935.*
> *Dear daughter, this letter is written by my own hand. The way things stand now I have my own cigar shop and so I hope in future I will be able to send you a bit of money now and then. I have seven decent suits and can wear a new one every day if I like. A man thinks of his loved one's even if it might not seem that way. Take care of your mother, she is a first class woman. If you cant read this letter you should ask her to read it to you.*
>
> *PS. I am inclosing a photograph.*

I read through the letter and put it in an envelope. Not a single spelling mistake. If I get a move on I can get down to Bruntell with the Kodak before the lunchtime rush.

I change into a clean white shirt and my Sunday suit from Herzog's Tailors. I spend an age dithering over whether to wear a waistcoat, seeing how I look with and without, but in the end I decide to simply button up the jacket to the very top.

With the letter in my inside coat pocket and Dixie's lead wrapped around my wrist, I shuffle down the stairs and go into Lundin's. I find him in the kitchen stooped over the classifieds in *Stockholms-Tidningen*. The coffee cups and schnapps glasses are still on the table. On the gas hob, a dented copper lid is rattling on a saucepan that occasionally gives off little puffs of steam. On the draining board is a keg of herring, ready to be cut up and fried.

'You have to put some make-up on my bruise.'

I notice that I'm slurring my words. Lundin gazes up at me with a giddy gaze and coughs. Outside in the yard, there's a racket when some snotty Friday truant climbs up on the dustbins to scale the fence into the next-door yard.

'Have to, do I? Why do people always expect to get something for free these days?'

'Bruntell's taking my portrait.'

Lundin points at the newspaper on the table.

'Listen to this, for example: "Girl asking those of better means for a little help with her teeth. Replies to *Poor*."'

'You're drunk.'

'Or this one: "Is there some humane person who wants to help two young people from going under? We lack even the basic necessities, don't have enough food to get us through the day, in fact we have nothing except the love we have for each other. We need help." Yes, so they do for all I know. But at least they can afford to pay for the advertisement.'

Lundin looks up from the newspaper with shiny, red-rimmed eyes: 'The make-up for the corpses is costly. I only use powder imported from France.'

'Put it in the book.'

The undertaker taps his snuff tin against the table a few times before he stands up with a sigh: 'Take a seat, then, you miscreant! I'll see to it that you're fairer than Queen Nefertiti.'

Losing his footing, he grips the edge of the table with bony fingers, his rangy body shaking for a moment, and I worry he's about to have an attack of his falling sickness. But he stays upright, and I let out a sigh of relief: I won't have to see him thrashing on the floor, foaming at the mouth like a hound of hell.

He straightens the lapels of his jacket and disappears into the kitchen. I sit on one of the wooden chairs, tipping it against the wall. The occultist next door to my flat starts tormenting his trumpet again, but after a few blasts he rounds off the performance with a prolonged, braying note. Dixie, who has placed herself under my chair, looks around in confusion.

Lundin returns with a brightly coloured make-up box. He opens it and makes his selection from brushes, pots of colour and powder. The pipes sigh when someone makes use of the water closet in the corridor.

'Last year I painted a driver from the brewery, who'd been kicked in the face by his horse. If I managed to make him presentable, I should be able to handle your mug.'

Squinting, he leans up close to my face. I feel his heavy breathing; the smell of schnapps, coffee and throat lozenges.

'But there's not much can be done about your nose, and your scars will have to stay where they are. Close your eyes.'

Lundin applies some sort of salve to my eyelids. It stings my skin. Maybe they use different face-paints for stiffs than for poor bastards still walking around on their own two legs.

'Did you know that Beda sent Petrus to school for two years?'

'I don't expect she got much benefit from it. Keep still now.'

A brush dabs my sore skin. A scent of roses seeps into my battered nose.

'The Asplunden Institute for Deaf Mutes or something like that. That was more or less everything there was in the Parish Register.'

'Let go of what's in the past, damn it. You're going to be a bloody till rat now. You want some colour on your lips as well?'

I run my hand across my Sunday-best trousers and feel the hard, round contours of the pistol bullet in my pocket.

'A promise is a promise.'

'Handsome as a prince on a black Arab steed with a gold bit and a silver saddle.'

Lundin's American timepiece strikes half past ten. I rise and go through the dimly lit vestibule to the undertaker's, where there's a mirror. Dixie limps along behind me; the lead drags along the floor behind her. She runs her nose over the floorboards and manages to walk right into the urn with the sad-looking palm in it, by the front desk. She lowers herself onto her rump and wags her tail half-heartedly. That animal's about to drink herself to death, mark my words.

I take one of Lundin's tearful-relative tissues from the box on the desk, fold it into a triangle, then tuck it in my breast pocket. After adjusting my tie I scrutinise myself in the mirror. Not bad at all. The skin under my eye is whiter than the rest of my face but it probably won't show in the photograph.

Outside, the grey clouds have mopped up the sparse sunlight of this morning. With Dixie in tow I cross Roslagsgatan and head south towards Bruntell's. Further down I see a couple of navvies from the tram company, checking the rails between the cobbles. One of them thumps the right-hand track with a mallet, and a ringing sound travels along the rail.

In Bruntell's shop window is a handwritten sign: JEWS AND HALF-JEWS BARRED. The deuce knows what he and his kind have against them. They've never done me any harm, and the only one I know sews the best damned suits in town.

Inside the shop, the ladies are lined up behind the counter, their aprons bunched up around their stomachs like sad, limp sails. The proper lunch rush hasn't quite started. I tie Dixie's lead to a lamp post.

Inside the shop, there's a jumble of conflicting smells: herring, roasted coffee, lip snuff, cleaning agents and cured pork in a net at 2.75 kronor per kilo. On the other side of the counter are shelves and little drawers of everything from horseshoe tacks to gift items. From the ceiling, a couple of pairs of boots are hanging by their straps.

Bruntell himself is on duty between the scales and the till. In front of him, the large customer ledger weighs heavily on the counter. His eyes are red, and there's a crumpled white cap on his head. Just behind his jawbone, on his emaciated neck, is a little sticking-plaster. A wedding band gleams on his skinny left hand. His wife is usually found sitting somewhere in the back of the shop, gluing the bottoms of the grocery bags.

'Still having trouble with that shaky left hand, are we?'

I nod at his plaster. Bruntell makes a wheezing sound. I think he's laughing.

'Th-that was a nice party the other night. P-plenty of folks booked themselves in to have p-pictures taken.'

I count out the money and put it on the counter.

'I was going to ask you about Beda…'

'A s-sad story. I always thought a b-b-bit of excitement would be good for business, but it s-seems not.'

'Did you see them when they came to pick up Petrus?'

'No, I was here.'

'Did any of your customers see them?'

'N-n-not as far as I heard. Apart from Ström, that is. He spoke to one of them the d-day after.'

I push my hat back with my finger and look around the shop: 'Say, I'd like my portrait taken.'

Bruntell squints at me.

'I h-have a few pictures left on the roll before it needs developing.'

'Splendid.'

'Y-y-you can have them by the weekend, but it'll c-cost you.' Bruntell wheezes again. That sod is even meaner than Lundin.

'Whose names do you have in that book there? There must be a few of them that don't pay up.'

'Ho-how do you mean?'

'Who owes you the most?'

'That would be O-o-olsson a few d-doors up, but he is sick with TB.'

'Who else?'

'The Lapp woman.'

I nod and get out my notebook.

'I was thinking we could take that portrait outside the cigar shop. I'll keep my hat on.'

Just before lunch, Dixie and I stroll the short distance down to the corner where Standards is. There's still no rain, but it's cold, and I wrap the coat tightly around myself. I should have put on my long johns.

The doorbell tinkles cheerfully. I look around. Elin Johansson is standing at the far end of the boutique. She's wearing a finely checked city dress, which clings to her voluptuous figure. Her red hair is neatly parted to the right, although it looks slightly fuzzed up. She's showing a young man a poplin overcoat.

'Obviously there's no smoking in here!'

A gangly girl with a boyish face has sneaked up on me. She's wearing a green dress with a wide sash. Her left eye seems to move a touch slower than her right.

'I do apologise.'

My cigar bobs up and down in my mouth as I speak. I open the door and toss it out into the road.

'Much better. How can I be of assistance?'

'I was going to invite Miss Johansson for lunch.'

The boyish face bursts into a full smile. Her teeth shimmer against her red-painted lips. Both eyes start glittering at the same time, much to my relief.

'Elin is busy with a customer for the moment. Do you have time to wait a moment?' the assistant twitters, putting her hands together across her bust. Her bony fingers have well-manicured nails, painted the same colour as her lips.

'Naturally. Maybe you can help me, while I'm here. I was going to buy a suit for my nephew.'

'Of course. Standards is a fashionable choice for young people. Is he coming out?'

I shake my head.

'He just needs a proper suit, simple as that.'

'Everyone needs a proper suit. What size does your nephew wear?'

I rub my chin. At the other end of the boutique, Elin recoils when she catches sight of me. She smiles in confusion at her customer and glances over at me with a raised eyebrow.

'He's a bit shorter than me. Slimmer.'

A double furrow appears between the assistant's eyes.

'He's blond.'

The assistant shakes her head, smiling: 'You really should find out what size he wears.'

'That could be difficult.'

'Maybe you should just try on something while you wait. At the moment we have promotions on old boy suits in both wool and serge, topcoats for sixty-five kronor and trench coats for sixty-nine.'

'Thanks, but I already have six decent suits at home.'

'I think Elin has finished with her customer now.' The sales assistant leans forward and lowers her voice: 'She's fond of cut flowers. Preferably hyacinths. Difficult this time of year, but have a try in Klarahallarna.'

She leaves me with an imperceptible nod. I tighten my tie.

The two women meet halfway up the narrow shop and have to twirl around each other, as if in a dance. They exchange a meaningful look. The boyish assistant laughs. A slight scent of herring reaches me before Elin does. It must be her favourite food. She wrinkles her face into a frown and rests her right hand on the daring curve above her hip.

'Lunch? What is this idea you and Alice have cooked up between you?'

She purses her mouth. I attempt a smile: 'You have to have something to eat either way…'

'I hope you're not getting the idea that…'

'It's only a question of a friendly lunch, nothing else.'

'What for?'

She turns her head, as if this might improve her hearing.

'Lunch and an amicable conversation…'

'You're just the same, the whole lot of you. You bait the hook with flattery and gobstoppers.'

'Gobstoppers?'

'And then once you've made a mess of things you scarper.'

'I can assure you that—'

'Nonsense! Let me get my coat.'

Elin bends her neck slightly and turns on a sixpence.

Her fat behind sways to and fro as she clears a path back through the shop. Her colleague, Alice, inclines her head and shoots me a certain kind of glance. I fold up my collar, open the door and step out into the overcast November day. I met another Alice once. A bandy-legged carpenter's daughter who was whoring on Kungsgatan, had a liking for Madeira wine. Our story didn't have a very happy ending.

A horse and cart are parked outside. The chestnut mare scrapes her hooves impatiently against the cobblestones. My extinguished Meteor lies on the pavement. I snatch it up while pretending to do up my bootlace.

At the beer café on the crossing of Roslagsgatan and Odengatan, a mouthy waitress tries to direct the flow of lunch guests. Her rumbling laugh cuts through the clatter of crockery and the diners' raised voices.

On her tray: stacks of chipped sandwich plates and greasy soup bowls.

'I'll wager two cards.'

'I'll pass!'

Four men in City District postal-delivery uniforms are playing auction behind me. The cards make a thumping sound every time one of them slams them down on the table.

'I'll pass as well.'

At a table next to us, an old-timer with blue-veined cheeks fills his glass of pils to the rim. He nods to himself, fully satisfied, and opens his newspaper, *Social-Demokraten.*

Behind Elin's back, a gang of lads from Norra Latin are making a ruckus. They all wear the grammar school badge on their caps; they're drinking milk. One of them is clumsily rolling a cigarette when his friend thumps him on the arm. The bottling machine gives off a dull thud at regular intervals.

'So, how long has Miss been working at Standards?'

I take a bite of my egg sandwich. Elin brushes a few crumbs off the table.

'Too long.'

'And in the meantime you had no idea that your mother and half-brother were living only a few blocks away?'

'Like I told you earlier.'

Elin takes a sip of coffee. Outside Oden-Bazaar on the other side of the street, old Johnsson is limping about with a broom in his hands. He's had that limp ever since I paid him a visit. The number 57 bus pulls into its stop. At the café entrance stands a gang of grubby vagrants with weather-beaten, furrowed faces under their king-of-the-road Borsalinos, gesticulating wildly as they argue some point.

'Laying it on a bit thick with your spades, aren't you?' hisses a throaty voice from the card game behind me.

I take a puff on my Meteor and rub my chin: 'Do you live around here?'

'What concern is that of yours?'

Elin's eyebrow is raised again.

'Just an innocent question.'

The beer is lukewarm but refreshing. I drain my glass in two gulps and refill it. The vagrants have come to the end of their negotiations, and they sway in through the door. Their commander wears his cap cocked at a three-quarters angle; there's a fag butt behind his ear, and traces of a nose bleed dried into his moustache. The leather uppers of his boots have split, and each of his laces is decorated with four or five emergency knots.

'We have to get a move on,' one of the grammar school boys exclaims behind Elin, and there's a hustle and bustle as the lads stand up and put on their coats. I have another sip of beer and clean off the foam around my mouth with the back of my hand. Elin leans forward slightly.

'So, Mister Kvist, tell me about Beda.'

I turn on the charm: 'I liked her a lot. You've been graced with her green eyes.'

Elin's mouth forms itself into a thin streak above her broad chin.

'What was she like?'

'Confused, at the end. Some say she was a compulsive liar but I don't know if that's anywhere near the truth.'

'Damn it!'

I gaze at her, feeling my smile falling off my face; but I manage to stick it back on: 'Everyone in Sibirien knew who she was. She was well liked.'

'And the other one?'

'Your brother?'

'Half-brother, thank you very much.'

'They say he was retarded but I don't think so. Just unusually good-hearted. A deaf mute, though. He helped as far as he was able. Beda used to say he came into the world back end first.'

'I don't understand what the purpose of this is!' Elin clenches her fist on the table. Her cheeks are flaming. 'First you near enough scupper my sale and then you turn up out of the blue and make the most chilling insinuations.'

I try out another smile. The muscles are straining in my face. Elin flushes with anger.

'I reckon Joel's sitting on the diamonds,' hisses the drunken voice behind my back.

I rummage in my trouser pocket while she catches her breath.

She raises her coffee cup to her mouth, with a shaking hand. There's a ringing sound as I reach across the table and let the little lead bullet fall onto her saucer.

'What's that supposed to be?'

'It's a pistol bullet. I dug it out of the laundry wall last night.'

'Put it away.'

'Excuse me?'

'Put it away. At once.'

Her voice aches with held-back tears. I do as I'm told. My manoeuvre hasn't quite gone to plan.

'I don't understand. Last night I was out having a good time with Stina at the old Fenix, and now I'm sitting here with you, and… I don't understand.'

'Your mother. She made me promise something, and a promise is a promise.'

'What?'

'That I'd look after Petrus if anything happened to her.'

'And now?'

'Now something has happened.'

'Jesus bloody wept!'

This boutique assistant curses more than many sailors I've met.

Beside us, the old man with his *Social-Demokraten* chuckles loudly at something in the newspaper. I inhale deeply on my cigar and wonder where I should begin when giving her the whole story. Elin shakes her head when the waitress approaches with the coffee pot for a refill. The tramps have sat down behind Elin and pooled their collective assets on a handkerchief on the table. They order two bottles of pils and three glasses.

I choose my words carefully: 'When I came home a few days ago from a lengthy trip, I learned that your mother had died about a month back. People said Petrus had crushed her skull, which sounded unbelievable. He couldn't even kill a sick rabbit. And she was going to die before long anyway. She had cancer.'

A shiver runs through Elin's stout body.

'It started in her eye but before long it spread.'

I get out Beda's letter and hand it over.

'When I was released this was waiting for me.'

'Released?'

'Came home, I mean.'

Elin looks as if I just handed her a dead latrine rat by the tail, but she grips the envelope and slides out the letter. I have a sip of beer and watch her while she reads. The sheet of paper starts to tremble slightly; she takes a deep breath.

'*I have seen to it there's a monthly bob or two for Petrus,*' she quotes.

'Precisely. Yesterday I checked the Parish Register to see if the father was named, but he wasn't.'

'Was there anything about me?'

'Regarding your father?'

The words get stuck in her throat; she swallows a few times, then finally manages to whisper: 'Yes?'

'Don't know a thing about it. What I do know is, the police came to Roslagsgatan in the middle of the day to pick up Beda's

111

body and Petrus, but no one saw them being brought out, at least not close up. A jumble dealer by the name of Ström spoke a few words with a plain-clothes officer when they came back the day after, and he found out that Petrus had crushed Beda's skull with a stone from a mangle. Or an iron. It's a little unclear.'

I take a deep breath – I'm not sure I've ever said so many words in one go. Elin grows pale and looks as if she's had one cup of coffee too many. I have a mouthful of beer to wet my whistle.

'And?'

'And there's not a trace of anything in the laundry to show that anyone had their skull flattened in there. On the other hand I did find, like I said, a bullet lodged in the wall.'

'Who would put a firearm in the hands of a retard?'

I push my hat back.

'There's no bloody way it was Petrus.'

'What do you mean?'

I raise my voice: 'I mean someone is letting a deaf-mute bloke, who maybe's not all there and can't defend himself, take the blame for a murder he never committed.'

'I'd say you're the one who's not all there.'

Elin puts on her beret and picks up her handbag.

'Your brother is locked up in Lunatic Palace.'

'Half-brother, if you please. And as far as I can see it seems the right place for him.'

'The problem is he hasn't even been put on trial.'

'What do you mean?'

'I spoke to a senior constable I know. No crime scene investigation has been carried out, no post-mortem or interrogation. That goes right against everything I know about coppers. Within twenty-four hours, Petrus was locked up in Konradsberg.'

Elin sinks back into her chair.

112

'Do you have a cigarette?'

She sounds very tired.

'Sorry, no.'

Looking out of the window, she mumbles: 'Stina's fiancé is a policeman.'

'Stina?'

'We share a flat.'

'So check with him, then.'

I stub out my cigar and look out of the window. A few drops of rain have streaked the glass. A tramp ambles along the pavement. A horse-drawn cab brakes hard for a stray dog crossing the wide street.

The three vagrants behind Elin get their pils bottles at last. They share the contents between them.

Elin sighs desolately: 'It's not long till advent now.'

I bite the end off a new cigar.

'That's right.'

'I've never liked Christmas very much.'

'Father Christmas and all that crap.'

'Who would kill an old lady in that way?'

'Haven't got a clue.'

Tears gleam in Elin's green eyes when they look into mine. For a moment I think of Beda and the way she kept rubbing her running eye until they cut it out.

'The man mentioned in the letter. If we assume he's Petrus's father… Maybe he's married to someone else? Maybe he's the one who's behind all this? It wouldn't be the first time some rich swine left an impoverished woman with a baby on her arm.'

Elin's eyes burn behind their veil of tears.

'Maybe so,' I said.

'Men will be men. You can never keep your hands to yourselves.'

I fumble with the matches before I manage to get the cigar going. The coarse smoke fills my mouth. I let it drizzle out of the corner of my lips.

'As I said, no father is mentioned by name.'

Elin peers at me. She puts down the handbag, takes off her beret and breathes deeply. Then her gaze meets mine with a different sort of light in it: 'So how do we go on from here?'

'What do you mean?'

'Surely you don't imagine you can just show up and tell me these stories, and that's the end of it?'

'Listen to me. I wanted to know if you had any information about the case. I've worked on private investigations for dozens of years and the last thing I need is a...'

'A what?'

'This is a man's job, simple as that.'

'She was my mother.'

Elin glares at me defiantly, bursting with conviction.

A sudden headache cuts through my skull. I shut my eyes tight and massage the thick bridge of my nose with my thumb and forefinger: 'Petrus spent a couple of terms at the Asplunden Institute for the Deaf, Mute and Blind. That trail's been cooling down for the last twenty years, but I was going to see if anyone still remembers him there. Above all I plan to speak to Petrus himself.'

Elin puffs up her unruly hair with one hand. Again her herring-breath cuts through the smells of cooking and tobacco. For the first time I see her smile. Her top-left incisor is chipped.

'You're planning on having a word with a deaf mute who's banged up?'

'I know one of the asylum nurses. A drunk, a neighbour of mine.'

Elin opens her eyes wide and stares dumbly at me.

'And you waited this long to tell me?'

She picks up her handbag, pushes back her chair and offers me her hand. There's something very mannish about her, although not quite in the way I can usually appreciate.

I stare at her hand. Her nails are dirty.

'Come on! Too damned right I may not have known my mother, but maybe I can do something for my poor sod of a half-brother.'

I push my hat up even further with my finger, then put my cigar in my mouth and give her my hand. She shakes it firmly.

'Let me call Alice and ask her to cover for me this afternoon, then we can take the number 4 to Fridhemsplan and change to the number 2.'

'Wallin might not even be at work yet. Sometimes he does the night shift.'

Elin stands up and smiles again:

'So much the better.'

Wallin's bedsit is acrid with a smell of sweat and stale hangover. Across the room runs a washing line, empty apart from a couple of pathetic grey clothes pegs. On a bureau is a crystal transistor marked with the manufacturer's name: DUX. By its side, a sunken leather armchair is surrounded by empty bottles. One of them has been shattered, and blood is visible on the jagged glass of the broken bottleneck.

The dirty wallpaper, which has come away from the wall along the edges, is covered in brown blotches from squashed wall-lice.

He's nailed up a bookshelf that he's cobbled together from a few sugar crates. A couple of years' worth of *Sports News* is kept there. The twat often brags about some nephew who, apparently, plays as centre half for Djurgården.

Wallin is in need of a couple of hours of sleep and a few cups of hot coffee before he goes to work. His left hand is swaddled with a dirty piece of cotton. We take a seat around the kitchen table on some chairs with high armrests. The blinds are down but in the middle of the table is a lamp, which is switched on, and next to it an enamelled tub filled with grey soapy water, and two detachable celluloid shirt collars floating on the surface.

'Well, I have to apologise for the state of the place. I don't often get womenfolk visiting here.'

Wallin slurs his words and rubs his unshaven chin. God only knows when he last saw hips like Elin's swaying through his room.

'No need to apologise on account of that.'

Elin's twittering tone has something brisk and hearty about it. It doesn't quite suit her, but it brings a smile to the face of the asylum nurse.

'I can go down to Nisse's Eva and make a few purchases. They have decent buns. Nice big ones.'

'Don't you worry about that.'

Elin gently pats Wallin's uninjured hand on the tabletop. I peer at the studio photograph on the window shelf. I assume that the pale-faced teenage lass is that daughter of his who committed suicide. She looks alarmed, almost as if the photographic flash has caught her unawares. They say Wallin himself had to tug her out when the midwife showed up late, which left her with a pitted skull and crooked spine; apparently the lass never learned from experience, and it was on account of an unwanted pregnancy that she walked into the sea many years later. The letter that I wrote earlier suddenly burns inside my coat pocket.

'Are you visiting that film star, Kvisten? Is that why you want to come with me to work?'

'The film star?'

I can feel Elin's eyes on me. I avoid them. Wallin's mouth twitches: 'Hasn't he told you? Kvist was a friend of Doris Steiner, from the movies.'

'We want to visit Petrus,' I interrupt.

'Petrus? He's not at Konrad?'

'Not for more than a month. Not at the Stora Mans clinic anyway.'

'They're probably keeping him in isolation, then. I had no idea. Well, I can't turn up with the pair of you in tow. I hope you understand, Missus…'

'Miss.'

'Miss, you must understand, we have all sorts there, and outsiders can't just walk about without good reason.'

'Of course. I suppose it takes quite a strong man to wander around there at night with all those freaks and morphinists and retards.'

'It's not for your average person, it really isn't.'

'I should think not.'

I chuckle silently and glance at Elin. She rearranges her red hair behind her left ear. Without any great fuss I haul out the litre-bottle wrapped in crêpe paper that I picked up at Lundin's place before our visit, and put it on the table. There's a glint in Wallin's eye. He rubs his chin and smacks his lips.

'You don't even need to come with us,' I say. 'All you have to do is lean back in your armchair and listen to the world singing, with your one and only best friend, Mister Kron.'

Wallin peeks shamefacedly at Elin from under his fringe, and gives me a crooked smile. I twist the bottle top so he can smell the vodka. He flinches at the sound. We've got him now, he's caught in the trap.

FRIDAY 22 NOVEMBER

Despite a few rain-heavy clouds hiding the moon, and the lack of lights in the yard out front, I can see enough to understand why they call the asylum Lunatic Palace. The towering building squats like a heavy throne in a large grass-covered field; you can make out the yellow façade between the bare trees. The lantern on top of the main building is crowned with a crucifix. The chief physician lives at the top of the hospital, with the other doctors in the flats below. The most difficult cases are placed at the far ends of the wings so the learned men don't have to be disturbed by their screaming.

There must be room for a couple of thousand miserable sods in there.

I reach into the pocket of Wallin's uniform, which I've borrowed, and get out a Meteor for myself. The trouser legs are a couple of inches too short. I turn away from the sentry box by the entrance as I light the cigar. Lundin's hearse is sitting back in the yard; I can just about make out Elin's silhouette in the driver's seat. A hell of a woman just like her mother was. More stubborn than death itself, with a mouth on her that's too much at times.

The gravel of the yard squeaks under my shoes as I turn and walk towards the looming hospital. I weigh up how I'll get past the barrier and the sentry box. Wallin's uniform is magnificent, of course, but it won't fool the bloody guard.

I'll probably have to follow the perimeter fence north, away from the new Väster Bridge, the Field Telegraph Corps and

Marieberg munitions factory, to find a place where I can climb over. I let my eyes rove, seeking a tree growing close to the fence.

A bony man is approaching me across the yard, scattering the gravel with his rapid steps. He's walking with a stoop, lugging a well-filled briefcase. A pair of half-moon glasses glint under the brim of his bowler hat.

'Now you have to watch your damned step, Kvisten.'

The man seems to be heading directly towards me, and it's too late to turn round. I tuck my Meteor into the corner of my mouth, hide my face under the brim of Wallin's uniform hat and rummage in my pockets as if looking for something. It's my usual strategy in these kinds of situations; I should probably try to come up with a better one.

The steps slow down at the same time as my pulse picks up. He stops in front of me. I force myself to smile and raise my eyes: 'Evening.'

'Good evening,' he croaks in response. He looks about sixty. His tongue flicks across his thin, bloodless lips as he hauls out a cigar of his own from his unbuttoned overcoat. His moustache is tinged tobacco-yellow. I offer him my box of matches. He's wearing a pair of elegant, polished boots. I catch sight of a waistcoat under his thick woollen jacket. I can't quite make a decision about this issue of waistcoat or no waistcoat. I have to ask Elin about it, after all she works in a boutique. The man takes the matches: 'Why thank you. You must be the new employee, I take it? You do know you can't bring matches into the hospital; they have to be handed over to the guard when you check in.'

'Of course.'

'Obviously, why else would you be standing here? Oh dear, quite a wind tonight, try again. There.'

I get my matches back.

'Lindström, chief physician.'

My heart does a somersault. I'm standing in front of the very doctor who signed the order for Petrus's transfer into mental-health care. I take his fragile little paw in mine. I have to use all my powers of self-restraint not to squeeze it to bits.

An hour of one-to-one with the bastard. Or fifteen minutes. It wouldn't take much blood-letting before this white-frock started talking. He lets go of my hand. I swallow the drool that's filled my mouth.

I've always had the lust for violence in my blood. Doughboy used to plead with me to take it easy; I was always getting into trouble with the screws and ending up in solitary. His anxiety was justified. There's many a story of uncooperative prisoners who've been tortured to death with whip and rod in the cellars, or ended up in the sickbay and never came out again. But changing my ways was never an option.

It's difficult to deny such a deep-rooted desire. But now I don't have a choice.

'Out and about very late, Doctor.'

'Problems at Mans. Herr Jäger had a negative reaction to the insulin. I've had to delay an invitation for supper.'

'I haven't learned all the names yet.'

'Naturally you haven't. All in good time, all in good time. Unlike the milk delivery, which should have been here two hours ago. And now the kitchen staff have gone home.'

'Surely the night shift can take care of it.'

'It seems you're a game chap, which we appreciate. Look here, have a cigar, as a welcome.'

Lindström offers me a cigar case well stocked with Havanas.

'There, sometimes a cigar is just a cigar and no more than that,' he adds, and lets his thin lips form themselves into a dry laugh. I can't quite see what's so funny.

'My thanks, Doctor.'

'Chief Physician.'

You bloody rat. I nod, smiling again: 'Pardon me. Thank you, Chief Physician.'

Lindström nods a goodbye and walks off towards the cars.

I see Elin ducking down in the front seat of the hearse. At the same time as the doctor starts his Ford, there's the sound of another engine approaching from Mariebergsgatan. I listen out in the dark November night, and let my cigar die under my boot heel. When I strain my ears I can make out the familiar rumble of the milk van.

The little truck turns into the hospital yard and slows down. There's no cover on the trailer. The driver's face lights up with a red glow when he takes a pull on the cigarette dangling in his mouth.

He's a young bloke. Beardless, blond, well scrubbed. He scrunches up one eye to avoid getting smoke in it. The truck has no wing mirrors. Crouching, I run alongside the vehicle until it starts slowing down by the sentry box. My back protests as I take a long step, jump and just manage to hang onto the edge of the trailer. The rough planks creak; a splinter pierces deep into my palm. I try my best to tuck my legs up under me.

When the truck stops I sway slightly, hanging there from the edge of the flatbed. I hold my breath while the driver and the guard exchange a couple of words. The gearbox grinds angrily but finally the kid finds the slot with his gearstick, and we slowly roll into the hospital grounds. The splinter in my hand is hurting me, my muscles are burning, but I don't let go. I hang on tight as if I'm clutching the railing of a ship in a storm.

We rattle along the road towards the massive building. My heart is thumping in the palm of my hand. The wind is ripping through my uniform. Every tree we pass has nesting boxes nailed into its trunk, sometimes as many as three or four. I jump off the truck, land awkwardly and take a tumble onto the roadside.

While the milk truck is parking up by the gable at the far end, I brush off my uniform and pull out the splinter in my hand using my teeth. According to Wallin I have to enter via the main entrance and head to the left until I can't get any further, then down a flight of stairs to the section for those in solitary confinement. The big bunch of keys and whistle jingle against my thigh as I stroll up to the main entrance. I feel like a screw, wearing this fucking outfit. I clear my throat and gob out my self-loathing.

The guard post in the central hall is empty. I follow Wallin's instructions, and head down a long corridor to the left, its dimly lit, wall-mounted shell lights with green hoods casting a sickly glow ahead of me. I meet a nurse in a light-blue cotton dress, an apron and a starched bonnet tied under her chin. I nod at her and continue on my way. I hear her steps slowing down; her eyes burn a hole in my back. The keys thump harder against my leg as I involuntarily quicken my pace.

To avoid calling too much attention to myself, I unlock a door to my right with the master key and enter a large, gloomy room. Along each side runs a line of white cast-iron beds, a metre's space in between them.

The mattresses stink of piss-soaked shredded-wood fibre. In each of the beds a head sticks out from beneath a blanket strapped to the mattress using a system of eyelets and hooks on the lower parts of the bed frame. One or two are sleeping, others turn their heads and look at me with dead eyes. Someone gives a muted cough, another weeps gently. In the second bed to the right from the door lies a younger, unshaven man; the taut blanket jerks violently as he tries to pleasure himself. He lies with his head on one side and his eyes tightly shut. A string of saliva runs from his mouth, seeking its way through the stubble on his chin.

In the far right corner of the room, one of the patients has managed to slip out of his bed. He stands there in his nightshirt and long johns, pulling at the fingers of one of his hands and making a clicking sound.

'I don't understand why you had to take my dolls away from me,' he whispers to me, in a tender voice. 'I'm an adult, am I not?'

He cracks his finger joints again.

'You have to lie down now.'

My eyes look into his, bloodshot from crying. He looks away.

'Of course. How silly of me. I apologise.'

He lies back on his bed, clasping his hands together over his chest. I leave the room, lock the door behind me and look around. The corridor is deserted; I continue towards my goal. On the floor above someone starts howling like a mangy street-dog. A shrill whistle cuts through the noise, and I hear soft-spoken men's voices. I walk faster.

After managing to reach the left-hand wing without running into any other staff, I arrive at a granite stairwell. According to Wallin, the more disruptive patients are kept in the isolation cells below.

My scalp is sweating under my peaked cap. Instinctively I bite the end off a Meteor, but I get a hold of myself and put it back in my pocket. Instead, I take out my little notebook and aniline pen and walk down the dark staircase, which makes a half-turn as it descends.

My progress is blocked by a steel door inset with a small glass window. Along the corridor are ten more doors on each side, all with sturdy locks and observation slits. At the far end, a screw is on duty in a sentry box. Through a rectangular glass window he can keep the entire corridor under surveillance, but he's holding a copy of *Stockholms-Tidningen* in front of his face – I recognise the typeface.

A brown head of hair sticks up from behind the newspaper. A pair of worn shoes are propped up on the desk. The desk lamp is on. Behind that damned screw is a telephone, bolted to the wall. I take a deep breath, push the door open and slip into the corridor. Quietly, but as casually as I can, I walk up to the first door on the right. With a trembling hand, I pull the catch and slide the little hatch open to have a look inside.

A naked bulb on the ceiling spreads a sickly light in the sparse cell. The furnishings in there are easily summarised: nothing but a bed equipped with sturdy leather straps, on which a poor, emaciated, lifeless sod is lying. I glance at the guard, still immersed in his newspaper about seven metres away, while I carefully bolt the hatch back into place.

The next cell is empty and, as the guard turns the page, I go to the third door. With a slight screeching sound, I force the hatch open.

My heart aches as if it was my turn to be shoved into the back of the hearse. My tight collar is damp with sweat.

The bulky body is resting heavily on the bunk, like the carcass of a bull on a butcher's block. His head, with its unruly blond locks, lies directly on the mattress. Petrus is awake but strapped down. The whites of his eyes gleam in the semi-darkness. He stares up at the ceiling.

I glance over at the guard's cubicle. I am so close now that I can read the headline of the newspaper's front page: 'Italian Aviators Hunting the Emperor of Abyssinia'.

'Petrus,' I whisper ineffectually through the slit to the deaf man, while fumbling with the keys. 'Petrus!' I blink the sweat out of my eyes and, trembling, manage to get the first key halfway into the lock before it jams. When I snatch it back, the entire jingling bunch of keys hits the floor.

'Fuck it.'

I curse silently to myself as I pick the keys up. The guard is still reading his newspaper behind the window. I straighten up and try another key. While I'm trying the fourth key Petrus suddenly flinches. I hold my breath. He lifts his head as well as he can and looks into my eyes. I snatch off my cap so he can see me better, and point idiotically at my face.

Before I know it, the deaf mute opens his mouth and brays deafeningly.

My blood curdles. The guard's gaze is on me. He's a young lad with his eyebrows halfway up his smooth forehead. He opens and closes his mouth twice before he throws himself at the telephone on the wall behind him. Petrus lets out another awful yell. His massive body tugs and strains against the straps. I fumble with the keys, calling pointlessly through the hatch: 'What happened to your mother? What happened to Beda? Who did it?'

Petrus is shaking, his bulk vibrating against the bunk.

On the other side of the glass, the guard hangs up and throws himself at his whistle instead. The shrill sound cuts through the narrow corridor.

'I'll be back,' I whisper through the hatch even though the lad can't hear me. 'In a while, when everything's calmed down. A promise is a promise.'

The guard opens the door of his cubicle and blows his whistle again. Before long the place will be heaving with screws. I turn my back on him, open the steel door and run up the stairs.

I need to cough, there's a fluttering feeling in my chest like a bird thrashing its wings, but I control the reflex and run up another flight of stairs. The large, silent building is suddenly filled with noise. Boots thump against floor tiles, the piercing sounds of whistles bounce between the walls, blending with the screams of terrified lunatics.

I throw open the first door on my left and jump inside, finding myself in a bathroom. The lights are off, the bathtubs lined up in rows. The walls are tiled from floor to ceiling. Each of the deep tubs is covered by a piece of cloth, more or less like tarpaulins thrown over boats. In the daytime, those who have taken shelter in madness can lie here and sweat out their delusions.

I lope quietly towards the door at the other end of the room, while the sound of feet on the stairs grows louder.

'Search every floor,' someone yells.

I try the door but it's locked. Like an old woman counting the stitches in her knitting, I check the keys on my ring, my fingers trembling.

'Every room! Don't let the swine get away!' the fierce voice calls out again, just outside the door.

I drop the keyring into my pocket and pull away the sheet covering the nearest bathtub. I step into the empty tub and lie down on my back. Using both my hands, I manage to roll the sheet back into place without making a sound.

Before I shut out the last bit of light, I check my timepiece. Almost half past eight.

Almost immediately afterwards, the door opens and at least two people come in. I cover the pocket watch with my hands to stifle the sound of the mechanism. If there's any trouble I'm in the worst possible position, lying at the bottom of a tub. One leg is jammed under the other and my left foot is already going to sleep. The steps come closer.

Someone sits down on the edge of the bath, which rocks. I think about Doughboy for a moment; he'll probably be alone and locked up in his night cell by now. I'm sweating and freezing at the same time.

'Who do you think it could be?'

It's a man's voice; a neutral tone, almost bored.

'One of the nuts in the laundry has got hold of a uniform. It's happened here before, before your time,' someone answers in an unmistakable Småland accent.

'Oskarsson?'

The bathtub rocks again as the person stands up. A corner of the sheet bunches up slightly, letting in a chink of light. Again I hear steps and the rattling of keys.

'You think that bastard would pull off something like this? I doubt it.'

The door opens and closes. As calmly as I can, I catch my breath. The sound of my beating heart seems to echo between the enamelled sides of the bathtub.

Gradually the noise dies away and soon all I can hear is the ticking second hand of my pocket watch, and the rain, which starts to fall against the windows. I am struck by an almost paralysing nervous exhaustion.

Even though I need a piss I decide to wait until nine o'clock before I get out of the bathtub. What I should do after that I just don't know. On the one hand I want to go back down to the isolation cells, deck that guard and find the right key. On the other hand I wouldn't mind just blowing off the whole damned thing, find a way out and lie low until it's time to meet Doughboy outside the gates of Långholmen. I check my watch again and shift my legs.

When my watch shows nine, I quietly get up. The rain has picked up in intensity, striking the window and drowning out the sound of my pissing into a drain in the corner. I button up Wallin's uniform trousers, go to the door and put my ear against it. Pressing down on the door handle, I open it carefully and peer through the crack.

One flight of stairs below there's a window; maybe I can open it and get out that way. As far as I remember there were no bars on it. Otherwise I'll have to hurry back through the corridor, get out via the main entrance and make a run for it across the lawns. What Elin will say when I come sloping along with my tail between my legs, I couldn't give a blind fuck about. Maybe I can persuade Wallin to contact Petrus instead. Shouldn't cost me much more than another litre.

I have my own business to think about now, whatever promises I have made. I slip out of the doorway and stop to listen again, hauling up a Meteor from my pocket and putting it between my lips to calm a raging need to smoke, which is flowing through my body.

As quietly as I can I go to the stairs leading down to the ground floor.

Every third step I stop and listen as hard as Job must have done for the voice of God. With only another five steps to go, I hear steps quickly approaching from the basement. Someone is jogging up from the cellar and the isolation cells. It's too late to turn back. I press myself against the wall and clench my fists, at the ready. I have the better position if they come up the second flight. There's nothing worse than fighting some-one uphill.

I take a deep breath and hold it while he hurries past just below, a squat bloke of about fifty, entirely dressed in black apart from a white shirt. His profile is flattened, not unlike my own, and there's a scar running through his eyebrow. His bushy white moustache is not unlike Lundin's. In his hands he's holding a handkerchief that was once white, but is now soaked with something red. The blood has spattered a good way up his starched shirtsleeves. My muscles stiffen. Even though he's only in sight for a few seconds, I know for certain that I have seen him recently, somewhere else.

Agile as a cat I dart around the corner and tumble down the stairs to the basement. A couple of the steps have red-coloured half-footprints on them. I press my sweaty hands against the door and peer inside. The guard's cubicle is empty but Petrus's door is ajar.

I press down on the door handle and swing the door open. Curled up and with my fists raised, I move gingerly towards the cell, all the time with my left foot before my right.

A pale streak of light is shining through the gap in the doorway. I push it open, then draw breath. The red gore has shot up against the walls and run onto the floor. Strapped onto his bunk, his wound looking like an extra grinning mouth, Petrus lies with his throat cut from one ear to the other.

Once more I have failed to keep a promise to someone I cared for.

Immediately I set off in pursuit of the man with the scar. The sound of my running fills the corridors. Again there's a cacophony of angry yells and sharp whistles against a background chorus of the wails and weeping of the lunatics. When I catch sight of the man in black, he's already running too. He has quite a head start on me, but I think I'm faster than him. I can't do ten kilometres in forty-five minutes any more, but I'm in better shape now than when they banged me up.

We're getting close to the main entrance when a young warder comes charging in through the door. He's a wiry type with a birthmark like a tear under one eye. He places himself in the path of the man in black and spreads his arms as if inviting an embrace. The poplin coat of the black-dressed man makes a slapping sound in the gloom as he slams into the youth with his shoulder. The youth cracks the back of his head into the door frame with a sharp smacking sound, and he's out of play before he's even hit the floor.

Outside, the rain is bucketing down. I slip and hit my knee on the imposing front steps leading down to the lawns, but I'm quickly back on my feet. The black figure still has a lead of twenty or so metres, and he almost disappears in the darkness, but I can hear the gravel crunching under his feet on the way to the main entrance. I grit my teeth and pick up speed. The raindrops lash my face under the peaked cap, cleaning the sweat off.

My lungs are screaming for oxygen. I bite my lip hard to give my muscles an extra push. I keep gaining on him, but when he jumps clumsily over the boom by the sentry box, there's still a gap of ten metres at least between us. I take a couple of long strides before leaping over in turn. In the street-lit yard I see him slowing down. The door of the sentry box opens just as I'm hurdling over the barrier, like some Swedish Jesse Owens.

'Start the car!' I roar, through the rain. 'Elin! Start the car for Christ's sake!'

I wave my arm over my head towards Lundin's hearse, at the same time as the man in front of me reaches a jet-black Rolls-Royce. He fumbles frantically in his pockets, unlocks and opens the door, then throws himself into the driver's seat on the right.

Just as the engine rumbles to life I take a huge leap and land at the stern end on the rain-drenched footplate of the luxury crate. I fumble for the handle of the back door and grip onto it at the same time as the car roars off, gravel smattering under the wheels like a double-barrel of lead. The door flies open and I lose my grip on the slippery door handle. For an instant I find myself in a state of weightlessness before I hit the ground hard, spinning round. Pain shoots through my worn-out shoulder joint. I raise my eyes and stare at the disappearing Rolls. A1058. I'm almost sure that the plate said A1058.

At that moment the hearse comes thundering along. I get up on all fours as Elin skids to a halt, no more than half a metre from my head, so that the gravel flies into my face; I give it a wipe with my coat sleeve as I'm getting up. The door opens and I crawl into the passenger seat next to Elin.

'What on earth…?'

'Drive!'

I whip out my notebook and aniline pen as Elin releases the clutch. Some way ahead of us the back lights of the Rolls disappear as it turns up towards the Väster Bridge.

'What's going on?'

Elin turns on the double windscreen wipers and changes gear. I catch my breath as I write down the registration number.

'That swine in the Rolls just sliced up your brother. And killed him.'

FRIDAY 22 NOVEMBER

Three times, Elin hammers the base of her palm against the top of the steering wheel, as if this might make the old ambulance pick up speed while it drags itself across the Väster Bridge. The Rolls has already increased its lead, and it's disappearing over the other side of the incline.

'Damn it,' she curses quietly to herself. 'God damn, damn.'

She whacks the steering wheel again. I peer at her. She's taken off her beret and her hair is glowing red in the darkness of the front compartment. She turns the wheel and overtakes an old crate.

The rain spatters against the bodywork. Between the lanes you can see the gleaming-wet rails of the number 4 tram.

We reach the top of the span, there's no sign of the Rolls. I glimpse the dark rocks where I was standing with the cheering people of Söder just a few days ago. Further ahead, the twin steeples of Högalid Church can be seen. I crane my neck and peer down at Långholmen Prison to the right. Doughboy is waiting for me in there. Five more days.

We pick up speed a little as we start to move downhill, and the sound of the engine rises by a few octaves. I lean back and light a Meteor. In the flaring light of the match, I see Elin's green eyes, seething with anger.

I take the cigar out of my mouth: 'There's no point. Not with this car. The Rolls is too quick.'

Elin thumps the steering wheel again and leans forward. She overtakes wildly again.

'Maybe the bastard will get a flat tyre. Or crash,' she hisses, her anger picking up steam.

'Or we will. Slow down.'

'What was that?'

Elin turns her head towards me. Her mouth hangs open, as if this might help her hear what I am saying. I'm starting to think that she's even deafer than her brother was.

'Slow down!'

'Never.'

On Långholmsgatan, close to the abutment, a little girl is leading Blind-Pyttan home. Pyttan is wearing dark glasses and a hat with a floppy brim. Every day they tour the streets of Söder from the saltwater to the freshwater side, the blind woman calling down a rain of five-öre pieces with her pure voice and heart-rending songs. People say that God took her sight but compensated her with a remarkable voice.

I close my eyes and massage the broad base of my nose. Inside, I can see Petrus's throat sliced open, the red goo over the sheets, the blood all over the floor and walls. I press my fingers so hard against the bridge of my nose that it hurts. The car slows down and I open my eyes. We turn into Hornsgatan. On the corner, a couple of slum sisters from the Salvation Army 4th Division stand under an awning. One of them is playing a guitar, the other shaking a collections box. The black bands of their bonnets are fluttering in the wind.

Elin shakes her head; she sounds desolate now: 'Why would anyone want to do anything like that?'

'If we knew that we'd have solved the case.'

'It has to be the father.'

'Who?'

'The man in the letter, it must be him who's behind all this.'

'If there's one thing life has taught me, it's this: never assume more than fuck all about anything.'

'It's always a man.'

I grunt: 'But not always a father.'

'Talk louder, please.'

'Makes no damned difference.'

The November evening has more or less cleared the city's inhabitants off the streets, and there's not much traffic. The rain sings its gloomy song in the gutters of Hornsgatan, and the stray dogs have taken refuge under carts and in doorways. Reluctantly, the streetlights penetrate the shadows.

We drive past the place where Maria, the covered market, used to be in the olden days. I slide my hand over my coat and feel the letter still there. I used to take my daughter there on Saturdays, if we could allow ourselves some toffee from the sweet stand. The place used to smell of raw meat, freshly harvested vegetables and the wood shavings scattered in the passages between the stands. One time Ida accidentally got her toffee stuck in her hair, and we borrowed a pair of scissors from the barber's opposite to cut it out. Emma was angry with me when we came home that time, but soon enough she was laughing about it. If I'd known then what I know now, I would have kept one of Ida's sticky locks in a box of matches. Something to remember my girl by.

I take a deep puff and exhale a leaden cloud in the driver's compartment. There are some memories that quickly fade away, while you end up lugging others around with you like a yoke. Elin coughs pointedly.

I get out my notebook and start humming as I write down a detailed description of the murderer, underneath his registration plate number: busted nose, scar through his eyebrow, moustache and a black poplin coat.

134

We cut through half of Södermalm lengthwise, passing the church and the Palace cinema in silence, turning off down into Slussen and its new roundabout. Elin suddenly starts sobbing and leaning over the steering wheel. She wipes away her tears with the back of her hand. I daren't look; I keep my eyes averted and stare out of the side window. Her crying soon stops as suddenly as it began.

'I got a couple of boxes of clothes, letters and other things from… Mother. I can look through it and see if I find anything that could help.'

'Do that.'

'For some reason I've been avoiding it.'

'It's natural.'

'Kvist, are you sure about the number plate?'

'More or less. Hessler can help us.'

'What?'

'My friend at the police can trace it.'

'Tomorrow?'

'Tomorrow.'

'Maybe the murderer got our number as well?'

'What do you mean?'

'You should be careful.'

I grunt by way of an answer. Elin steers the hearse along Vasagatan, past the Central Station. On the other side lies the exclusive Hotel Continental. Only three years ago I was dining there with the film star Doris Steiner; I even drove around in a sixteen-cylinder 1930 Cadillac for a few weeks. Now I'm rattling about in a hearse with this woman. I glance at Elin. Life: it's as simple as a square boxing ring. When you're in it, you can only fight like hell and hope you're still standing when you hear the gong.

Elin drives past Lennartsson's reputable shoe shop and Norra Bantorget. She continues up Dalagatan to the north and eventually stops in front of a glass-panelled oak door not far from Matteus's Church. The car doors creak; my cigar fizzles out in the gutter and bounces into a drain. I fold up my coat collar and Elin puts on her beret.

'It would be unseemly for me to invite you in, Kvist.'

The rain drips onto my coat from the brim of my hat.

I shrug: 'All the same to me.'

'Stina, the woman I share the flat with, starts work early. She might already be asleep.'

'I have a funeral tomorrow but I'll be in touch after that.'

I offer my hand. Elin takes it, wrinkling her nose.

'I stink of your awful cigars.'

'That's not the worst you've been through today.'

Elin gives a barely audible snort. With a cursory nod she goes to the front porch and pushes it, only to find that the caretaker has already locked up. She gets out a key from her handbag. I wait to make sure she gets inside all right. I catch myself eyeing her up.

'You're gawping worse than a schoolboy.' The fire is back in her voice. I prefer it to her weeping.

The door closes behind her. The rain keeps coming down. I shake my head and fumble for a Meteor. When she hits the light switch inside the stairwell, I can see that for some reason she's smiling slightly. I frown, and push my hat down over my eyes. There's a minor waterfall bucketing down over the road. The match rasps against the phosphorus strip and flares up as red as her hair. I shield the flame with my hand and get the cigar going. I run my eyes across the dripping house fronts with their hopeless rows of empty windows. The November wind roars in the cavities of the inset basement windows as if trying to compete with the din of the rain.

It's still raining when I turn into Roslagsgatan. The lantern outside Lundin's funeral parlour is broken. The boys from the gang often turn it out with a well-aimed kick at the pole, which makes the gas mantle collapse like cigarette ash.

I park on the other side of the street and get out of the car. My body is aching after all the evening's knocks and falls. Both the uniform and the coat will have to be cleaned. I look up. For an instant I stare at the dark windows of the laundry.

An unexpected wave of nausea convulses my stomach. I spit between my boots.

The drains are greedily sucking in the rainwater. I jump across the streaming gutter and amble across to the other pavement. A great tiredness is surging through my limbs, now that I'm so close to my bed. Lundin's sign screeches in the wind. Weathervanes and chimney cowls spin restlessly. There's a rattling sound from around the corner on Ingemarsgatan, as if someone just kicked an old tin can. Probably rats, digging about in the mound of rubbish that often builds up there.

I pause and turn my gaze to the laundry. A thought darts so quickly through my head that I don't have time to catch it. I stand there for a moment to see if it comes back. It doesn't.

'I'm worth a nightcap. What a damned Friday night.'

I'm deep in thought, but I still have time to notice a series of sounds that don't belong in a deserted autumn evening street: the clattering noise comes again from Ingemarsgatan, then a series of quick, light steps, followed by the unmistakable sound of an Italian flick-knife being opened – my brain kicks into gear.

I twist my body and turn towards the noise. A dull pain radiates from my left side. The blade of the knife flashes as it's drawn back for a second strike. I jump backwards, flicking a punch with my right hand and barely dodging the knife as it swings again. I'm rocking back on my heels and the force of the punch is lost, but at least I land it, hitting my opponent just below the scar that runs through his eyebrow: an old acquaintance, it seems.

His hat is knocked off. He stumbles backwards, pulling an ugly face.

'So you were going to kill two blokes on the same night, were you?'

I fire off a double left jab. He rolls his head away from the first but rather than chasing his ugly mug with my fist, I let number two land in the same place, so that he whacks his head right into it when he sways back, and his cold blue eyes open wide with surprise. He's had a bit of schooling but he's never boxed at any high level. For half a second I've got him in the bag. He stands there with his feet far apart. I can see his brain struggling to re-engage with his body's muscles.

Ten years ago this story would already have been over, but now I hesitate and back off a few steps. He's hefty but I've got him beat on both technique and speed. I circle him anticlockwise, away from the knife, which always feels awkward, but my old trainer taught me to change position from time to time and go in with my right if necessary.

It's necessary now.

Lundin's sign slams in the wind, and somewhere behind me a cat hisses. The blood warms my body down my left flank but I daren't check how bad the damage is. I keep circling and waiting. The murderer leads, I follow.

We dance a few slow turns in the rain. Over his jagged nose, his ice-blue eyes shine in the darkness, and mine lock with his.

An opponent with a weapon usually puts all his trust in it. He can't get it out of his head, which makes him predictable and for this reason vulnerable. I can feel my strength seeping out of the hole in my side, so I decide to make a firmer offer of a dance.

I move in closer and make a barely perceptible movement of my right shoulder as if I'm about to jab him in the face. A worse boxer wouldn't have noticed the movement; a better one wouldn't fall into the trap.

Straight away the knife comes slicing through the air. I duck the blow, charge forward and breathe out through my nose as I let him have my left over his extended right arm. My swing hits him on the temple. The impact travels down my arm bone and makes my sore shoulder joint jump with pain. He reels.

I take advantage of my momentum and thunder into him with all my strength. He gasps as he hits the ground with me on top of him. The stiletto clatters over the cobbles and come to rest about a metre away.

The murderer has his hand in my face and I hold onto his collar as we both desperately reach for the knife. His fingers press the inside of my lips against my teeth and a nail grazes my cheek. The rain-soaked blade, clean of blood, glitters against the dark stone.

Ten centimetres.

Five.

Groaning with exertion I reach the hilt with my fingertips and quickly gather it into my hand. Once I had a bloke on a boat to China, a big bastard cook he was, and he said you shouldn't make do with any less than ten stabs if you're looking to kill a man with a knife. The blade doesn't always go true; it'll glide off the ribs if you're not careful. He used to stand without a vest in the hot pantry, and judging by the scars on his massive body he knew what he was talking about.

I grasp the hilt so that the point of the blade points right down at my opponent. When I straighten my back and raise my arm, his eyes already look dead.

Ten times.

I clench my jaw and drive the knife down with all my strength.

The man in black tries to defend himself with his hands. He grimaces with pain when the point goes into his forearm. He grunts. I pull the knife out and raise it again.

'You don't know who you're playing with, you fucking queer.' The words wheeze out of his mouth.

Nine to go.

This time I find my target, and the blade sinks into his chest. Finally the bastard is yelling. His pupils dilate, as if his brain is trying to savour the last of the light still left to him before death sweeps him into the darkness. A raindrop falls right into his eye. He doesn't blink it away. His closed lips let out a final sigh. I'm salivating.

I twist the blade half a turn to the right and then back to the left before raising the knife again.

Eight.

Blood spatters up, glistening in the rain. With all my strength I drive the blade down and snatch it back. I hear the cook's voice.

Seven more.

Afterwards I'm left sitting on my arse next to the body. I lean my head against my pulled-up knees and try to get my breathing under control. My coughing comes back, tearing at my wound. I groan with pain, firmly pressing the palm of my hand against my side.

The rain washes away the blood around the corpse. The knife lies between us, its snapped-off blade buried deep in his belly somewhere.

'Five was enough.'

I breathe as lightly as I can, to avoid aggravating the coughing reflex. The ice-cold rain falls right down the inside of my collar, runs down my back and slowly brings me back to life. I raise my head and look around. Roslagsgatan lies deserted, but further south I can hear the number 6 tram whining across the siding. There's not much time.

I grunt as I get onto my feet and limp over to the door of the funeral parlour. Quickly I find the right key and open the door.

Still with my hand pressed against my side, I limp back and grab hold of the corpse by the armpits. The bastard weighs a ton. I moan as I drag the body the short distance. The red lights of the number 6 approach in a green rain of electric sparks. I bend over the corpse to avoid hitting the back of my head against the door frame. The bloke's boot heels thump as we go down the steps and then we're inside, in the warmth.

'What the hell…?'

A dazed-looking Lundin is standing in the kitchen doorway with his hair on end. Outside, the number 6 rattles by.

'What the hell are you doing, brother?'

'Shut your mouth and help me before me and this bastard cover the whole foyer in blood.'

'Dead?'

'Dead as a bearskin hat.'

'Chuck him in with the others, then!'

Lundin opens the door to the cool-room. We grab an arm each and drag the corpse over the floor, while from time to time I groan in agony.

The cool-room is fully tiled, with a couple of metal bunks for the corpses. Underneath are some large vats, which Lundin keeps filled with ice covered in a layer of wood shavings, to keep the cadavers cold during the summer months. Just as in the stiff-house there's a sweet smell of decomposition. On one of the bunks is a white coffin, a medium-size model belonging to the lad I picked up this morning. We let the body fall and it thuds against the floor.

'Well, then? What the devil's going on here?'

Lundin's all worked up, flapping his long arms.

'Calm yourself down and I'll tell you.'

Grimacing with pain, I take off the uniform jacket while rapidly summarising what happened earlier at Konradsberg: Petrus and the car chase. Hopping from one foot to the other, I fiddle about trying to get my trousers off, and describe the assault in the street. Lundin caresses his big moustache, periodically grunting in response as he listens. Now and then he slaps his legs to get the circulation going.

When I've got my rags off I examine the wound. It's not especially deep but it's opened up badly across my ribs.

'That needs stitches.'

'How the hell am I supposed to manage that? Should I just toddle off to the surgery and tell 'em I slipped and fell on a scythe?'

'Jensen, up in Katarina.'

'The abortionist?'

'One and the same.'

'That bastard's drunk by ten in the morning and now it's ten at night.'

'Nonetheless… He healeth the broken and bindeth their wounds.'

'The hell's that supposed to mean?'

'Just that it's going to take more than a bit of gauze to patch this one up. I'll telephone him and check if he can see you.'

'You stitch up men, women and children every day.'

'My left hand's too shaky and the thread's too coarse.'

Lundin goes out to make the telephone call, while I rip the arms off my shirt and strap a temporary pressure bandage around my chest. I can hear Lundin mumbling out in the foyer.

I examine the sturdy figure on the floor, his short hair and a moustache nearly as impressive as Lundin's. His cold blue eyes look almost the same in death as in life. He reminds me of old Hindenburg. Maybe that's why I feel I recognise him.

Exhaling sharply with pain, I bend down and go through his pockets. He has nothing on him except a pair of car keys, a pack of Negresco and a lighter. I put the keys on the bunk. The car should be parked somewhere in the vicinity.

Lundin comes back with two brimming glasses of aquavit. He hands me one of them. He's put on his big pigskin apron.

'This one's on the house.'

'Thank you kindly.'

We knock them back on the spot.

'The Dane can fit you in.'

'Did he sound sober?'

'Difficult to say.' He looks down at the body. 'Damned giant, he is.'

'And what am I supposed to do with him?'

I give the corpse a little kick with the side of my foot.

'I'll take care of him; he'll accompany the boy into the oven tomorrow.'

143

'You'll be needing a bigger coffin, then.'

'Or a bone saw, and I have one of those.'

After conferring for a few minutes, we lift the cadaver onto one of the metal tables. I take Wallin's dirty uniform under my arm and go through Lundin's rooms into the stairwell. With one hand on the banister I make my way up to my flat.

The neighbours have put their copy of *Social-Demokraten* outside the door: a hint that I might care to share their subscription like I used to. I pick it up with another gasp of pain.

As soon as I put the key in the lock, I can hear Dixie's claws against the cork mat inside. In a matter of seconds she's jumping against my legs. She follows me into the kitchen. I pour her some porter into a bowl, and mash a couple of boiled potatoes in a soup plate with a few scraps from the butcher. While my overjoyed mutt is eating, my thoughts once again return to the subject of Doughboy. In my mind's eye I see his pale neck with its red flea bites. I close my eyes and I can almost taste his salty tang. As usual, whenever I think of that youth, it sends my blood into a tumult, churning through my ventricles.

'Now then, Kvisten, you bloody rascal, you've really made a mess this time. How do you think you're ever going to get out of this one?'

Dixie's cropped ears point towards the sound of my voice. I sigh and walk out of the kitchen and into my walk-in wardrobe. A smell of mothballs and gun oil hits me. I choose a grey shirt that has always fitted me poorly, and a light summer suit, whose cut has gone out of style – just in case I bleed through. I was planning to let Herzog knock me up another one in the spring anyway. On the way out I pick up the box containing the pistol.

I feed the magazine with shells before slotting it back into the Husqvarna. After checking the mechanism by cocking it, I flick the safety catch with my thumb and drop the gun into my coat pocket. With Dixie tottering along behind me, I go back down to Lundin.

As we enter the flat I can hear that he's struck bone. The saw blade is rasping against the skeleton. The undertaker swears so fiercely that his voice bounces between the walls of the cool-room.

Black clothes stick out of a sugar sack on the floor. The pale pink body is lying on the metal table. It's fuzzed with fine grey hair, like the bristle of a hog.

Lundin's sweaty mug is speckled with red. Blood has spattered onto his leather apron and his lower arms, as if he was an old village butcher. His white hair stands on end, shining like a halo in the light of the ceiling lamp. Sweat is beading on his brow as he struggles to saw off the legs of the corpse just below the knees. He's already thrown the feet into the open coffin next to him. The bones stick out of the flesh like pale yellow reinforcement rods. Dixie sniffs the air with interest.

'Get me the axe by the cooker, and the shotgun and powder horn in the living room,' Lundin orders.

'What do you want with that?'

'You said you were going to stay out of Långholmen for a while.'

'What do you mean?'

Lundin's expression is impenetrable. He moves his lips about as if manoeuvring his snuff into position.

'Your place is here.'

I shake my head but wind Dixie's lead around the door handle, go into the living room and take down the muzzle-loader from the wall. The old-fashioned gun looks Napoleonic. I grab the axe from the kitchen and take both back to the cool-room.

'Take the clothes with you and get rid of them, there's not much room in the coffin as it is.'

145

I pick up the jute bag of clothes, and loop Dixie's lead around my wrist. For a moment I wonder whether I might hand in the suit to Herzog to see whether he could alter it for Doughboy, but I resist the thought.

I walk out of the door. The weight of the Husqvarna bangs against my hip. The wound in my side is throbbing.

On the way back to the hearse, the ground seems to move underfoot, like when you've got a proper concussion from one too many punches.

The small surgery at the far end of Tjärhovsgatan smells of blood, ether and alcohol. Whether the doctor himself or his equipment smells more of alcohol is difficult to ascertain. Jensen himself is a podgy, red-faced bloke in his fifties. Under his unbuttoned shirt there's a glimpse of a dirty vest covered in big grease stains. The Dane removes his round spectacles and mops a handkerchief against his sweaty forehead.

'It's an ugly cut.'

'Get it done.'

'Fifteen kronor for each stitch, that's what I want for it.'

I nod, lighting a Meteor. I'm sitting naked to the waist on a scratched table in the centre of the room. Two worn fabric straps hang down from the ceiling, where the ladies can hitch up their legs when they're lying on their backs. On a small sideboard are a number of instruments: forceps, a stethoscope, a vaginal speculum, an anaesthesia mask and a curette.

'I'll just go and get a pair of gloves.'

As Jensen straightens up he stumbles and grips the table. He mutters something to himself that I can't hear, then with a certain amount of trouble steers his steps to a cupboard next to a window with closely drawn curtains. I inhale deeply and look around the room. In the corner is a refuse bin filled with blood-soaked rags. There are no diplomas hanging up on the stained walls to testify to the reliability of this doctor.

Jensen fixes a head-mounted light around his great skull and puts on a pair of long operation gloves. Breathing heavily, he pours some clear liquid into a glass jar and comes back with a rag, which he dips into the jar and hands to me.

'Press this against your wound.'

I do as I'm told. I might as well have taken a swim in the Dead Sea. I grimace with pain.

'It's a shame to let the rest go to waste.'

Jensen takes a good pull at the jar and then offers it to me. I have a mouthful of spirit; it tastes of fusel. Jensen takes the rag from me and throws it towards the refuse basket. He misses by several metres. The rag hits the wall, which explains the rust-red stains in the corner.

While he's pinching together the open wound with his fat fingers and putting in the first stitch, he glances at the full-rigger on my chest.

'All seven seas, huh?'

I grunt and take another mouthful from the jar, while Jensen keeps stitching.

'My brother was a sailor. He drowned when they were torpedoed in the North Sea. Just as well. He never forgave me for what happened to his wife.'

Jensen puts in another stitch and mutters something else, which can't be understood. I try to relax, but I keep staring at those bloody rags in the refuse bin and thinking about Petrus.

Before the funeral tomorrow I'm going to walk around Sibirien until I find the Rolls. I could find something inside it to help me identify the murderer. But if I don't manage to find it, Hessler should be able to help me with the number plate. That is, if by then I don't have my hands full dealing with unwanted visitors searching the funeral parlour.

'Ninety kronor,' mumbles Jensen, who's now on his sixth stitch.

I take a deep puff on the cigar, burning my lungs in the process.

'One hundred and five.'

With a sigh, I exhale a great cloud of greyish-black smoke. My lacerated side has thrown in the towel and become insensible to pain.

'One hundred and thirty. We're done.'

The wound tightens when I peer down at the stitches. It looks like a blind old woman's embroidery, but the pink edges of the cut look reasonably clean. I wedge the cigar into my mouth. When I pull on my shirt I near enough bite it in two. But it's not exactly the first time I've been stitched up, and not the first time I've been knifed either. I probably have more stitches in me than a patchwork quilt. Injuries of that kind usually heal in two weeks if there are no fists involved. I take the Meteor out of my mouth: 'What do I owe you?'

With a grin, Jensen says in his Danish accent:

'A hundred and thirty.'

'What was that?'

'A hundred and thirty-five.'

I try to do the calculation myself but I soon give up. A whole heap of blokes have paid good money after I brought their women here when misfortune struck; very likely I'm getting a decent price. I walk into the room at the far end to fetch my wallet from my coat. Dixie whines with excitement and spins around my legs, snapping at my trouser legs as I enter the waiting room. She's probably in the mood for a porter. I pay the doctor what I owe, using money that I've borrowed from Lundin.

It's stopped raining. Slowly I drive back in the hearse along Katarinavägen. Behind me, the bells of Gabrielsson's church strike midnight. Far below, the cresting waves of the black waters of Saltsjön refract the city lights. On Stadsgård quay the cranes stand like emaciated, long-necked animals. A nightwatchman with a torch shines a beam of light across them. I wonder how far Lundin has got with the cadaver at home. The inside of a body is a messy thing. That damned coffin had better not start leaking in transit tomorrow.

I think about Petrus and I wonder who'd feel compelled to silence a person who couldn't even speak or hear. My thoughts flit on to Ploman, the boss of Vasastan's smuggler syndicate. About ten years ago he won a young lass in a game of cards, and as far as I've heard he still keeps her. She's not particularly beautiful but he had her tongue cut out and she's illiterate, so she can't easily pass on information. You'd have to look hard for a more cautious bloke than Ploman.

'How could Petrus have spilled the beans on anyone? He didn't even know how to write.'

I reach out with my left hand and give Dixie a scratch; she yawns lazily, curled up on the passenger seat.

Once I'm home I drive round the neighbourhood a few times to see if I run into a black Rolls-Royce with the number plate A1058. It's not the sort of car you often see in Sibirien. There's not a soul on the streets and no sign of a Rolls either.

I park a short distance from the funeral parlour. The lights are still on in there. I hold the door open for Dixie but she doesn't want to budge so I have to pick her up. I look around a few times before I bite the end off a Meteor and light it. I stand outside the

149

funeral parlour smoking while Dixie whines, then I press down the door handle and step inside.

The bell above the door tinkles, before giving way to a desolate silence. A wave of anxiety passes through my body. I hang Dixie's lead over the back of one of the visitors' chairs and slide my hand into my coat pocket, clasping my Husqvarna and flicking the safety catch.

The door of the cool-room is shut. It's dead silent in there. I put my cigar in my mouth and cock my pistol. My hand is trembling as I push the door open. For a moment I find myself staring down the barrel of Lundin's muzzle-loader. He's still wearing his messy leather apron and his white moustache is speckled red with blood. We both take a deep breath. Lundin lowers his gun.

'Fine time to show up, now that the boar is already butchered and packaged.'

'Did you get all of the bastard in?'

I peer over Lundin's shoulder. He points at the dripping axe, which is leaning up against the wall.

'I did, after I crushed his sternum with the blunt side of the axe.'

On the white tiles underfoot the blood is as bright as cinders on an engine-room floor, but the boarded-up coffin has been wiped down. It's ready for cremation. Perched on top of the lid is a half-full bottle of aquavit. Lundin scores the label with his thumbnail, to indicate how much is left, and then he leaves it where it is.

'I've done my part, you clean up. Throw a bucket of water over the pavement as well, to be on the safe side.'

'Don't you want to ask me anything else about what happened?'

'Tomorrow. Blessed is the worker's sleep.'

'I owe you one.'

'I don't want you going back to prison.'

'I'll do what I can.'

Lundin gives me a tired nod, then points with the gun barrel at a bucket on the floor: 'I cut up some of the giblets for the dog.'

I take a deep pull on my cigar.

'When are they being cremated?'

'Tomorrow at half past two. With Our Lord's blessing no one will come and start rooting about before then.'

SATURDAY 23 NOVEMBER

I'm lying on my undamaged side, my body still heavy and stiff from sleep. The tip of my nose is cold; the coal in the ceramic burner has run out in the night. The frost crystals on the windowpanes slowly melt away in the greyish sunlight.

The stitches in my side tighten as I reach for the pocket watch on the bedside table. I whimper in pain. Dixie answers with a yawn from the foot of the bed. It's past ten. I smack my dry lips. There were a few too many nightcaps and cigars yesterday. It feels like someone raked out the fireplace and poured the ashes down my throat.

Laboriously I roll onto my back. The wound thumps to life. As I'm winding up my pocket watch, I notice a couple of old splashes of blood that have stained the wallpaper. It's not the first time I've bled in this bed. I close my eyes and remember that messy story I had with Doris Steiner, the film star. I wish Wallin had shut up about it when me and Elin visited him yesterday. The less I hear about it the better. Now and then I think about that bony woman, I even miss her, but usually my bad memory takes care of that problem.

The bed is big enough for two, with proper bolsters and three real-down pillows. It's been a long time since anyone kept me company in it, though.

In Långholmen, Doughboy will already have been working for several hours. Most likely he's hungry by now; it'll be three-quarters of an hour before they start serving lunch. Time never passes so slowly when you're inside as the last few days before your release.

I raise my head and meet Dixie's jet-black gaze. Her head is resting on her front paws, her tail wagging with rhythmic lashes, like a two-stroke engine between the cast-iron bars of the bed frame. I throw the bolster to one side and swing my legs over the edge with a groan. My skin comes up in goosebumps. Usually Lundin keeps the boiler warm, but there must have been a cold snap. With some effort Dixie gets up on all fours and yawns excitedly.

The little hatches of the square-shaped ceramic burner make a screeching sound when I open them, squatting down naked to load its innards with newspaper, wood and a thick layer of coal briquettes. I strike a match. The fire sucks oxygen from the chimney stack. Before long, it's burning so fiercely that the hatches are vibrating.

Ignoring Dixie, who's whining at the edge of the bed, I go into the dressing room. I put on a pair of elasticated underpants, clip my sock garters to my shins and decide on a pair of grey wool trousers that sit a little lower around the waist than the others. With a grimace I put on my vest. Again I think of Doughboy and the suit I've promised him. Time is starting to run out. I could do with a bit of money coming in.

Dixie is still standing on the bed, hesitating like a child on the edge of a jetty. I pick her up and put her on the floor. Christ knows what's ailing her; three years ago when I took her in there was nothing wrong with her hips or her eyesight; maybe she's getting old. I read somewhere that for every year, seven years go by for a dog. It's beyond my understanding how this could ever be true.

I walk over to the big desk and with some effort open the large drawer, where I have a bottle of Kron, from which I fill the

153

schnapps glass on the desk. In the ashtray with the hula-hula-dancing figurine in the middle, I find a half-smoked Meteor.

While I let the acrid, heavy smoke fill my mouth, I peer into the drawer. I pick up Beda's letter and open the folded paper with my thumb.

'You can't get away from a promise,' I remind myself. 'It's always honour and glory all the bloody way, but when you think about it, those are the only things the poor have.'

I close my eyes and massage the top of my nose with my thumb and forefinger. That old girl always had a fire in her belly. I remember the way she used to bawl at me whenever I let a curse or two slip out. I can almost see Petrus sweeping the floor tiles with that broom of his as he constantly did; then, even though I don't want to think of it, the same Petrus strapped down in an isolation cell with a large red bib of blood on his chest and his throat cut open like the stomach of a gutted fish.

The room-temperature schnapps swills through my innards. I shiver and refill my glass. I just can't understand why anyone would want to kill off two such harmless figures as Beda and Petrus. On the other hand I've been in this game for long enough to know there isn't always any rhyme or reason to all the blasted things people do to each other.

I remember my first line-crossing ceremony. I wasn't much more than a child, working the coffee route from South America under a Norwegian flag. We passed the equator at night. I was standing by the gunwale when they sneaked up on me: the trade wind was caressing my face, the moon sprinkling its silver over the ocean dunes, when a pair of strong hands grabbed my arms and threw me down on the deck.

The drunken men put on quite a show; they were wearing dresses made of jute sacks and sailcloth. They forced me to drink a reviving tincture of castor oil and pig shit, cropped my hair and anointed me with a mixture of tar, eggs and chicken droppings. I was baptised in the name of Neptune; then, one by one, they came forward and gobbed in my face. Finally I had to go to the windward side of the ship and piss into the wind. The men cheered and raised their glasses.

On the way back across the pond, some other poor sod had the same treatment, and this time I was one of the men taking part in the ritual. It was the way of things. If I was to go around asking myself why one bloke harms another every time it happened, I'd go raving mad. Sometimes there are no reasons. It's just how it is. It's hard to resist the call of violence.

For a brief second I see the man in black, his ice-cold eyes; I hear his last hoarse words and then I see the light in his eyes going out when I stab his chest for the fifth time. I pick up the glass on the table and drain it again.

I'll give Petrus and Beda another three days. After that it's time for me to take care of Doughboy and let go of everything that's happened. That's what I'll tell Elin after the cremation this afternoon too. Three days and not a minute longer. She's not likely to be pleased about that.

'There'll be a hell of a racket,' I mutter to Dixie, who's hungrily spinning around my legs.

In the kitchen larder I don't have much more than a dry bit of bread, a couple of eggs and half a bucket of cooked human mess.

When as a child I was given anything at all to eat, I often got potatoes so old that they went black when you boiled them; so I wouldn't say I'm a fussy eater, but I decide against the contents of the bucket and opt for the eggs instead.

I get the wood-burning stove going, crack two eggs into the frying pan and put a copper saucepan of water on the other ring. I open a bottle of Carnegie and pour half of it into a bowl for Dixie. She drinks greedily with a splashing sound, while I sip carefully from the bottle.

When Dixie has slaked her thirst, I put down a soup plate of brownish slop. She doesn't sniff it, just dives in. I drop a couple of coffee beans into my grandmother's beaten-up grinder; then I watch the bitch wolfing down the human remains.

'That's what happens to you if you ask Kvisten for a dance with weapons drawn.'

My chuckle is joyless. I pour the ground coffee into the saucepan of boiling water and take it off the ring to let it brew. Dixie looks up with a shamefaced expression, her whiskers caked with brownish-red stickiness. She whines for more, and when she cocks her head like that I'm not man enough to deny her.

While I'm eating, I plan my day. There's a lot that needs doing before I meet Elin. First of all I have to get my boots shined, then I have to hand in Wallin's uniform for a clean, and lastly I have to pitch in with the funeral arrangements. I remember that Beda recommended a chemical dry-clean in a place on Observatoriegatan for bloodstains. The most important thing is that I'm not recognised, so I'll have to use a false name.

I mop up the egg yolk with the dry crust of bread and wash it down with the porter. If I have time, I'll use it to call in a couple of debts for Bruntell with the Kodak, as payment for my portrait in front of the tobacco shop, which will be sent to America. Debt collection is a nasty job, but this time there's a good reason for it.

I tear off a mouthful of hard bread with my molars. An icy pain radiates downward through my jaw. I go rigid, throw away the bread; it clatters against the draining board. Still stiff with terror, I finger my lower line of teeth.

One time when I was young, I spent weeks with a throbbing toothache before we put in at Casablanca Harbour. There, with another unfortunate, I went to the local dentist, an Arab in a full-length dress. A pedal-driven drill and a pair of pliers were his only instruments. He got us to inhale a treacherous smoke he called *kiff*, and before I knew it I was completely dizzy and couldn't tell port from starboard. Maybe I pointed to the wrong place and that was why he pulled out a healthy tooth, then sent me back to the skiff. From the corrupted tooth the infection spread through half my jaw, and I lay in a fever all the way to Hamburg, where a smith at the shipyard pulled the bad tooth from my gob. Ever since then I've dreaded dentists more than anything, apart from heights. But I've managed pretty well, all in all. They say a glass of schnapps helps keeps your chompers in good order.

Dixie has cleaned off her plate and lies stretched out on the rag rug with a swollen belly, as if she's about to have puppies. Maybe she's just tipsy? I ask myself if I should get rid of the bits in the bucket, but I decide to keep them and give her few more helpings later on. She seems to like the giblets and I have to save every copper I can. I'll have to live with the smell of the goo in the kitchen.

Once I'm dressed I call for Dixie, who limps over. I put her on the leash and take the package with Wallin's uniform under my arm. I thread the leash around my wrist and remove the empty bottle I put on the door handle last night as a safety measure before going to bed. I no longer have faith in Dixie's sense of hearing.

Only after stepping out of the door do I button up my coat and fold up the collar. Dixie's decrepit legs shiver. There's no trace on the pavement of last night's antics. I walk down Roslagsgatan and turn up on Frejgatan to see if the Rolls is parked there. Dixie limps along behind me like a consumptive kid.

'You're the gentl'man people call Kvisten, ain't you?'

The shoeshine boy looks up at me, his mouth full of wonky teeth. He's an agile youth with a strong jaw and inky black fingers. A pair of blue eyes glitter under the peak of his cap, and the cold has brought his cheeks out in a flush. I haven't taken my eyes off him since he started polishing. I take the cigar out of my mouth and wet my lips: 'Correct.'

On Sveavägen, the number 14 tram rattles past with three carriages. I'm sitting on a smooth-worn, three-legged stool just below the broad steep steps of the City Library. The youth is kneeling on an old newspaper in front of me.

Next to him he has a carpenter's box of brushes, rags and shoe creams. The smell of the coffee roasters a few blocks away hangs heavy in the air. A few metres to one side of us, a ragamuffin with a cap on his head and frayed trouser legs is minding the pump by the horses' drinking trough.

'My customers often say we 'aven't had a decent boxer since Kvisten and H.P.'

'H.P. never did so well against the Yanks.'

'Sanctions against Italy still in place,' yells a newspaper delivery man, waving an issue of *Svenska Dagbladet*.

An old Volvo, coughing like an old man with a weak chest, pulls out into the traffic. On the other side of the street, rays of sunlight are flashing from a gilded cow's head above the butcher's shop.

'It was a pity, what happened, sir, your havin' to give it up an' all. Point your foot up would you, please.'

I chuckle and do as I'm told. The lad has spirit, you have to give him that.

'Yesterday's news.'

The kid takes a rag in both hands, stretches it and starts quickly rubbing the top of my boot. The sock garters strain around my shins as I tense my muscle. He's got a handy pair of thumbs for his size.

'I used to box as well. At Linnea. But it got too pricey. Other foot now.'

'Skint, are you?'

'This jacket's borrowed.'

'There are cheaper clubs.'

'Not cheap enough. We'll be done here in a minute.'

Further down the street, a driver manoeuvres his piebald horse towards the drinking trough. The lad who's been leaning against the trough throws himself on the pump at once so the horse can drink. It raises its head again, champing at the bit, its muzzle dripping with water. A five-öre piece flies glittering through the air; the lad catches it adeptly in his cap and bows.

'Ten girls chosen for the Saint Lucy's Day parade!' roars the newspaper man.

Dixie tugs at her lead when a fat rat scurries past in the gutter below, its tail dragging behind. I take a deep pull on my cigar and look at the boy: 'What are you trying to say?'

His cheeks turn even redder. He concentrates on his work although we're pretty well done.

'I have a girl, you know… but I could do with some help.'

'Spit it out.'

The lad straightens his back and puts his dirty hands on his thighs. His eyes dart about.

'I was thinkin' maybe you could have a look at me. Give me a couple of pointers?'

'Here and now?'

'If sir gets the shoeshine for free?'

With a chuckle I put the Meteor back in my mouth. I pull Dixie back and make her sit next to me, then take another deep puff: 'Put 'em up then, boy! Let's see what you're about.'

The lad jumps to his feet and throws his cap on the steps. His head drops down between his shoulders; his hands shield his face. He's got dark armbands of shoe polish and dirt at the end of his blue shirtsleeves. He's carrying too little weight for his height, but so was I when I started. His build reminds me of Doughboy.

'Lightweight class?'

'That's right, sir.'

'Damn it, lad, call me Kvisten. And try to make it up to welter-weight if you can find enough to eat. Feet further apart!'

The lad is not slow to take orders; he's not wholly dim-witted, this one.

His black hands shimmer in front of him. I remember when I first decided to take up boxing: a smitten first machinist had invited me to come to the ring at Lorensberg to see Jack Johnson, must have been just before the war. I'd already been prize-fighting in various ports, although I hadn't been schooled at all; I'd smacked around mess waiters and other ship's boys until they were black and blue.

We had the cheapest seats. The sweat was pouring off Johnson's black shaven skull; the crowd was booing him. 'Send that nigger home in a cage!' they bawled. Johnson's gold teeth flashed like tracers in the dark as he smilingly demolished his opponent, while the first machinist's hand caressed the small of my back under my jumper. In that moment I understood I wasn't much other than

160

an unusually pale Negro, and that there was one world inside the ring and another outside it.

I smile. 'Good,' I say. 'Shadow-box for me, I want to see some combinations.'

I reach down and scratch Dixie behind her ear while the kid starts firing off punches into the air. He's got fast hands and he can put together basic combinations, but he hardly moves his feet. Most likely his trainer put him on a sack and forgot all about him. An elderly couple stop to watch. They're joined by a couple of small lads on their lunch break. A couple of them start laughing, but the kid doesn't seem to notice them.

It's something I never learned. A good sign.

'That's it!' I holler. 'Always at least three punches, block at the end of every series. No, no! Hands above your eyebrows, deflect with your elbows. A little quicker, good. Twist half a turn on your front foot and go for another combination. That's it! Again! And again! Every time you turn the other bastard has to think again.'

I slide forward on the stool and try to direct the lad with my cigar waving about in the air.

'Where the hell are your feet, lad? Wide apart! Dance, you sod! That's it! No, you're crossing your legs! What's the matter with you? That's better, now roll your upper body. Now follow up with your jabs! Never give the other bastard a breather!'

I smile and slap my hand against my thigh. Sparks and smoke whirl into the air. I feel a sensation almost like music in my chest. A good glass of rye now would hit the spot like a knife in the county constable. The old bloke who's there with his missus leans over to tell her something. A heavily made-up woman with wavy dark hair and worn heels also stops to have a look. Her eyes are shiny, almost fevered.

161

'Roll your whole shoulder into the uppercut! Legs, lad! Legs! One step forward for every jab now. Elbow pointing down at the ground every time you pull your arm back! That's it! No, damn it! Forward with the left foot every time. Let your right foot drag behind. Like this!'

I laugh, let go of Dixie and stand up to show him how to move forward. He looks quite giddy but he does as he's told. A couple of National Socialists with fliers in their hands join the group. Under their coats they're wearing brown shirts and black ties, both of them with leather belts across their chests. On their armbands, yellow swastikas stand out against a blue background. They're drawn to people like lice.

Soon others join the group as well, there must be ten or fifteen people standing there. A sigh of admiration runs through them when I show off and demonstrate to the boy how it's done. My stitched-up wound is howling with pain but I ignore it. The lad imitates my moves as well as he can.

I let him keep working after the round has finished. When at last I call out to the lad that he can have a breather, there's scattered applause from the audience. I'm almost as out of breath as him, with all the yelling I've been doing. I offer him the stool and before I know it I'm massaging his neck with one hand. He's soaked with sweat; he smells good.

'Thanks, Kvisten.'

He pants for air between the words.

'Don't give it a thought. You're not so unlike yours truly when I was young.'

'Quick?'

'Penniless.'

The lad gives me a crestfallen look. I laugh, ruffling his hair and adding: 'And fairly quick too.'

His crooked teeth flash a big smile. He says eagerly: 'Maybe we could do it again some time? In case Kvisten needs his shoes polished again?'

I give it a bit of thought while I get out a box of matches to relight my cigar. I rub my unshaven chin. It's a tempting proposal, at least no less tempting than he is himself. Any old sod knows you can read a man's situation in life by looking down. In the first years of my life I had to share a single pair of shoes with my twin brother. Damn it, Kvist, you're coming up in the world.

'I can take you on once a week or so, on certain conditions.'

'Are you pulling my leg, Kvisten?'

'You haven't heard the conditions yet. Do you have a name?'

'Hasse. Or Hans.'

'Okay, Hasse. I need to hand in this package to the laundry on Observatoriegatan today. Can you do it under the name of Zetterberg, and take a receipt? I'll pick it up myself tomorrow. How tall are you?'

'One sixty-eight.'

'Perfect. This afternoon you're to go to Standards and try on a suit. Ask them to put it aside and pass on my best wishes.'

'A suit?'

'For my nephew. I think you're about the same size. You're a Söder lad, aren't you?'

'Mariaberget.'

'You lug all your stuff here and back every day?'

'My opening hours are the same as the library's. The caretaker lets me keep 'em locked up inside.'

'So run like you've got the devil on your heels.'

'What's that?'

'I want you to run every day. I liked the mornings best. The day you manage to keep up a good speed all the way here, you do a hundred press-ups facing down the steps.'

'A hundred?'

'And the day you manage that you give me a ring.'

I rip out a page of the notebook with Lundin's number written on it.

'Eat everything you can lay your hands on in the meantime. Everything.'

'Any old thing?'

'You have to be in form by early March and ready for your first match in the summer. July.'

I get a five-krona note out of my wallet: 'And buy yourself a skipping rope. It helps hands and feet to get along.'

Hasse takes the bill and makes a bow. I haul in Dixie, wink at the lad and turn away. The only spectator still there is the made-up woman with the glazed eyes. As I draw closer she stumbles on her narrow heels as she's undoing the belt of her overcoat. A sigh slips out of her red-painted lips, and she pulls an irritable face. Under her coat she's wearing a black velvet dress. A cloth rose is fixed in her décolletage. Her lips part in a greedy smile:

'Does the gentleman like roses? Would you like a smell of it?'

'Go to hell.'

I brush past her, putting my newly polished boot on a flier proclaiming, 'End the class war! March on with National Socialism!'

'Piss off home to wifey then, old man,' she hisses throatily at me, as I take Dixie and steer my steps back to Sibirien, whistling 'Ole Faithful' as I go. The morning has gone considerably better than I expected. Once we've got the dead boy and the man in black safely cremated, I can meet with Elin this afternoon.

I peer over at Standards on the other side of the big crossroads where the small-time gangster Fridolf Five-Bob reputedly bled dry in the winter of '29, but I see no sign of her.

I turn around and see Hasse still standing there huffing and puffing by his stool, a couple of black smudges of boot polish on his forehead where he wiped off the sweat. I think about Doughboy. Four days left.

Loneliness tightens across my chest like a badly tailored shirt.

According to Bruntell the grocer, his two biggest debtors are the Lapp's widow and Olsson on Roslagsgatan. There's nothing to be had from the widow. She cleans at the jeweller's without charging for it, then brings the dirt back home and strains it for flakes of gold. Olsson has admittedly been bed-bound for a while, he's sick and frail but nonetheless my best chance. He lives a couple of blocks to the north, in the last house on Roslagsgatan. It's a tatty building with the brickwork showing through where the pointing's peeled off.

I leave Dixie tied up around a drainpipe and push the door open. From the elementary school opposite, I can hear the shrill tones of the student orchestra in the middle of their Saturday rehearsal. The stairwell smells of damp and boiled turnips. Olsson lives one floor up. My stomach starts growling as I walk up the stairs. I take off my tie and put it in my pocket, then crack the joints of my fingers.

Above Olsson's nameplate another ten or so names have been glued to the door. I hear the mumbling of several voices inside. I take a deep breath and steel myself.

'I'm doing this for you, little Ida…'

My voice echoes desolately in the stairwell. I bang on the door. The sounds on the other side quickly stop. I wait a couple of seconds, then bang again. Someone coughs raspingly, then I hear dragging steps approaching.

The door opens narrowly, just a small slit. I grab the door handle and tug it open.

Olsson's sickly greyish-yellow skin stretches over his skull like weathered sailcloth. A coughing fit passes through his rickety body, making him twitch like a broken jumping jack. He's an emaciated bloke with white locks of hair around his ears. A lifetime of resentment and disappointment has twisted his wrinkled mouth into a permanent frown. One of the spent cogs of the machine; I heard he used to be a boiler-man at the wool factory in Söder before his sickness caused him to lose his job. The rings of soot under his eyes seem never to have disappeared.

He rests his arm and forehead against the wall. With the other hand he's holding up his trousers. He doesn't have a belt or braces. If I nail a bloke in this condition, I'll be risking a murder prosecution. I have to take things easy here.

While I'm waiting for Olsson's cough to settle down, I peer into the one-room flat. The dirty walls are completely bare, and there's no furniture. Most likely he sold it all, or pawned it. It's a trial by fire, getting ill in this country.

There's a stink of humanity and tobacco smoke. The broken window at the back of the room has been plugged with newspaper and glue, and there's not a lot of light coming in, even in the middle of the day. The entire floor is covered in old newspapers and filthy pillows. This is where they all sleep, men, women and children. Pale faces stand out in the gloom.

There are plenty of these kinds of lodgings in the tenements of Sibirien. They're all similarly short of hope and oxygen. I've seen my fair share of them, either when tracking down missing persons or just collecting unpaid rent. But if Olsson has people dossing on his floor, he ought to be making a bob or two, surely?

'Kvisten,' Olsson wheezes once he's recovered. 'It's been a while. What can I do for you?'

His Scanian burr is more or less intact, even after all these years in the city. His eyes are filling with tears. Another rattle passes through his ramshackle body.

'I'm here on a job.'

For half a second, Olsson's bronchial tubes stop whistling. He looks down at his torn socks. There's a slight tremble in his hand as he points into the room: 'Who's it about this time?'

'You, Olsson. Bruntell wants his bread.'

Olsson's lower jaw drops and judders up and down twice. He snuffles. His limbs start shaking as if there's an earthquake in the offing, and his eyes tear up. I clench my jaw. He tries a smile, but his trembling lips only manage to pull his mouth out of shape.

'Sad to hear it.'

'You heard about Johnsson, on the corner? What happened to him when he got difficult with me?'

'Certainly I have, yeah.'

Tears fill the furrows on Olsson's face and drip onto his dirty linen shirt. He snuffles again.

'I wouldn't want to take it as far as that this time.'

'But… I don't have that much money. If I could have a bit of an extension…'

'You've had months of extension. Bruntell's fed up with it.'

'Couldn't you be a bit nice about it, Kvisten? Think about—'

'Think about Johnsson.'

Olsson keeps shaking. He rubs his hands together, but soon has to catch his trousers when they start slipping down. He's not wearing underpants; his grey pubic hairs stick out from beneath the waistline. Disgusted, I take a pull at my cigar and glance down the stairs.

'But what has Kvisten got in mind for me? Can't you show a bit of mercy? I'm sick and—'

'Stand up straight, for God's sake!'

'But what will you do to me, Kvist?'

'Straighten up! At least show me you're half a man, will you!'

'I don't have that much money. I know what Kvisten likes. If you let me… we could go somewhere…'

Olsson puts his emaciated right hand on my arm and caresses me with shivering, convulsive movements. I stare at him, nauseated, then take his hand and throw it aside.

On the floor inside the flat, people are lying immobile under their blankets, grey bundles resting like stones on a barren shore.

'Get your mitts off, will you!'

'So tell me, then! Tell me what you're going to do, Kvisten!'

For the first time his eyes, red from crying, look into mine; his head leans to one side, and then I see a sort of glint in his gaze, like when a whippersnapper comes up with an idea for some foolery.

Before I know it he's put the fingers of his right hand into the door frame, while with his left he grabs the door handle. This is not looking good. I freeze for a second, then leap forward: 'Wait!'

He doesn't listen to me. He clenches his jaw, and then slams the door as hard as he can. There's a crunching sound followed by a high-pitched yell which two or three other voices echo in fear. The door slowly glides open again, revealing Olsson kneeling on the floor of the hall, rocking to and fro with the bleeding knot of his right hand inserted into his left armpit. His trousers have slid halfway down his thighs. He whimpers, looking up at me with his red-rimmed eyes. I take half a step back, stumble and almost fall.

'Is it good enough for you, Kvisten? If I pay Bruntell what little money I have?'

Olsson sobs. I stare at him.

'It should be good enough, yes.'

I turn around and rush down the stairs so quickly that the back of my coat flaps in the tailwind. When I reach the ground floor I stop, push my hat back, wipe the sweat off my brow with my sleeve and sink down on the first step. Upstairs I can hear Olsson whining like a little boy who's been slapped.

With a shaking hand I light a phosphorus match and put a fresh cigar in my mouth. It's a hell of a job, this.

Father and mother are following their son to the grave in a rusty Oldsmobile. I can see them in the rear-view mirror as we slowly approach Norra cemetery. The mother, a middle-aged woman with a sharply cut profile under her veil, stares fixedly out of the side window. The father squeezes the steering wheel with his sausage-like fingers. Now and then he comes too close, and I have to pick up speed. Not that it concerns me. The quicker we dump the cadaver in the oven, the better.

'The pall-bearers know they're dealing with a very corpulent boy.'

Lundin slurs his words, sitting next to me and massaging his skinny legs. He's wedged his pocket-flask between his thighs.

Once more I peer into the rear-view mirror, while accepting Lundin's proffered flask with my left hand. I have a sip and then another to calm my heart, although schnapps has no effect on a day like this.

'My brother, I told you loud and clear, stay out of trouble until you've worked off what you owe; then the first thing you do, you take a bloke and turn him into blood sausage.'

'I didn't have much choice.'

I keep my eyes on our escort in the rear-view mirror as we go round a bend in the road. At the back is a lorry that seems to be loaded with furniture. A matt-black Ford has also joined the cortège. Instinctively I pick up speed slightly.

Lundin clears his throat: 'I'm dying one day at a time.'

'We all are.'

'It's gaining on me from the feet up. It takes me forty-five minutes to get out of bed in the mornings. Not to mention the pain in my hands.'

'You want me to bring you a cup of java in bed? I could dress up like a maid on Saint Lucy's Day.'

'Forty-five minutes! And dying for a piss the whole time.'

'White slip, candles in my hatband.'

Lundin laughs, making a wheezing sound.

'That would be a sight.'

'I'd rather call Welfare and get you into a home.'

'Forget about *that*, you hear me?'

We turn off into the churchyard. I keep my eyes on our escort. In the back, I can hear the white coffin sliding across the floor. I don't even want to think about what would happen if the boarded-up lid was removed. The lorry carries on without turning off, but the Ford stays on our tail. My knuckles turn white around the steering wheel; the red scar tissue stands out even more. I breathe deeply.

Lundin raises his voice: 'Are you listening?'

'What did you say?'

'I said, we'll go to the bank on Monday, on Tuesday afternoon I have to go to the doctor's about my blasted hand, and on Wednesday you become a till rat.'

'And a boxing trainer, if all goes to plan.'

'What was that last bit?'

I catch a glimpse of the dome of the North Chapel through an alley of bare elms. I take a last look in the rear-view mirror before I peer across at Lundin, who's twisting the ends of his moustache.

I reach for the hip-flask between his thighs: 'We have company.'

'What do you mean?'

'The coppers in that damned Ford.'

The chapel smells of lilies and cut spruce sprays. The dead boy's parents sit in the first row, straight-backed and dignified. In a monotonous voice the priest tries to explain why God had to have their son killed.

Not a lot of people have taken the time to be there, although possibly more than usual on a Saturday – after all, they are bury-ing a boy who'd hardly turned fourteen.

I sit with Lundin and the other pall-bearers in the back pew. Lundin holds his personal brown leather-bound Book of Psalms in his gnarled hands. We wait patiently for the next hymn. The people in the Ford haven't come in, and I didn't dare look too closely at them when we carried the coffin up the front steps of the chapel. Still, I can feel their presence more strongly than God the Father's, that's for sure. I shake my head, counting the seconds till the coffin is lowered through the floor and burned to cinders in the cremation oven below.

When I close my eyes I see Doughboy standing on his own, waiting outside the prison gates on Wednesday. I shudder invol-untarily and the pew creaks.

I look at the coffin at the front. One of them ran into a tram, the other ran into me. The outcome was the same.

The pastor stops preaching. A pair of water-combed church-goers, stiff and God-fearing, shift in their seats. Their pew creaks in response. Someone blows their nose loudly. Lundin's fingers drum gently against his Book of Psalms. The first organ tones of 'Children of the Heavenly Father' resound between the walls, and Lundin and I lean our heads together to pick up our conversation where we left off. The pastor gives the last psalm everything he's got. The little congregation murmurs along. Lundin's breath, soured by schnapps and coffee, wafts into my face from only a few inches away.

'So we're agreed, then?' he says. 'We played cards all night?'

'At my place. Mainly poker.'

'Who won?'

'I did.'

'Hardly credible.'

'What difference does that make?'

'So I won, then?'

'Okay.'

'And if they open the coffin?'

'We deny all knowledge.'

Lundin coughs, scraping his foot against the floor. He leans towards me and goes on: 'And the dog food?'

'What do you mean?'

'The bucket of slop for your bitch!'

'Her name's Dixie.'

'Is there anything left in it?'

'Just a bit in the bottom.'

'How much or how little is hardly very significant.'

'It's boiled to shreds.'

'Can they establish its blood group?'

'Don't ask me.'

The music stops. After some further words, the pastor gestures for the next of kin to come forward. The congregation stirs all along the pews.

Everyone takes a turn around the coffin. The mother curtsies, and the father bows. Those with bouquets in their hands lay them down. Farewells are mumbled. A sob or two echoes through the chapel.

The parents are the first to walk back down the central aisle. The father's fat face is scarlet, as if his starched collar is a size too small. He squeezes a snuff handkerchief in one hand. His wife supports herself on his other arm. She hasn't cried a tear. I nod appreciatively at her. I can't stand women when they start crying. I'll go along with anything to make them stop.

Outside, the bells start up. The few fellow mourners stumble along behind the parents, looking disconcerted and confused. This was no funeral to write home about, not as heart-rending and beautiful as it's meant to be when some poor sods bury their little darling.

'Let's get a bloody move on.'

Lundin stands up with a certain heaviness; I do the same. There's a bit of muttering and bickering among the pall-bearers. I step into the central aisle and let my eyes wander towards the square doorway of the chapel, the doors of which are wide open to the falling dusk.

The church bells fade away. We gather around the coffin, our bowler hats in our hands. My palms are sweaty.

'Where the hell's the sexton who's working the hydraulics?'

Lundin looks around. I see the tension in his face. The furrows on his brow are deeper than ever. Outside, I hear a car door closing. A chill runs through my bones. I turn around. The man in the doorway, an old acquaintance of mine, is wearing an elegant overcoat and a bowler hat. His name is Berglund, a detective superintendent. He has the same little grey moustache as the last time I saw him. I hate him. As far as I can tell, the feeling is mutual.

Fear churns inside me. I'm trembling. I think about Doughboy. I think about the suit I've promised him. I think of him in that damned cigar shop.

Berglund has brought along two uniformed constables.

They keep their hands on the hilts of their sabres as they come down the central aisle. Berglund already has the cuffs ready in his hand. A dog barks twice. Lundin passes his hip-flask around the bearers. The blokes raise it to the coffin before they take a pull at it. Lundin imbibes another mouthful as it comes back. I lean towards him, my eyes fixed on my newly polished shoes.

'There's a suit in my name waiting at Standards. Would you be good enough to pick it up?'

'Certainly I can.'

'It's for Doughboy. He should come by the funeral parlour looking for me in four days.'

'I'll see to it.'

Berglund and the other coppers are halfway down the central aisle now. He's smiling, that same old stiff grin. Somewhere beneath the coffin there's a clicking sound. The hydraulic lift huffs and puffs. The wooden base trembles.

'And give him my best too.'

Lundin raises his eyebrow quizzically: 'What?'

With a scraping sound, the coffin slowly sinks through the opening in the stone floor. I seem to feel the heat of the oven under the soles of my shoes. Sweat flows from my prison haircut and down over my brow.

'What do you mean?'

'What should I say?'

'Just give my best to Doughboy.'

'Here come the pigs now.'

The pall-bearers scatter and head for the exit, avoiding the detective superintendent's path as you would a sharp reef in open water. Anger surges through me, the vein on my forehead pulses and my nails dig into my palms.

Berglund stops in front of us. His handcuffs dangle like a hangman's noose in his hand. Lundin tries to barge in between us, but I push him aside. The policeman grins, his lips cracked from the cold: 'You'll have to accompany us to Kungsholmen, Kvist.'

The detective superintendent's voice is taut and high-pitched. 'What's this about?'

'An assault on Roslagsgatan, apparently Kvist was involved.'

'Like hell I was.'

One of the constables grunts. At last Berglund's copper's grin fades. He leans towards me and lowers his voice: 'Kvist obviously feels at home with all the sodomites at Långholmen,' he hisses. 'He's hardly had time to be released before he has to crawl back inside.'

SUNDAY 24 NOVEMBER

I'm shuffling back and forth in my socks, between the graffiti-covered walls of the remand cell. To keep warm and make the time go by, I practise a bit of gentle shadow-boxing. When my inner tension becomes unbearable, I give my muscle memory free rein, releasing lightning-quick combinations, mixing all sorts of punches, going in low, then high. It gives me a momentary relief.

'Harry Kvisten Kvist in a magnificent comeback.'

I shiver, double my jab and release a heavy right at chest height. Then withdraw quickly and accidentally put my heel on the rim of the plate I just put down by the heavy wooden door. It clatters. The remnants of my breakfast porridge splash over the floor. I lower my fists.

The cell doesn't measure much more than five square metres, with a barred window at the short end. Under the window a latrine bucket spreads its stink. Along one of the long walls, there's a bunk bolted into the stone, on it a mattress stuffed with compressed wood shavings. If you're lucky you get a blanket of uniform cloth. I'm rarely lucky, I'm just not the type. Not this time either.

I scrape at a couple of the night's flea bites and resume my pacing. They still haven't interrogated me. This is how they work. First you have to sit alone all night in your own thoughts, you have to get your thoughts all in a tangle, your nerves taut as violin strings. It's hard not to fall into it. You scare yourself, like a horse.

The faces of the dead tumble through my consciousness: Beda, her skin as wrinkled as a dry apple, laughing with her toothless mouth; Petrus, the large-hewn bloke with the mind of an urchin, blushing under his blond mane of hair; the man in the poplin coat, his eyebrow scar, his ice-cold blue eyes and the splashes of blood on his face.

My plan, and Lundin's also, must have gone wrong. Some curious neighbour who saw the knife fight probably took the chance to avenge an old injustice.

I let my fists explode in the air before me, a furious flurry of blows. A sour exhalation for every punch. Hooks and uppercuts, my whole arsenal in action. The wound in my side smarts. Sweat breaks out, makes the flea bites sting. My shoulders go numb.

Panting, I back into the wall, sink down on the floor with my knees in front of me, burying my face in my hands.

Doughboy comes into my mind, and for a moment I feel the temperature of my blood rise. The worst time of the day for the Långholmen convict is the moment between work and bed, when there's time for thinking and yearning. But the worst of all is the day off, Sunday. Wherever you look, your eyes collide with the damp grey walls.

The only human contact is the prison chaplain, who makes his weekly visit only to tell us again that we're all sinners. Well, at least it's Doughboy's last Sunday on the inside.

They bring another dollop of porridge before two uniformed screws cuff me and bring me up through the system of stairwells in the large police headquarters, fairly empty on a Sunday. With heavy steps I allow myself to be shepherded through a bare corridor. Visual memories of Doughboy flash through my head like lightning. Doughboy with his neck full of raw, scratched flea bites. Those smooth fingers of his. His soft mouth.

One of the screws shoves me between the shoulder blades: 'Get a move on!'

Somehow that boy gave me a new lease of life. Cleaned out my polluted innards. For the first time in years, something other than fury pulsed through my blood. I promised him a new suit and a warm bed with proper bolsters. Now that I'll fail to keep my promise, rage is once again pounding in my veins.

'You can go to hell!'

We enter something more like a meeting room than one of the small chambers where interrogations are usually held. The room is dominated by an oblong table with some ten chairs around it. In the middle is an empty but dirty ashtray. A row of windows runs along one of the walls.

The screws press me down into a chair. The stitches over my ribs smart; I groan, keeping my mouth closed.

There's a click when one of the handcuffs is released, only to be locked again with a rattling sound. They've shackled me to the back of the chair.

'The hell's the point of that?'

'Orders.'

I grunt by way of an answer. Something warm is running down the ridges of my ribs. At least one stitch has gone, maybe more.

On the table in front of me, someone has placed a thick file, a notepad and a pack of Carat cigarettes. I crane my neck to get a better view. On top of the file lie an elegant fountain pen, a torn-off cinema-ticket stub, an enamelled tiepin with a swastika, two fifty-öre pieces and a gas-metre counter.

'Apparently the criminal division has picked someone up for the murder of that pedlar,' one of the screws says to the other, who sighs wearily.

'They must have stumbled across the right person, I suppose.'

'A vagrant.'

'One-way ticket to Långholmen. At least he'll have a roof over his head.'

The first screw gurgles, a laugh of sorts. I close my eyes. I hope with all my heart that Doughboy has the sense to seek out Lundin and get his suit, when I'm not there waiting for him.

'Didn't Berglund say half past?'

'He'll come.'

'Why do we both have to wait here?'

The bunch of keys hanging from the screw's belt rattles when he takes a couple of steps. The whisper that follows is too low for me to make it out. One of them stifles a laugh.

'Well, you can always hope,' adds the comedian.

I sit in silence on my chair, while the blood drips down my side. Using one arm, I try to pull the jacket around me so the blood can't be seen, but it's difficult when I'm locked to the chair. I clench my fists behind my back. I'd do anything for a last cigar.

The door opens and closes. I look up. Berglund saunters into view with the same damned smirk on his mug as always. The screws linger: it's the final round, my opponent is keeping his seconds in the ring. Outside the ring there's no justice. Inside there's no difference between one man and another. Two blokes can meet there on equal terms.

Berglund sits down opposite me. He's wearing an impeccable charcoal-grey three-piece suit and holding a leather briefcase in his bony fingers. His nails are short, perfectly white against his fingertips. There's a click as his briefcase is opened; Berglund picks up the little items from the top of the file and puts them away. He leaves his bag on the table, caresses his grey moustache with an affected gesture and then drills his gaze into me: 'So, we meet again.'

'We wouldn't if it was up to me.'

Berglund chuckles and opens the file. I keep repeating my alibi in my head: poker with Lundin in my kitchen; Lundin won. Drank vodka and sugared soda. A short evening walk with Dixie. Early to bed. If the coffin made it into the oven, I might still be in with a chance.

Berglund puts on a pair of gold-rimmed spectacles: 'Harry Kvist, born on the thirtieth of December 1898 in Torshälla parish.' He lifts my file, as if gauging its weight: 'Quite a bundle.'

One of the screws laughs but stops short when Berglund gives him the eye. The detective superintendent purses his mouth slightly and hauls out his timepiece. The lid opens with a click. He scrutinises the watch face and then snaps it shut.

'Your name comes up in a dozen different investigations, and your bail was once paid by the Swedish consul in France. You have been sentenced for your anti-social tendencies. We have here a fine of seventy-five Swedish kronor for deviant behaviour in 1924, a prison term for assault in 1925, and another in 1928. To which we must add the most recent stretch for illegal intimidation.'

'I'm not a lucky man. I learned that early on.'

My vest is sticking to my skin. The gold mussel in his hand clicks again as he opens it; then he closes it with a snap, before gripping his pen.

'You and I met for the first time when you figured in a murder investigation concerning a certain Zetterberg, on Kungsgatan. Some three years ago, that was. The case remains unsolved to this day. I looked through the investigation this morning and some of the documents seem, highly mysteriously, to have gone missing from the file. For instance, I am quite certain that I interrogated you on a few occasions between Christmas and New Year in '32.'

'I don't think so.'

'I'm not the sort to forget. And this is the reason for the presence of these constables here today.'

'My memory is not what it used to be.'

'Your old friend Oskar Olsson is the head of the city police corps now. He's not here to make sure you're comfortable, Kvist.'

Berglund leans back in his chair and tucks his thumbs into his waistcoat. He lowers his chin to his chest and stares at me over the top of his spectacles.

'So you were released from Långholmen around the 20th. Which would usually mean you were let out around lunchtime, as I understand it?'

'What has that to do with anything?'

'Anything?'

A little rivulet of blood seeks its way down under the lining of my trousers. They took my belt when they locked me up. I strain to keep smiling at him.

'You mentioned an assault?'

'Be good enough to answer the questions. What did you do after you were released?'

'Went and gawped at the King, but I don't know if he'd back me up if I said I was there.'

'What are you going on about?'

'The opening of the bridge. Bloody bad weather, but plenty of people anyway. A load of kids, singing away.'

'And then?'

'I went to the Toad. It's a betting shop...'

'And after you got home? To Sibirien? On the evening of the 20th?'

'There was a house party next door. There always is, every November.'

'How long did you stay?'

181

'I went home early, but I can't remember what time it was.'

'Did you see anyone on your way home?'

'I bumped into Rickardsson. That's one of Ploman's blokes.'

'I know them, all right.'

'You have a very colourful circle of friends, Detective Superintendent.'

'I know *of* them.'

Berglund bends over his notepad. His pen scrapes across the paper. He looks up: 'No one else?'

I think. My muscles relax, I release my neck with a click, a honey-sweet feeling of peace spreads through me, and a sense of calm blows like a soft breeze through my veins. I feel a little smile coming on. I lean towards Berglund until the chain rattles and I come to a stop.

'No one.'

Berglund rifles through his papers and finds the one he wants, then pushes up his glasses with his finger. I can't stop smiling.

'We have had an assault reported by a certain John Kullberg. On the given date at nine in the evening, Mister Kullberg without any apparent reason was attacked by a man of your description outside business premises at Roslagsgatan 48.'

'I didn't see anything.'

'A man not even known to Kullberg beat him so badly that he received a fracture to his rib, and when the victim duly attempted to escape, he was kicked in the crotch.'

'Most likely I was sleeping off the vodka.'

Berglund sighs and leans back again in his chair.

'Kvist, I know that in your time you were known as a technician, but I'm inclined to believe that you've become a damned slugger. Kicking a man in the crotch!'

The commissioner shakes his head like a giddy old bat.

'Any witnesses?'

'So, you have hardly been out of prison for eight hours before you have a punt at a man who was not even known to you. And you end up with a black eye to prove it.'

'So… no witnesses, then?'

'I suppose a nancy boy like you, Kvist, actually likes being in prison.'

'Remove these handcuffs and fetch my damned coat with my cigars.'

Berglund tucks his thumbs back into his waistcoat, and sighs. He nods at the screws.

'Well, Kvist had better be bloody clear about one thing. We've got our eyes on you. If you make the slightest false move, we'll have you back inside before you know it.'

'And you, Detective Superintendent, should be bloody clear about one thing too: waistcoats are no longer fashionable in America.'

With a grin, I nod at his well-tailored suit.

The sun is turning to ash. In the failing light of dusk, Roslagsgatan shimmers as if metal flakes were falling from the sky. The pink rays are reflected against enamelled shop signs and plate-glass windows. Outside Nyström's barber's a gang of navvies are repairing the rails, but they're not the same blokes who were here before. Hammer strokes ring out, and bounce between the façades. The acetylene flame hisses and throws up sparks as it attacks the metal.

A discordant clattering of hooves can be heard when a stout working mare pulling a cart-load of planks shies away from the sound. The driver, who's leading her by the bridle, struggles and forces her to keep moving. One of the navvies sits up on his knees and grimaces, his hand against the small of his back. He removes his cap and mops the sweat off his forehead.

On the street corner there's a tramp with a violin, a mess of fleas and rags. His only garment that's not full of holes is a sturdy striped farmer's vest. The violin's out of tune, as is the tramp, but I stop for a moment, because it's my favourite song:

> *He owns neither father nor mother,*
> *And through his life there's no one to keep him fed;*
> *Like a needy child at yet another*
> *Rich man's table he begs for his bread…*

I hum along for a while, then take out my wallet.

> *And so he becomes a man of the road,*
> *Seduced in his most youthful days;*
> *His name did find its charted abode*
> *Among Stockholm's criminal ways.*

I find a five-öre coin, flick it through the air and manage to hit the violin case on the button. The tramp nods at me and I continue homeward, singing as I go.

Little clusters of ragged-clothed children are hanging about on the street, free to do as they please on a Sunday. Their pockets are bursting with marbles. A couple of the older boys have ripped out a page of a newspaper with a photograph of Hitler, which they've nailed up on a tree outside the widow's cigar shop. At the head of the group stands a spotty lad aiming a dart with red tail-feathers at the German leader.

'It's Allan's turn,' says a little lad in a red hat.

'Allan's out,' answers the snotty kid holding the darts. 'You have to hit him right in the peepers. Allan hit the eyebrow.'

I smile and light a second Meteor off my first. My stomach is rumbling with hunger. Police porridge is hardly a filling meal.

I still can't get my head around the coppers letting me go, and them not even wanting to question me about the man in black – only about that other incident from several days before. I tip my hat back, shove my hands in my coat pockets and keep walking north.

I find Lundin in the little workshop attached to the undertaker's, where he's assembling one of the prefabricated sections of the coffins that are delivered to him a couple of times every month. The various sections are laid out between two trestles, and he's busy trying to fit the base onto one of the side panels.

'Well, I'll be damned.'

Lundin straightens up, and stares at me as I stand there in the doorway. His bushy eyebrows shoot up on his high forehead. I lean against the doorpost.

'Do I look as bad as all that? I suppose I need a bath and a shave?'

I rub my chin and step in the poorly lit workshop. It smells of pitch pine and paint.

'When did they release you, brother?'

'I came straight here.'

'I'll be damned.'

The undertaker leans over the wooden coffin again. He's all smiles under the moustache.

'It was about something completely different. Nothing big.'

'And now it's time to put all that business behind you, I hope? Pass me that wooden mallet, will you? The one with the rags around the head.'

185

'You weren't bloody serious about that cigar shop, were you?'

'Of course I was. Keep this lower part steady, the sod keeps jumping out at the joint.'

I feel I ought to take off my hat and thank him.

'There's one thing I can't understand. If they shot her in the middle of the day, the shots would have echoed all through the street, and people would have come buzzing around like flies.'

'Forget about that damned mess, now. Hold it firm.'

The muted blows vibrate through the wooden planks of the coffin, travelling through my palm as I hold the side panel in position.

'The junk man Ström saw them when they took out the body, although not up close. They carried the corpse out by the arms and legs, and loaded her and Petrus into an unmarked car. A black one.'

'You know what they say about Ström, my brother. That he was Petrus's father. Now we change places. Hold on as tight as you bloody can.'

'Have you seen Dixie?'

'Twice. Her food's run out.'

'It was the coppers that put a slug in the old girl.'

Lundin straightens up and stares at me; a glint of fear shows in his iris.

'Something's amiss in your head, my brother. Beda wouldn't have harmed a fly. A sick old woman. True to her word and always a good egg. Why would the authorities do away with someone like that?'

'You can't get away from a promise.'

'What was that?'

'Nothing.'

Lundin sighs.

'Anyway, that carrot-top is waiting in your flat.'

'Elin?'

'Been sitting up there for hours. Intending to give you the suit personally. I said you'd probably be delayed. Very delayed.'

'My God.'

'She was very determined. As carrot-tops often are.'

I let go of the coffin and head for the door. I'd arranged to meet Elin yesterday. If I know her right she'll make me feel the sting of that.

'Brother?'

I turn towards Lundin once more. He's standing there with the mallet in his hand, his cravat hanging from his neck like a sleepy bat. With an almost timid glance, he says: 'Shall we say I'll take eight per cent of the profits instead of ten, once the debt is paid? From the cigar shop, I mean. To make sure you keep out of prison.'

I need to clear my head with some fresh air before I meet with Elin. I button up my coat and fold up my collar. On the slope of Ingemarsgatan, I see Nisse's Eva making her way to the bakery, with the last of the evening light on her back, and a shawl over her head.

I throw my cigar end into the gutter and cross the street. Outside the laundry I stop and peer inside through the window, my hands cupped around my eyes. I can just about make out Petrus's old broom. From some nearby courtyard, a fiddler starts to play.

I turn around and look at my own building. The man in black must have seen our registration plates and checked the number within the space of ten or fifteen minutes, then parked somewhere and lurked in the shadows of Ingemarsgatan until I came home.

'Where the hell did that damned Rolls go?' I mutter to myself, getting out my third Meteor of the day. I light it and look up at the façade. My flat is dimly illuminated. A shadow is moving across the bedroom ceiling, as if Elin is pacing to and fro in there. Better not say a word about being attacked out here that night. The fewer who know about that the better.

Filling my lungs with smoke, I turn south towards the general store. A couple of kids cycle past. They have both taken off the company signs from their delivery bicycles so they can use them on a Sunday. One of them is peddling along on a three-year-old Crescent, the other has an Adler which must be a new model, because I don't recognise it.

There's an evening rush on at Bruntell's. Both he and his wife are running between the shelves, the till and the scales. The fat grocer is sweating under his folding cap, and his wife has a strained smile fixed on her face. She's a tall, quiet woman. Thin as a poker, even though Bruntell has given her six children.

The women form a long, winding queue in front of the counter, carrying baskets and cloth bags filled with all sorts of shopping. They hardly pause to draw breath as they gossip about everything from food prices to the rotten weather we've been having, and the tragic story of the Jewel's baby, which actually she left deliberately in a draught to make sure that it died. There's no way of getting the slightest word in, so I just have to wait my blessed turn at the back of the queue. I've been kicking my heels for a minute or two when a voice rises above the hubbub: 'At least my Ove doesn't go for the booze like your bloke does!'

A sudden silence falls in the shop.

'Don't you go getting on your high horse now!'

'He's pickled so often his long johns get tangled on the clothesline by force of habit.'

'Why don't you just worry about your own dirty hovel!'

A tall, emaciated woman has tears of rage in her eyes as she spits her reply at a large-busted lady. The former looks like she'd like to stab the latter with her hatpin. Their neighbours in the queue start to tug at their sleeves, hushing and tutting.

'Drunkenness is a self-inflicted foolishness.'

The first woman turns back towards the counter, her lanky frame shaking with anger. I have to suppress a chuckle. At first only the odd mumble can be heard, then a general hum of chatter develops, and soon the sound level is back to what it was before.

I have a headache. I need a drink or two, a bit of food, a bath. A decent night's sleep. The wound in my side needs dressing. I catch the grocer's eye and nod. He smiles cautiously under his ludicrous postage-stamp moustache, and leans over the ledger on the counter: 'O-olsson came down and p-paid off half his debt.'

'Well, I'll be damned.'

'If Kvist t-takes his other hand as well, I m-m-might get the other half.'

'That wasn't me.'

'I hear he's offering l-lodgings to gypsies.'

'Maybe so.'

'Beggars.'

He spits out the word with disgust, as if he's just noticed a rancid pork chop among the meat on his counter.

'I'll be taking charge of the cigar shop.'

'Oh really? I heard it was f-for sale. I should wish you welcome, then. I'm the s-secretary of Roslagsgatan's Merchants Association.'

'Christ.'

'Beg your pardon?'

'Nothing. Has the portrait been developed?'

'It's v-very good.'

Bruntell bends down behind the counter and, humming to himself, puts the photograph in front of me. It's a half-length portrait, taken from the front. My eyes are shaded by the brim of my hat, but you can make out the cigar shop in the background.

I buy potatoes, eggs and American back rashers for my dinner, but when I ask to have it on credit, Bruntell won't hear of it and gives me the groceries free of charge. His wife packs it all into a rustling paper bag.

'You-you came in the o-other day asking about Beda and Petrus,' says Bruntell in a low voice, just as I'm about to leave. I stop and turn around again.

'That's right.'

'I developed the ph-photographs from the party and the p-portrait, and there were a couple of other negatives th-thrown in as well. I-I-I don't know if they're of any use to you.'

'What, exactly?'

'I'm n-not quite sure, but I th-think it was the same day they picked her up.'

Bruntell roots around behind the counter.

'I h-had to feed the film through and I cli-clicked a few times just pointing the camera through the shop window.'

I put my shopping bag down.

'And I th-think, soon after that Ström c-came and t-told me what he'd seen.'

He hands me a photograph.

'I d-don't know who they are.'

There's a blurred image of my own house, I recognise the sign over the funeral parlour. On the pavement in front of the house stand two figures wearing black, their eyes directed at the street. From what I can make out, the first figure looks like a man, partially obscuring a lady who's pointing at the laundry.

Bruntell stammers: 'A m-man and a w-woman?'

'Looks like it, judging by their hats. They seem to be walking arm-in-arm…'

'No one f-from around here?'

'Hard to say.'

I study the picture more carefully. At the right-hand edge, I can see the back end of a passing car but it's impossible to make out the registration plate.

I turn to the line of gossiping women, stretching back through half the shop. I hold up the photograph and raise my voice over the general din: 'Ladies! This is very important. I'm going to show you a photograph. If any of you recognise the people in this photograph, you must contact me urgently.'

Elin is sitting in the warm kitchen, waiting. On the table are two food cartons from NORMA and a couple of bottles of pilsner. She's gone for the octagonal plates. The table is laid for two but she's already eaten. A fire crackles in the hearth. Cheery jazz tones can be heard from the neighbour's transistor.

'So what sort of time is this to turn up?'

Beda's illegitimate daughter rises from her chair and puts her plate and cutlery in the sink. She's wearing a green dress with a pleated skirt. Pinned to her large bust is a brooch set with purple stones. The colour of her lipstick doesn't go with her hair. She has plucked her eyebrows to a fine line. They curve over her green eyes as if scratched in with a seven-inch nail.

'I completely forgot.'

'Been on one of your benders, have you?'

She turns on the water, and starts noisily washing the dishes. I shake my head.

'No, hard at work. Late to bed, early to rise.'

I take the big copper saucepan and go over to her: 'Water.'

She turns the tap and slowly the saucepan begins to fill up.

'You stink,' says Elin in a low, sharp tone. 'Your suit needs pressing.'

I don't know how I should answer her. Either I have to tell her I've been in the clink or keep quiet about it. I keep quiet. The water trickles unbearably slowly. The brooch rises and falls violently with her breath.

'Have you spoken to your friend at the police about the registration number?'

'It's Sunday.'

I put the saucepan on the ring.

'Horseradish beef with mash.'

Elin nods her broad chin towards the NORMA carton on the table.

'Thank you.'

'It's gone cold.'

'That doesn't matter at all.'

'I can heat it up.'

'No, really.'

I sit down and open the carton, shoving the food onto a plate and opening a bottle of pilsner.

'Shouldn't we report it to the police officially?'

'I don't think they'd put any time into it.'

'What do we do if the registration number doesn't match any of their records?'

'Well, then we've done what we can. Damn, this is good!'

'What about that school? The Asplund Institute for the Deaf, Mute and Blind?'

'Your brother went there twenty years ago. What would be the bloody use?'

'So, what next?'

'What's next is I'm opening a cigar shop and becoming a boxing trainer.'

The clattering of dishes stops all of a sudden. The air is thick with silence. Elin wipes her hands on the towel hanging on the wall, then turns to me.

'What do you mean?'

'The widow's cigar shop down the street is for sale. I'm borrowing some money from Lundin. It'll go through tomorrow or on Wednesday.'

'You going to run it all on your own?'

'My nephew's helping out.'

'You said it yourself, Kvist, a promise is a promise. My mother put all her hopes on you.'

I carry on wolfing down the meat and potatoes.

'There's a limit to everything. I've done what I can.'

'Is the suit for your nephew?'

'Yes, I need to pay you for that.'

'No need.'

Elin sits down, facing me. I have a couple of big gulps of beer.

'What do you mean? Course you have to get your dough.'

'I've got a steady job and a fair amount in my bank book since the sale of the laundry. Not too bad for an orphan.'

She brushes some crumbs from the table into her cupped hand. 'I've always had a good head for figures.'

'Well, thank you.'

'Spent half my life standing at a till, and the figures always add up to the last penny at the end of the day after cashing up.'

I help myself to another couple of spoonfuls of mashed potato with sauce.

'Thanks for the food, it's so good. From the NORMA on Kungsgatan, isn't it?'

'Giving the right change, calculating rebate percentages; it's hard finding staff. You can't count on young people.'

'The one on Vasagatan isn't much good. Kungsgatan is better.'

Elin takes a deep breath. She looks out of the window towards the reservoir in Vanadislunden. I go on eating. Half a minute passes in silence. Then, to my surprise, Elin starts to sob.

'But it never goes away. The loneliness. Once you've grown up alone you're never rid of it.'

I stay in my seat, staring at her, and take a long, slow swig of beer. On the hob, the water is slowly simmering in the red copper saucepan.

'Yes, I suppose…'

'It becomes a part of you and in the end you hardly notice it, like a tramp walking around stinking to high heaven but completely oblivious. You don't notice it but it's right there.'

'Well…'

My headache becomes a bellyache. I refill my glass.

'I know she must have thought of me sometimes. A mother does think about her child even if she's had her taken into care.'

'That may well be so.'

'Why did she never come and find me?'

'The days go by, and with every day it gets harder.'

'Poverty and disgrace.'

'A nice combination.'

For a while I follow her gaze out into the night, then I take out Bruntell's photograph from my breast pocket and slide it across the table. Elin tears her gaze away from the window and looks down at it, her eyes all shiny with tears.

'Who are those two?'

'I've asked around. Nothing.'

'And?'

'It seems it was taken precisely when your mother was being carried out of the laundry. You see how that woman's pointing?'

'Christ Almighty. We have to—'

'We'll never be able to find them.'

Elin's cheeks are flaming red.

'You must have taken a punch too many.'

'The hell's that supposed to mean?'

'God damn it, Harry. Sometimes you can't even see it when you're looking right at it. Like today, for example.'

A tear is running down Elin's cheek. Angrily she wipes it off with the back of her hand, then stands up so violently that the back of the chair is thrown into the wall behind her. She snatches up the photograph and storms out into the hall.

'Elin?' I slap the table so hard that the plate jumps into the air. 'What the bleeding hell is going on?'

I hear the door opening and then slamming behind her. I push back my chair and shuffle into the hall. She remembered to take her shoes and coat but her hat is still hanging on a hook.

'Well, she's quick off the mark, anyway.'

I go back into the kitchen and half-fill the bathtub with cold water from the tap, then put it down on the floor and top it off with the contents of the saucepan.

I have to rip the blood-blackened undershirt off my skin. A couple of the stitches have opened up; the wound across my ribs yawns like the gills of a freshly caught perch. Nothing that a new plaster and a tub of Sister Ella's Ointment can't fix. I remove the rest of my clothes and open another pilsner, then throw a bar of soap into the water and step into it myself. The wound stings even when I keep it above the water but the warmth soothes my sore muscles. I'll be having an early night tonight.

I put the beer bottle on the floor and soap my body. When Doughboy comes out, I'll take him to the Central Baths. I go there myself for a thorough clean now and then. Of course, there are other reasons to go there too, and I'm not talking about their twenty-five-öre cups of hot soup: 'Shapely youths, well-off gentlemen. And then Harry Kvist, of course, the cigar shop owner and boxing trainer.'

I rinse myself off as well as I can and have another few pulls at the beer. The water is murky with soap, prison dirt and blood. I take the scrubbing brush and run it across my nine remaining fingernails. The stub of my little finger tingles.

Suddenly I hear the front door open and close. I flinch, sending water sloshing over the edge of the tub. A pair of heels click on the floor and Elin comes back into the kitchen. Her eyes open wide when she sees me sitting there in the tub like a humiliated dog. I bend forward and wrap my arms around myself to hide my knife wound. Elin slaps the photograph down on the draining board. She glares out through the window over my head.

'I may be a cast-off from a sodding orphanage who didn't get very many years of schooling, but that doesn't mean I'm a fucking moron.'

'Pardon me?'

One hell of a woman for cursing, is Elin. I snatch up a towel and drape it over the tub. Elin turns her fat posterior towards me, picks up the poker and gives the fire in the grate a good raking. Her suspender belt is showing through the fabric of her green dress. There's a clanking of metal against metal. A couple of jaded trumpet blasts can be heard from next door. She continues in a calmer voice: 'I've always had my head screwed on. If you have a jug of some kind, I can help you rinse out that half-kilo of pomade you've got in your hair.'

'There on the wall.'

'This one?'

I nod and adjust the towel.

'What do you mean? Head screwed on?'

The pipes sigh as Elin fills the jug with water.

'Didn't you notice the way they were dressed?'

'In the photograph?'

Elin circles me and stands behind the tub.

'Look up.'

'What do you mean by—'

The cold water hits me right in the face, running through my beard stubble, down my neck and over the wound. I clench my jaw until I can hear a crunching sound in my head.

Its iciness nips at my skin.

'Did you show Lundin the photograph?'

'What would that half-blind twit have to say about it?'

'Only that the couple are known as the Rymans.'

'The Rymans. I'll be damned.'

'You have dirt behind your ears. They live on Vattugatan.'

'How do you know all this?'

Elin rubs a finger against the ridge behind my ear. She slides her hand down and starts to knead my neck. Something releases there, with a cracking sound. Elin lets go and before long another spout of cold water comes down over the top of my head. I splutter and cough. Elin grabs my scalp and starts massaging it.

'They're in mourning: in other words, they're clients of Lundin's. A couple of months ago he buried Mrs Ryman's old father. Mister Ryman is a postman, and his wife works in Klarahallen. We can find them.'

'I'll be damned.'

MONDAY 25 NOVEMBER

Two days to go. The kitchen window is wide open, I'm shaking with cold as I crawl about with a bucket of soapy water, scouring the floorboards with a brush. My damp knees are aching but I only have a little bit left to do. I straighten my back and bend down again, keeping one of my eyes clamped shut against the smoke, and grunting when ash from my cigar tumbles over the clean floor. The eleven chimes from St Stefan's Church break through the sound of my scrubbing and, before long, the bells of Johannes join them from the south. On the eighth chime I put one foot on the floor and on the ninth I stand up, taking the cigar out of my mouth: 'Harry Kvist in a magnificent comeback.'

I mop up the remaining water with a rag and wring it out over the bucket. My cracked cuticles sting. I have to get myself down to the Toad, and make arrangements for my bare-knuckle fights. Only a few more weeks till the first dust-up. I should invite Hasse, the shoeshine boy, to show him how it's done. No one has ever knocked me down.

'Never taken a count.'

Maybe I should start going for runs, work on my fitness a bit. Until I knew better I thought it would be enough to take Dixie out for long walks, but she limps along so slowly that it's impossible to keep up a decent pace without strangling her.

I shake the rug out of the window. Dust, dog hair and crumbs rain down into the courtyard. I whip it up and down a couple of times, making a cracking sound. A black alley cat darts off, her belly dragging against the ground. A smell of fried herring wafts on the wind from some neighbour's kitchen.

I lay out the rug on the floor and admire my handiwork. Doughboy shouldn't lack for anything. It's been six months since he was allowed to move into the cell next to mine. I kept my eye on him from the moment I first saw him, and I couldn't have done otherwise – a beautiful lad like that.

It was less than a week before the kid started running errands from the kitchen staff to a gang of bootleggers on the East Wing. After a few days of running back and forth with corn gruel – which can be fermented with yeast – he started trying to sneak a share of the goods for himself. If I hadn't stepped in at that point and taken him under my wing, he would have found himself in trouble.

When love entered the picture it felt as natural as putting my left foot forward in the boxing ring. We spent the nights in an ecstasy of desire, moulding one another according to our passions, but after two weeks there was no longer any need for this: each of us knew exactly what we wanted. The last six months, which are usually so slow and tedious, flew by.

Every morning I woke with joy in my breast, my blood warm, a silky smooth feeling in my heart. Soon after the debacle of the mashing operation, he started making rat traps using shoe soles from the cobbler's workshop and steel springs, which he sold to the other prisoners. There's no doubt about it, the lad knows what he's about, and I'm sure he'll be handy around the cigar shop.

I walk out of the kitchen, lift the mattress and pick up a pair of trousers which have been in the press to sharpen up the creases. I make the bed with clean linen. There's a growing mountain of dirty laundry. Christ knows what I'll do with my dirty laundry now that Beda's gone west. I'll have to find a new washerwoman. The main thing is that it's clean and tidy here for Doughboy when he's released in two days' time. That is, if I dare trust him and his promises.

Unfortunately you can't always trust smooth-cheeked cabin boys. The same old story repeated itself to damnation during my years at sea: first I'd sit with one of them, wasting time and money for a half-eternity in some dingy drinking hole in a port somewhere; then we'd set up a meeting for later on in some dark corner or alleyway, but they'd rarely show up as agreed; and when they did some of them would make the mistake of trying to rob me. The first few times I set to worrying, imagining they'd been shanghaied or thrown in jail. I'd spend hours looking for them in bars and whorehouses, but it wasn't long before I started wising up and would slope off back to my ship instead, cursing under my breath.

But there ought to be a difference between a couple of hours propping up a bar and several months in the slammer. We were able to talk when the screws weren't listening; we told each other all there was to tell. I know everything about Doughboy: I know about his drunken father and his dead sister looking down on him from heaven. In a way he reminds me of myself when I was young, although in my case it was my twin brother that died, and I never saw hide nor hair of my father, drunk or sober.

'He'll probably keep his promises. Where else would he go?'

I speak these words to myself to soothe my uncertainty. I take the hanger with Doughboy's serge suit from the kitchen door handle. It's black with wide lapels and it smells spanking new. I remove a couple of hairs from the shiny cloth, then hang it up again and run my hand over it.

The soot-speckled windows could do with a going-over but that will have to be done in the spring, after I've removed the inside windows so they can be opened. Maybe we can give each other a hand with it. I put on my hat and go downstairs to give Lundin a lift to the bank.

The stairwell smells of lunchtime. I grip hold of the old banister, polished smooth by trouser seats and coarse working hands. On the way down I caress the glistening wood with my scarred hand.

'With this twelve hundred today, you'll owe me three thousand, one hundred and thirty-six kronor and fifty öre.'

'It's been worse.'

I steer the hearse down Birger Jarlsgatan. Outside the pawnbrokers on Norrlandsgatan, the Monday queue stretches a good way along the street, exposed to the cutting wind. The sky hangs like a lead roof over the city. Most of the women have tied shawls tightly around their heads. Someone has already opened an umbrella, even though it hasn't started raining yet. Next Friday, when it's time to get their rags out of hock with the old man's pay packet, they'll all see each other again. They stand about nattering, most of them seem to be acquainted. I take my eyes off them and change down a gear.

Lundin gets out his nickel-plated snuff tin and taps it with his finger.

'If your figures add up, my brother, you'll have to pay off the debt in weekly instalments of around two hundred and eighty kronor. And after that you'll be paying me about sixteen kronor a day.'

'For all eternity?'

'Amen.'

I take a left into Stureplan. We pass the Hotel Anglais, and the wheels thump against the double tram tracks. A newly made coffin, required for the following day, thumps around in the back.

In the middle of the triangular plaza, a customer is sitting in a hut, having his shoes polished. That would be a good spot for my boxing talent from outside the City Library. A hut of his own to lock up at night. I glance at Lundin, who's kneading himself a decent wad of tobacco with a shaky left hand. He shoves it under his lip.

'Maybe we should get it all down on paper?'

'By God, yes, of course we should. You pick up the funds this evening and I'll arrange it. Have you spoken with the widow again?'

'Haven't had time.'

'But it's yours if you want it? The shop?'

'Got till Wednesday morning.'

Lundin rearranges the snuff in his mouth with his tongue: 'So the Devil got you in order at long last. Who would have thought it?'

I brake to let two elegant youths in brushed top hats cross the road in front of the Royal Dramatic Theatre. They've carefully done up all the buttons of their overcoats; I can't tell if they're wearing waistcoats.

Birger Jarlsgatan merges into Nybroplan. Crates, kegs and piles of birch wood fill the quays. Some of it's being loaded onto ships, some of it's coming off. Stevedores are running up and down the gangplanks. A sack of potatoes or brown beans has split and scattered its contents over the muddy paving stones of the quay. A couple of lads with pale noses are crawling about on all fours, trying to salvage what they can. Lundin seems to have dozed off.

I turn right and then left where a faded metal sign nailed into a façade announces the beginning of Kungsträdgårdsgatan. In the summer months, Kungsträdgården with its trees and wooden benches is the cauldron in which much of the city's gossip is both boiled and salted; I often sit there in the sun, feasting my eyes on bare-breasted sailors walking under the trees with a swing in their step. Now it is almost deserted here apart from a couple of loud-mouthed lasses, who perhaps haven't understood that the weekend is over yet, stumbling about in the slight shadows of the lime trees.

A tall lad, hanging about outside the bank, lets his tongue whip across a cigarette paper. I glance at him as I brake. He's wearing plus fours, with a big beret on his head. Possibly a waiter with the Monday off. He leans nonchalantly against the wall, one of his boot soles also resting against it. I hold my breath; there's a tickling sensation in my crotch immediately followed by a mouldering guilt.

Doughboy just cannot get out of prison quick enough. I need the angular outline of a bloke in my bed as soon as possible.

Lundin wakes up with a start, coughing. He nods at the fuel gauge, I nod back at him, acknowledging that I will have to fill up.

'Don't you bloody forget now, the automobile has to be back for the funeral tomorrow morning, nine o'clock at the latest.'

He peers up at the flint-grey sky, steps out into the traffic and hurries towards the bank. I release the clutch and continue on my way, to pick up Elin. We're on the trail of the Rymans. The steering wheel shudders as the engine splutters and chokes, but I press the accelerator and pick up speed, passing the statue of Charles XII at the southernmost end of the park. He's pointing stoically towards the Russians, but the pigeons have gone for the warrior king in a big way and covered him in shit.

I stifle a yawn. The shoulder holster with the Husqvarna chafes against my ribs. I adjust it. On the corner of the Norr Bridge stands a lone angler with his line in the water, and a faded leather cap on his head. The skin of his creased face hangs loosely like the folds of a turkey's throat. I don't know if I've seen him before or if I am having some sort of dark premonition. I shudder in my seat and turn right by Gustav Adolf's Square to make my way back to Sibirien and Standards.

I've turned up Sveavägen and I'm just nearing the columns of the Handels High School when I catch sight of a back that I feel I recognise. I step on the brakes, move to the kerb and crawl along behind the kid. Damn, surely that's him? The worn jacket, the stained beret and the shiniest boots in town. He's limping, but he's running all the same, even if the pace leaves something to be desired.

I smile to myself, thinking of my future as a boxing trainer. It's been almost fifteen years since I last set foot in a boxing club. Maybe they've forgotten all about me by now. I pull up alongside the shoeshiner. He's sweating, his head hanging low between his shoulders, but he keeps pushing himself on.

I'm just about to wind down the window and encourage him to keep it up for the last hundred metres, when Hasse looks up at his finish line. He sucks in his lower lip and picks up speed, his cheap boots clattering against the pavement. I remember my glory days, pull away and leave him behind. If I had strength enough to knock out one well-prepared opponent after another back in those days, then surely I can also squeeze a bit of information out of a postman like Ryman?

The great windows of Saluhallen Market let in the washed-out late-autumn sunlight, illuminating the lunchtime rush. Business is brisk after the morning's wholesaling, and everywhere you can see women bargaining for flowers and root vegetables. From time to time the whistles of the steam trains can be heard through chattering voices, pulling into and leaving Central Station. The massive siding is only a stone's throw to the north.

Mrs Ryman brushes off discarded leaves and stalks from her stall with her slim hand. Her greyish apron is stained with soil. She's thrown a man's jacket with a frayed collar over her shoulders. Her features are unmoving, frozen on her face. Maybe it's the loss of her father that's turned her to stone.

Elin and I are inside the market's own Restaurant NORMA, watching her through the window. We sit next to each other, so we have a clear view. The café is half-full of people eating their lunch. Elin slurps her coffee without taking her eyes off the florist. Mrs Ryman sits behind the table, her hands clasped in her lap.

'Stina works in the fish market next door.'

Elin's cup clinks as she puts it back on the saucer. I tear my eyes away from Mrs Ryman. Elin is wearing a navy-blue casual dress. A fashionable colour, she claims. Her shoes are brown, like the leather gloves lying on the table.

'Who?'

'Stina. My flatmate.'

'Explains why you smell of herring.'

Elin bites her lip, folds her bun wrapper down the middle and then into a triangle, before she starts drumming her fingers gently against the tabletop.

'What do you think of my hat? It's new.'

I glance at her cloche hat with its blue band.

'It suits you. And Mrs Ryman?'

'She's waiting. We're waiting.'

'For what?'

'It's almost one. I bet her old man comes to see her if he finishes his round early.'

'Another drop of coffee?'

Elin nods.

'I wish I had a cigarette to go with it.'

I grunt, peering again at Mrs Ryman from under the brim of my hat. Just then I see a small, thin man in a uniform approaching her stall with sprightly steps. He's carrying a black-lacquered postbag. The strap has worn a smooth diagonal line across his chest. His small eyes are too close together, and there's something bird-like about his face. For the first time since we caught sight of her, Mrs Ryman breaks into a smile as she stands up and runs her hands over her apron. He gently touches her arm in greeting, but no more.

'Will you bloody look at that.'

'What did I tell you?'

Elin gives me a wry smile. I fumble about in my inside pocket for the leather cigar case.

'And now?'

'More waiting about.'

I grunt as I take out a Meteor.

'That's my speciality.'

'I'll bet it is.'

'No one beats me on that score. Patient as a bloody night fisherman.'

The Rymans are each tucking into a sandwich. Sitting beside one another, their eyes seem to be looking right into the café through the plate-glass window. I quickly look down, covering my eyes with the brim of my hat, and, out of the corner of my eye, I notice that Elin is doing the same. Another locomotive yells out a warning signal from the siding. I whisper: 'Did they see us?'

'What bloody difference does it make?'

I let out a hoarse, involuntary cough. The sound explodes like dynamite through the premises. I clear my throat: 'No, of course, what do they know about us? What do we do afterwards, when they're done?'

I strike a match and get the cigar going. Elin brushes crumbs off the table.

'I suggest we split up if they go their separate ways. You take the husband and I'll have a word with the wife?'

'Okay.'

Elin touches up her lipstick and blots her lips on a tissue, then checks the result in a mirror.

'Go easy on the poor sod, and meet me later by the car?'

'Of course.'

We remain there in silence, and when the gaunt Mr Ryman at long last takes his farewell of his wife with a cursory nod, I pick up my cigar case from the table. With a parting wink at Elin, I follow him out of the café.

I take off my tie, roll it up and put it in my trouser pocket. Ryman walks out of the back door and cuts through salesmen, lorries and porters. I keep about ten metres behind. His uniform hat is an excellent marker.

At the north end of Saluhallen market, some blokes are unloading big blocks of ice. Just as I'm passing, one of the blocks hits the floor with a crunching sound. Fragments of ice fly through the air like transparent shrapnel.

Ryman turns around.

For a second or so I get the idea that he's staring right at me. I slow down, look the other way and start rooting about in my pockets. Ryman carries on, but he seems to be moving faster now. We emerge into the heavy traffic of Vasagatan and turn off towards Central Station. I've let the distance between us increase a bit. Ryman steps aside for a man pushing a cart of flour sacks, touching the brim of his uniform hat as if he knows him.

If he's on his way to the central Post Office depot, a little further up on the other side of the street, I don't have a lot of time to play with. I crack my finger joints and quicken my pace. When I've almost caught up with him, I take a quick look around me. Two wrinkled old bats, with wicker baskets hanging from the crooks of their arms, are waiting to cross Vasagatan. Wrapped in aprons, scarves, cardigans and shawls, they both look like colourful versions of Karloff's mummy. On the other side of Bryggargatan, a tramp has laid out his wares on a blanket: boot straps, safety pins and other bric-a-brac. In a telephone box behind him stands a copper; he gives himself away with his uniform trousers. I have to go easy here, for the sake of Ida and Doughboy if no one else.

I follow Ryman as he crosses Bryggargatan. Once we're on the opposite pavement, I glide up on his right side. He's just about to turn his head when I grab his ear, slap my other hand over his mouth and drag him along behind me. The heavy Husqvarna bangs against my ribs. Ryman's postman's boots bump along the pavement, a couple of muted shrieks of anguish slipping through my right hand.

I kick open the first door on the left and toss Ryman inside, following him into the gloomy stairwell. If I'm not mistaken, this was where the editorial department of *Stockholms Dagblad* used to be. I feel as if I can still hear the thumping of the presses, and the reek of printer's ink in the air. Maybe another newspaper has moved into the premises.

I put my left hand around Ryman's throat and press him up against a wall from which most of the plaster has fallen. He collapses like a pocket knife when I give him a sharp jab in the stomach. I straighten him up again and take a firm grip on his testicles. He knocks my hat off with his left arm. He's as weak as a fly. I chuckle.

'You ought to calm yourself down,' I say, gripping even harder on his crown jewels. 'You want me to tear off your balls?'

I consider whether I should snap his collarbone with my right. It's easily done with shorter blokes, because you can punch from above, doesn't cause a lot of damage, but hurts enough to persuade them to betray their own mothers if that's what's required. No need for it this time, though: Ryman's already whining piteously. I have him exactly where I want him. Limp as a midshipman after a litre of vodka and two hours with the harbour whore.

'A couple of months ago you buried your father-in-law. The undertaker was Lundin on Roslagsgatan. Do you remember?'

'The Mora grandfather clock,' hisses Ryman. By now his mug is as red as his ear. He gags for air. His gob is moving like the mouth of a babe on the breast. I slacken my grip on his throat.

'What are you on about?'

'That heirloom. You can take it if you want.'

I grip hold of his jaw, pull his face forward and drive my elbow into his solar plexus, all while squeezing even harder around his balls.

'On the way to Lundin you saw something. A black car. Didn't you?'

'I don't remember. Is it my brother-in-law what sent you?'

'Compose yourself! Think about it. A black car. A couple of men carrying out a body, or taking a large man away?'

'I remember! I remember!'

'Start with the car. What model was it? Do you remember a number plate?'

'The car was black.'

'Aha?'

I squeeze even harder. It's not entirely unpleasant feeling the weight of the seed-basket in my hand. Work and pleasure at the same time. Ryman whines like a street dog outside the abattoir.

'My wife. My wife thought it was suspicious.'

'What was, that the bloody car was black?'

'Those blokes.'

'Description?'

'They took out a body, a woman I think. They threw her into the car.'

'What did they look like?'

'Both of them wearing black.'

'Poplin coats?'

He shrugs, terrified.

'Anything that stood out?'

'One was smaller than the other.'

I sigh and tense my jaw.

'That's all I know. I swear.'

I glance briefly into the street before I look into Ryman's eyes again. I've been in this game for long enough to register the slight glint in his iris. He's preparing himself for some desperate attempt to escape. It's not a question of courage, only the dumb despair that absolute panic gives rise to. Inexperienced people can come up with all kinds of nonsense when they're in a tight spot.

I let go of his balls and block the knee that comes flying towards my crotch. Then I pile an uppercut into his chin. There's a crunching sound as his teeth snap together, and the back of his head thumps into the wall. The postman goes out like a candle in the wind and collapses on the floor.

A little cloud of pulverised plaster hangs in the dark air where his head was a moment earlier. I clutch my aching right fist, grunting to myself.

Ryman lies on his side, red blood flowing out of his broken gob. His uniform cap has rolled into a corner by the stairs. One of his feet is twitching. Blood and dust from the floor are all over his bird-like face. I resist the urge to search him for his wallet. Can't be bothered.

'This codger won't be waking up for a while. You have dynamite in your fists, Kvisten, even if some might say you're thick as two short planks.'

I disappear out the door before I'm caught red-handed. Calmly I walk back to the car on Norra Bantorget, as agreed. I sigh loudly, dusting off my hat and pressing it down over my cropped Långholmen hair. I doubt Elin has had any more success than me, which wouldn't leave us very much to go on. Just as well. I think we have taken this as far as it'll go. It's time to drop it.

There's no Elin waiting for me in the car. I turn up my collar and make myself comfortable in the driver's seat. In the square, the tram tracks glitter, green rivulets running between cobblestones, rubbish and horse manure. There's a large crowd waiting at the bus stop for the number 56. The queue for the hot dog stand of the bloke who was knocked down by Prince Gustaf Adolf's car a couple of years ago is almost as long. His sports car skidded, they said. Good for business, but not so good for the hot dog man himself, who was left with his legs all twisted at the end of it all. I let out a sigh so long that it seems it will never end.

I push my hat forward and close my eyes. In my dream I hear Doughboy calling out my name. An old woman, so badly disfigured by chickenpox scars that you'd think someone must have tortured her with a fistful of cigarettes, is keeping him prisoner. I can't help him.

Despite the icy air I wake bathed in sweat like an old carthorse when the car door is opened.

'You look like you've seen a ghost.'

Elin smoothes the back of her coat and gets into the passenger seat. She's bought a bunch of flowers wrapped in brown paper. I catch the smell of hyacinths.

I shake my head to chase away the images from my dream and clear my throat: 'Must have nodded off.'

The sweat stings where the prison fleas have ravaged me. Elin takes off her gloves and puts them on top of the dashboard.

'The old man was taken by lung fever. One week he was fit as a fiddle and the next he was dead. Seventy-six years old, but still. Life is hard to fathom.'

'I don't understand.'

'Her father. Apparently he had a cat. It was meowing so pathetically after he died. That was how they found him. Hadn't been fed for days, poor little thing.'

For the second time in two days I burst out: 'How do you know all this?'

'Had coffee.'

'Coffee?'

'Did you find out anything yourself?'

'Not a lot.'

'I found out quite a bit. She sketches in the evenings, goes to classes at the Workers' Association.'

'Really?'

'I think she's got a good memory.'

'Let's hear it.'

Elin takes a deep breath. From the dairy on Tunnelgatan a girl, her long hair all tousled with sweat and dust, comes running with a jug of cream. An emaciated horse hitched to a cart slowly raises its head and follows her with pleading eyes as she passes. The nag should have been sent for slaughter long ago.

'Just like we thought, the Rymans were on their way back from Lundin's when they brought out my mother. The car had Stockholm plates. She was sure it was a Rolls-Royce. Her brother has a car workshop.'

'But he doesn't have the Mora clock.'

'What was that?'

'Go on!'

'There were four blokes involved, but two of them were standing on the other side of the window with Petrus and she didn't get a good look at them.'

'And the other two?'

I pick up my notebook and the pen.

'She remembers them as looking very different. She even joked about them being like Laurel and Hardy.'

'One large bloke and one smaller?'

'One of them looked like an old boxer. A big fellow. With a smashed nose like yours. And a bushy white moustache.'

I stop writing. That bloke is an old acquaintance: the same man who cut Petrus's throat at Konradsberg and later assaulted me outside Lundin's. Now his ashes rest in consecrated ground one fathom down, with the remains of a fourteen-year-old lad.

When my day comes I wouldn't mind a similar resting place.

'And the other one?'

'Short and slim. About one metre sixty-five tall, about the same height as her husband. He had a hooked nose, and he was a bit slow, had trouble keeping up with the others, he was following behind.'

'And they didn't find it at all odd to see them there?'

213

'As far as they were concerned everything was in order. There's another detail, you see: there was a constable in uniform patrolling up and down Ingemarsgatan.'

'What did he look like?'

'She couldn't say. He was quite far away and she only saw his back.'

'Someone from the Ninth District. You said they were on their way back from Lundin's?'

'That's what she said.'

'So they saw nothing on their way there? Did they hear anything?'

'I didn't ask.'

'Shots, for example.'

'She probably would have mentioned that.'

I hum to myself as I jot some notes. At last the number 56 bus comes chugging along. Passengers alight and get on.

'So, you had coffee with her?'

I think about Ryman's bleeding, unconscious body in the dark stairwell. Someone should have found him by now. I hope I didn't cause any lasting damage.

I start the motor car and put it in first gear. After checking behind me, I pull out and drive off towards Vasagatan, heading for the electrically lit King's Bridge to Kungsholmen.

'We had two cups, drank 'em from the saucer with sugar lumps. Sweet buns too.'

I rub my chin and root out a cigar from my coat. I push down the accelerator; the tyres sing as we cross King's Bridge.

Elin holds onto her new hat as the hearse sways from side to side. In the back, the coffin rattles about. A rhythmic thumping of wheels against the welds in the track can be heard as a fast train pulls into Central Station from the north.

'What was that?'

Elin leans towards me.

'What do you mean?'

'You said something.'

'Did I? I don't think so.'

Women have got something wrong with their hearing, I'm sure of it. I spin the steering wheel and turn right. On the corner of Scheelegatan and Fleminggatan, the number 2 tram has collided with a horse-drawn carriage. A shiny brown mare lies on her side breathing heavily, with distended nostrils. Her right back-hoof scrapes against the paving stones. One of the wagon's shafts has broken off and pierced deep into her side. Life is slowly draining out of her, filling the gaps between the cobblestones with blood.

The gawping passengers press their hands and pale faces against the misted windows. The driver limps back and forth in front of the horse in his dusty leather boots, tears running into his beard as he slaps his cap against his thighs again and again.

Elin gasps and I slow down. As I turn the steering wheel to overtake the wagon lying halfway across the lane, I see a motorcycle policeman unbutton the holster of his service pistol. Just as I'm turning into Agnegatan by the old lunatic asylum, I hear the shot, to put the animal out of its misery. It echoes all over the block. Elin flinches in the passenger seat. I take a deep puff on my cigar.

'Not like in the cinema, is it?'

'What do you mean?'

'Makes more of a noise than you think. It would have been heard halfway across Sibirien.'

'I read a serial in the Sunday supplement of *Social-Demokraten* once: the murderer muted the sound of the shot with a pillow.'

215

'We'll have to ask Hessler the copper about that,' I say, pointing at the large police headquarters building looming up ahead of us. We park and go into the lion's den, waiting for a while in a room filled with secretaries and clerks before the head of the spirit-smuggling unit can receive us.

A constable in uniform leads us through an anteroom full of typists clattering away at their machines, then a hall dominated by a gigantic oak table surrounded by chairs. None of the group of dumb coppers sitting there pretending to work has the energy even to look up.

'There's more brass here than on Karlavägen when the May Day parade goes by,' I mutter to myself.

Hessler has his own office at the back of the hall. He's been promoted since the last time I saw him, as if he didn't already rake in enough, including bribes from the gangster syndicates organising vodka smuggling. The chief constable is in uniform sitting behind his desk, which is crammed with piles of documents and papers, all of exactly the same height. There are a few crow's feet around his blue eyes and the well-trimmed little moustache on his thick upper lip is shot through with grey streaks. He's pulling a comb through his pomaded hair when we walk in, but stands up when he sees Elin. He gives me a meaningful pursed-mouth glance as they shake hands. He turns to me.

'Harry. Been a while. Three years?'

'That's right.'

The last time we saw each other was in the remand cells at the bottom of the building. Hessler was drunk and in need of some company. I get out my notebook from my pocket and he breaks into a smile. I've never been able to make head or tail of the bloke.

'Eighteen months at Långholmen. Intimidation, wasn't it?'

'All in the line of duty.'

Hessler sits back down behind his imposing desk and drums his fingertips together. Elin chooses the chair on the right.

'The plaintiff was only twelve years old.'

'Old enough to hear the truth. And see his old man escape through the kitchen window.'

'And may I ask who the lady accompanying you is?'

With a nod at Elin, Hessler straightens his back in his chair and folds his hands. The smile is beginning to sag, like a pair of old braces.

'Miss Johansson. A client.'

Elin's chair scrapes. Hessler leans towards me.

'Harry, it's bad enough just my talking to you.'

'It's all in order.'

'But mightn't it be better if Miss Johansson waited outside?'

'You have my word that you can speak in front of her.'

'This is men's business.'

'Damn it, Hessler!'

I take the cigar out of my mouth and raise my voice. Hessler averts his eyes and adjusts one of the paper piles in front of him. Elin's chair scrapes again. I daren't look at her. Maybe by now she has unpicked the truth about who I am, maybe it's quite clear that Hessler and I have a past.

I rifle through my notebook and clear my throat: 'It's about a car with a Stockholm registration, a Rolls. Ten fifty-eight.'

Hessler nods stiffly: 'One moment.'

He stands up, slides his hands over his uniform trousers and leaves the room. I look around for an ashtray but can't find one. I hold the cigar vertically to balance the tower of ash. Carefully I drop the notebook back into my inside pocket.

'What a bloody stuffed shirt!'

'Don't worry. I'll be in his debt for this, not you.'

I sigh when I think of it, then strike the ash off into the cupped palm of my hand.

'Ask him about the pillow when he comes back.'

'The pillow?'

'If a pillow can smother the sound of a shot. Like in that serial.'

'Ask someone else.'

'Why?'

'He who has no debts is a rich man.'

'A bit late for that. You said so yourself just now.'

She's getting on my nerves, and I'm about to reply when the door behind us creaks. I sit there with the ash in my hand. I feel Hessler's weak fingers on my shoulder. He leans forward next to my ear, smelling faintly of hair tonic and flat pilsner.

'Nothing, Harry.'

Hessler squeezes my shoulder, then takes his hand away. He goes around the desk, pinches the creases of his trousers and sits down again with a smile on his face.

'Nothing?'

'The number plate in question doesn't exist. These things happen.'

I close my fist around the pile of ash in my hand.

'What about checking for similar plates on a Rolls?'

'Tomorrow.'

'I don't have that much time.'

Surreptitiously I let the ash sprinkle over the rug between my fingers.

'What do you mean?'

I stand up and put my cigar in my mouth. Elin moves forward in her chair, her hands on her handbag.

I button up my coat and I'm just about to leave when she stops me with one hand on my lower arm.

Hessler twists slightly in his seat: 'I'll be here till late. If you come by in a couple of hours, I may have something for you, Harry.'

'I'll see.'

'Our informers are going on about some kind of comeback for you. A series of illegal matches arranged by Lindkvist at the Toad?'

'Not worth your while thinking about it.'

'Is it possible to silence a gun by using a pillow?'

Hessler recoils at the sound of Elin's voice. His little moustache trembles, a fleeting smile. He stands up for the second time, comes round the desk and holds out his arm towards the door. He doesn't even look in her direction.

'To some degree, but it's not as effective as with a Maxim silencer.'

Elin stands up and buttons her own coat. She takes her leather gloves in her right hand.

'What's that?'

'Miss is obviously not very familiar with firearms. A Maxim silencer is a device that's screwed onto the barrel of the weapon. It makes the sound of a shot no louder than, for instance, the pop of a champagne cork.'

'A champagne cork?'

'Ah, there's a phrase that Miss understands. Watch out for that one, Harry. She seems to have expensive tastes.'

The joke tumbles out stillborn from Hessler's pilsner-stinking gob. He isn't even smiling about it himself as he ushers us towards the door with outstretched arms. Elin slaps her gloves into her left palm.

'The cheek!' she hisses.

'Yes, quite incredible, isn't it? Apparently the American secret police have been using them for ten years,' says Hessler.

'The chief constable should watch his behaviour,' Elin goes on.

Hessler reaches the door. He turns to me and looks into my eyes: 'I'll be staying here till eight or nine tonight. Ten if I have to. If you telephone me I'll make sure they let you in.'

The door creaks and Hessler strokes his ridiculous moustache. He smiles foolishly at me. I let Elin out first.

We pass through the hall full of the blank-faced coppers and then the second room, the typewriters chattering louder than a shoot-out in the gangland war of '23. I lead the way, sticking my cigar in my mouth and buttoning up my coat on the way out.

At the desk nearest the far door, a brunette stands up abruptly when she catches sight of me. She must be a bit over twenty. Her thick woollen dress is dark green. From her left shoulder some five white buttons seek their way diagonally across her modest-sized bust, down towards her slender waist. She's slightly under medium length, possibly about one metre seventy. For a moment she looks as if she's prepared to run out of the door, but she stays at her post, her eyes gazing down at her desk. Maybe I had to rough her up at some point in the past? I rarely have to work over women, though, and I think I'd have remembered it.

I slow down. She runs her hands over her skirt and takes a breath so deep that I can hear it over the chattering typewriters. Full lips, broad hips. The sort of filly that sometimes makes me want to reconsider my ways.

I touch the brim of my hat as I pass. She meets my gaze with her brown eyes and smiles stiffly. The scent of a musky perfume finds its way into my many-times broken nose, and then the door shuts behind me and Elin.

Still thinking about that typist, I wander back to the car with Elin clattering along behind me on her heels. The hearse is parked by a run-down building on Bergsgatan. The car seats are ice cold.

'Loathsome person, that Hessler.'

I stifle a yawn in the driver's seat: 'So we've come to the end of the road.'

'What do you mean?'

'That was the last lead. Time to let this thing go.'

'I don't think so.'

'The day after tomorrow I'll be the owner of a cigar shop. I also plan to train a couple of lads to box, if I have the time.'

'The day's not done yet.'

'We have nothing else to go on.'

Elin frowns, then comes to life suddenly and slaps me hard on the thigh. I jump in my seat.

'Petrus's school!'

'Which one?'

'Asplunden Institute for the Deaf, Mute and Blind. So you're forgetful *and* dozy, it seems! It's just around the corner.'

Why the hell doesn't that woman give it a rest? I grip the steering wheel, and snap: 'I'm tired and I've a lot to get done by Wednesday. There's a funeral tomorrow.'

'Do me this last favour. Then you will have more than kept your promise to Mum.'

I grunt in response. Darkness falls as a polluted rain comes down over the city, already overflowing with water. A gang of sparrows mob a radio aerial on the building above.

'This'll be the last thing I do. After that you'll have to go on alone, if you have anything else to work with, which I doubt.'

The smell of herring and perfume washes over me as Elin leans forward and pinches my cheek, like I was some lad in short trousers. My knuckles turn white around the steering wheel, my scars glowing red against the white. Elin warbles: 'You'll see, Kvist. I have good instincts and, as the last few days have proved, I'm usually right.'

221

MONDAY 25 NOVEMBER

The gravel groans under the tyres of the hearse as we drive into the Institute's courtyard. The school lies hidden in the park behind the Garnison Hospital with its green-coloured roof; not far at all from the stiff-house where I picked up that boy last Friday. The main building measures some forty metres across the walls covered in decorative curls. The wings are simpler in style and seem to have been built much later.

I turn the crate around, reverse and park with my nose facing the exit beside some old red-painted sheds. Quite honestly, I can't wait to knock off for the evening.

'Good instincts,' she said. Walking across the gravelled court-yard, my instinct is that we're wasting our time.

Elin's shoes clatter up the broad front steps and the doorbell buzzes.

'I'm afraid I have to ask you to put out your cigar,' says the superintendent, when the door opens.

He smiles broadly, holding out a damp hand for me to shake. His sensual, feminine lips would not look out of place on a fat cherub in an Italian painting from long ago. He wears a daringly cut wool suit in black, which hugs his narrow shoulders. The perky, bright tie matches the silk handkerchief in his top pocket. No waistcoat. This bloke knows how to dress. I feel a pinprick of jealousy. I push the door open and flick my cigar down the steps.

'Not a problem.'

'Excellent.'

The superintendent's smile gets even more effusive as he claps his hands together in front of his chest, showing off the watch from under his shirt cuff. Gold: this sod makes money. He has weak wrists. I'll wager they've never done any real work, but I suppose they'll do for giving some blind lad or other a beating. Like Petrus I only had two years of schooling. All I ever learned was the feeling of an iron ruler across my fingers.

I look at the superintendent again. The skin of his face is smooth. There are countless grey wisps in his carefully coiffured dark hair. I wonder who cuts his hair. I wonder what it costs.

We're standing in a palatial lobby with a high ceiling. From a large portrait to the left of the reception desk, Gustaf V gazes down on us through his rounded spectacles. He's wearing a dark-blue suit with a high collar. Under the painting is a brass plate, but I can't see what's written on it. There are staircases on both sides of the room.

Dead ahead runs a corridor with a cross-vaulted ceiling and globe lamps lining the walls.

'Sorry, I didn't catch your name?'

'Kvist,' says Elin, tucking her arm under mine. 'Harry and Elin Kvist. We'd like to take a look around if that's quite all right with you. Our daughter is deaf and we've heard such good things about your school.'

I glance at Elin out of the corner of my eye.

'The Kvists. Excellent. Of course I would be happy to show you around.'

'I hope you'll excuse us coming unannounced like this, but we were in the area. My mother owns a haberdashery on Hantverkargatan. She asked me to keep an eye on it while she went to the doctor. She's tormented by gout in her toe, I'm afraid.'

I glance at Elin again. Her bright-red lips shine as she smiles; her eyes sparkle.

Lying comes easily when you're a survivor. I should know that better than anyone.

'That's no problem at all, Mrs Kvist.'

The superintendent babbles on about the merits of the school as he takes us up the stairs on the left-hand side. His compact little buttocks move in front of me, at eye-level. Two apples wrapped in a snuff handkerchief with a walnut in between.

It must be bloody Christmas.

'We're very proud of what we do here at our school.' The superintendent's voice rings out in the stairwell. 'Currently we have ninety-eight students in three separate streams. Our work is supervised by six teachers in academic subjects, two in workshop activities and two female teachers in sewing. Including our support and service staff, there's a grand total of nearly a hundred and thirty people here during the day.'

We walk down a corridor where there's such a crossfire of whining, screeching and banging that the superintendent has to raise his voice to make himself heard.

'On this level we have the shoemaking workshop, the tailoring class and the woodwork room, but let's go to a quieter part of the building.'

The superintendent throws out his arm and takes the lead. Elin looks at me, rolling her eyes, nodding at his back, but I don't understand what she's driving at. We're hardly in a position to interrogate the bloke in the middle of the corridor.

'Naturally all our members of staff are well versed in sign language. Here we are now.'

The superintendent puts his ear to the door and listens. He pushes it open and we walk into a gym with a scratched floor.

Along the short wall runs a line of wall bars, the lacquer worn from years of use. Six ropes hang down like lianas from the ceiling. There's a heavenly smell of sweat and Sloan's liniment. I breathe in deeply through my nose. The rhythmic sound of swinging skipping ropes and the thumping of sandbags echoes in my mind. I'm tired and my thoughts are wandering, but the silly fop interrupts my musings.

'I can understand that like most any other parents you want the best for your daughter. At this school your child will not merely receive a thorough vocational training. We also attach great significance to recreation and physical activities. Strong body, strong mind, as we like to say.'

The floor seems to flex slightly under our feet as we go into the gym. The superintendent's voice echoes between the walls, but I'm no longer listening to him. Something has made my thoughts turn back to the port in Gothenburg, almost twelve years ago.

It's the last time I see my daughter.

My work boots make a hollow ringing sound against the gangway. Flags are flapping in the breeze. My mouth tastes of salt. I have Ida on one arm and a suitcase on my shoulder. In my trouser pocket: a folded handkerchief containing tickets, food coupons, a visa and two unfolded ten-dollar bills. Ida is weeping with hunger and tiredness. The ship sounds its steam whistle. With a thump I put down the suitcase on the deck.

Ida is wearing her golden-brown hair in pigtails. She sniffs and wipes her snotty nose. I want to hold her one last time but she reaches for her mother. I hand her over to Emma.

'Give my very best to your uncle when you get there.'

'Do it yourself when you come.'

'Three months.'

'Don't forget we're owed five kronor by the Svenssons.'

The steam whistle sounds again. I take the handkerchief from my pocket. She leans towards me with Ida on her arm. Her hair smells soapy clean. I run my calloused hand over it.

'Three months goes by quickly.'

I attempt a smile and give Emma the handkerchief.

She briefly caresses my cheek: 'Keep yourself in order now.'

I nod and then pull at the lapels of my coat, before I turn my back on them.

I turn my back on them.

'Sir?'

A penetrating note in the superintendent's voice snatches me out of my memories – I'm back in the gym. I blink.

'As I have explained, smoking is not permitted on school premises.'

I stare, first at him and then at the burning match between my thumb and index finger. I quickly blow out the flame before it burns me, then remove the unlit cigar from my mouth.

'An old bad habit of mine. Sorry about that.'

I shake off the memories like water from a wet dog's coat. Elin gives me a puzzled glance. The superintendent smiles hesitantly, splashing his hands together once more. Damn how I hate this Sunday school whelp. If I didn't have Doughboy less than two days away, I'd have crushed his hand under the heel of my boot against the floor, and got him to reel off all the information he had about Petrus, as if reciting the multiplication table or the Ten Commandments.

That damned multiplication table.

I tuck the cigar back into my pocket and force a smile, which rests uneasily on my lips. The beating of my heart begins to slow. A drop of sweat runs slowly down my spine. I fumble in my inside pocket to check that the letter to my daughter is still there. I must remember to pass by a postbox.

The fop tightens his impeccable tie, a double Windsor knot, and nods to gloss over the matter. He gestures at the door and walks on ahead. Elin whacks me gently on the arm with her handbag and frowns. I shrug and shuffle along behind her.

'Let's continue into the wings now and inspect the dormitories. Since we began to admit girls we have separated them from the boys. The boys sleep in the north wing, and the girls in the south, so there's no cause for concern there.'

We go back down the same corridor. Elin walks arm-in-arm with me. She keeps me in a firm grip, as if she wants to stop me from putting a stop to the fop's insistent drone with a well-aimed punch. Otherwise a few blood-spattered teeth might be just the thing for this varnished floor. I also wouldn't mind having an expensive timepiece on my wrist.

'So they find themselves good jobs after their education, then?'

'Obviously it's not something we can guarantee, but I believe that our pupils' prospects of finding employment are considerably improved by our efforts here.'

'Next time I'll be sure to hire a blind cobbler.'

Elin tugs on my arm as we turn left into yet another corridor.

'It seems you're a difficult gentleman to convince, but the fact is that many people, out of a sense of benevolence and goodwill, choose to give their support to more exposed groups in society.' The superintendent stops, turns towards us and adds, with a note of seriousness in his voice: 'I know I do.'

'That may be so.'

I indicate that he should keep moving. He purses his fat lips, then goes on.

'Here are the dormitories.'

We go into a darkened room. On the short side is a little window. It's almost completely dark outside now. There are about twenty iron bedsteads in all, arranged in two rows. They're neatly made up, with white sheets folded over grey blankets. A notice on the wall lists the general rules.

'We have no fewer than three similar rooms for the boys, and two for the girls. Obviously the pupils are monitored at night by staff.'

Elin looks around.

'It seems a little impersonal. Don't they miss their families?'

I can hear the emotion in Elin's voice.

'The pupils' personal belongings are kept in boxes under their beds, so they can look at them whenever they want to remind themselves of home.'

Elin takes a couple of deep breaths, then runs her finger along one of the bedposts to check whether it's been dusted.

The superintendent smiles cautiously: 'All parents want the best for their children, wouldn't you agree?'

I glance over at Elin. Her hand trembles as she smoothes back a lock of hair behind her left ear.

'Of course it's hard for all involved when a family is broken up. On the other hand we have generous visiting hours and the pupils spend their vacations at home.'

'There are some things one can't do anything about.'

With this Elin gives a little sob and digs a handkerchief out of her handbag. She seems a better actress than Greta Garbo to me. Or Doris Steiner for that matter. But her looks might count against her.

'Your daughter's handicap is hardly your fault, my dear lady. How old is the girl?'

Without thinking about it I spit out 'fifteen' at the same time as Elin says 'twelve'. In the silence that follows I catch myself thinking I can even hear the indistinct mumbling of deaf children in the corridors.

'My husband was thinking of our eldest.'

'Twelve, then?'

The superintendent's gaze passes fleetingly across me. My chest is more painful than when I had to go through those last few rounds with 'The Mallet' Sundström in '22, and at that point I did have three broken ribs.

Or was it four?

The vein in my forehead is thumping to life. I clamp my jaws together so hard that it hurts: 'Twelve.'

Elin tucks her handkerchief back into her handbag. She turns around and goes into the corridor again. The superintendent and I stay where we are for a few seconds before following her. We go back to the entrance and reception area. The fop walks ahead of us, throwing out his arms now and then, as if guiding us through a museum filled with priceless art.

'How are the fees arranged?'

Elin's voice echoes over the sound of our feet on the stairs. The superintendent lowers his voice as if he's just about to reveal a secret, and I notice Elin leaning forward so she can catch his words.

'The cost per pupil is six hundred and ninety kronor per year, of which the state makes a contribution of two hundred and fifty. For children that cannot be provided for through private financing, a few are admitted by means of a grant from the school's own support fund. The greater part of this is provided by the royal household.'

'Royal household?'

'His Majesty is a generous benefactor.'

The fop makes a sweeping gesture at the portrait on the wall.

'I have a feeling that our neighbour at home in Roslagsgatan had her son here for a few years. Petrus. Petrus Johansson,' Elin said.

The superintendent checks his wristwatch. It's almost gone five. He pulls at his ear lobe and clears his throat.

Just like me, he wants to call it a night.

'I read somewhere that the level of civilisation of a nation should be judged by how well it cares for the weakest of its people. I am convinced that His Majesty shares that view.'

'Maybe you remember Petrus?'

In the corner of my eye, I can see Elin flashing the same sort of smile she gave Wallin. It suits her about as well as a ball gown on a gnarled peasant wife.

'I don't have extensive contact with the pupils.'

'He was here during the War.'

'Before my time, I'm afraid.'

'Is anyone still working here from that period?'

'I don't believe so.'

'What was the name of your predecessor?'

'Why do you ask that?'

Elin catches her breath.

The superintendent needlessly adjusts his tie. I look him in the eye and cut in: 'Just plain bloody curiosity I'm afraid.'

I feel Elin grip my arm and she carries on: 'We just want to know as much as possible about your school before we put our faith in you to care for our little girl.'

'My predecessor's name was Erik Gyllenbrandt. A pioneer in our field. Unfortunately he's been dead for many years. What is your daughter's name?'

'Ellinor.'

'Ellinor. A lovely name. When was she born?'

'The twelfth of March, 1923.'

I glance at Elin and try to do the mental arithmetic. She wasn't exaggerating when she said she has a good head for numbers. That's damned quick.

'Is her deafness acquired or did she have it at birth?'

'She was born that way.'

'Better born deaf than dead.'

I laugh hoarsely at my own joke. Both Elin and the fop stare at me blankly. I crack my finger joints and rock back and forth on my feet. Not long now until I can have a cigar. The superintendent's gaze passes from my hand to Elin's.

His eyes narrow; a twin furrow appears above the top of his nose.

'Have you both misplaced your wedding rings? Excuse me for asking…'

Elin gasps but she recovers: 'Handed in for a clean. It will be our fifteenth wedding anniversary next week.'

'Well, then congratulations are due.'

The superintendent bows slightly:

'Would you just allow me make a call and fetch some applications, and then I think we're all done here. Roslagsgatan, wasn't it? What was the surname again?'

I sit on the driver's side with Elin next to me. The car is already heavy with cigar smoke. Keeping my eyes on the rear mirror, I quickly change my tie knot to a double Windsor.

The front steps of the school and the heavy copper doors are illuminated by a faint, half-moon-shaped light. Somewhere nearby, hoarse factory whistles announce the end of the first working day of the week.

'You didn't think he was flustered when I asked about Petrus?'

'Not exactly.'

'You come on to people like a bloody buffalo.'

'What sort of buffalo would that be, then?'

'You might find you'd get further if you were a bit more pleasant.'

Elin raises an eyebrow and surveys the dark courtyard. I mutter: 'If you hadn't given away our names the first thing you did, I could have squeezed one or two things out of the bloke.'

'Squeezed, huh? You'd enjoy that, wouldn't you?'

I fix my eyes on the grey pillar of ash at the tip of my cigar. Elin sighs.

'I suppose this is the end of the line?'

'Suppose so.'

'I'll go to the police tomorrow.'

'Good luck with that.'

'Sometimes, Harry, you're completely bloody impossible.'

An approaching motor makes itself heard over the churning sounds of the city. The gravel crunches under two pairs of tyres. A double beam of headlights sweeps across the courtyard. The leather creaks as Elin and I instinctively slide down in our seats.

A car pulls in and stops by the steps some ten or so metres away. Its black-as-night paintwork melts into the dusk. I remove my cigar from my mouth: 'Rolls.'

'Are you sure?'

Elin grasps hold of my lower arm.

'That damned fop and his telephone.'

'Can you see the number plate?'

'Not from here.'

My nerves are yelling for tobacco but I daren't have a puff in case they see the glow. A car door slams, then another. Slowly the cigar goes out between my fingers, it'll be sour now when I relight it.

I crane my neck and peer over the steering wheel. For every step they take, the two men in black grow clearer in the light. They're strapping fellas, of similar height. If they were boxers they'd both be heavyweights, but they look agile and quick with it. They both wear identical black poplin overcoats with belts.

'Maybe my instinct was right again! Can you see anything?'

I hiss: 'Shut your big mouth!'

The two men step into the faint half-circle of light by the door. One of them rings the doorbell. The other takes off his hat and turns towards us. I quickly slide down a few centimetres. As if the hearse was not already eye-catching enough without occupants. I wish we could just disappear.

The bloke has close-cropped hair and a small, rounded head. His dark eyes are far apart and he has a thick-set neck, like a bull.

A cake slice of yellow light cuts into the faint semi-circle when the door opens. The bull turns around and follows his companion inside. When the door closes, Elin sits up. I puff intensively on the cigar, inhale and blow out a half-kilo of smoke: 'Christ Almighty.'

'What did you see?'

'Fucking poplin overcoats.'

'What did they look like?'

'Can you see the plates?'

'Not from this angle.'

'Wait here.'

Quietly I open the door and let my cigar drop to the ground. I put my foot on it, and then I'm outside in the November cold. Leaving the door ajar, I squat behind the bonnet. Listening.

Nothing.

233

Staying low, I move in a half-circle across the courtyard so that I have the school building and the car right in front of me the whole time.

The gravel makes a racket under my feet. Gradually the digits on the rear-end number plate loom into view, one by one, and every time I see another I gasp as if I'm watching a muscular sailor removing his garments. Finally the trousers come off.

One, zero, five, nine.

A1059.

Even though I'm halfway between the Rolls and Lundin's hearse without so much as a dandelion to hide behind, I can't stop myself from lowering one knee to the ground and rooting about for the hard outline of the notebook in my coat pocket. I quickly find the right place, angle the book to catch some light and peer at the page. My heart leaps.

One wrong digit. One damned digit. Otherwise Hessler would have been able to identify the car earlier this afternoon.

The hinges of the heavy door screech about five metres in front of me. I throw myself flat on my belly and bury my face in the wet gravel. My heart thumps hard against the damp ground. Steps tap against the stone steps and one of the doors of the Rolls opens and closes. I raise my head and catch a glimpse of the other man: the bloke has an almost triangular head. The high, wide forehead tapers off towards a weak little chin. The tips of his moustache are waxed. He quickly tightens the belt of his overcoat before putting his hand on the door handle. The passenger door closes behind him; then the courtyard gravel glitters in the sudden glare of the headlights. The motor starts up with an angry sound. The driver releases the clutch and the little pebbles spray over my head like a double-barrel of lead when he pulls away with a wheel spin and disappears onto Pilgatan with screaming tyres.

Elin has already started the hearse, and I throw myself into the passenger seat as we start moving off. She turns first left and then right, and we exit through the gates. The empty coffin in the back of our car bounces from side to side. I'm practically hyperventilating. I manage to get out a cigar even as I'm struggle to find my balance in the seat. As the match flares I see the grim expression on Elin's face.

'Is it them?'

'All the numbers except one.'

The red tail-lights of the Rolls disappear round the right curve towards Norr Mälarstrand and I tumble against the window, as I draw the Husqvarna from my shoulder holster.

'It's them?'

'Too bloody right it's them.'

'So in the end I was right!'

The way this harpy goes on, you'd think it was some sort of bleeding contest. I grunt instead of answering. My thumb slides over the engraved emblem of the Swedish Royal Navy; I flick the safety catch and feed a bullet into the chamber.

The dark waters of Mälaren reflect the lights lining the quay and hanging from the sterns of the skiffs. Waves are breaking hard against the dock. A seagull cries somewhere. The hearse speeds along, following the shoreline towards the west. I look up at the red-painted hovels on Mariaberget, across the water. I lived there with Emma and Ida before they took the ship across the ocean. I squeeze the butt of the pistol and concentrate on the Rolls instead. Elin turns abruptly to the right, into St Eriksgatan. The coffin strikes the left-hand side of the car with a hollow thud.

'Don't lose them now, for Christ's sake.'

'What did you say?'

Elin leans towards me. Maybe I should have enrolled her in the school for the deaf?

'Don't lose them like you did on Väster Bridge!'

'No risk of that. Not again.'

The traffic gets heavier as workers pour out of Kungsholmen's many factories on their bicycles. Under their peaked caps you can see the whites of their eyes gleaming in their sooty faces. Frozen fingers grip the rain-soaked wooden handlebars.

On the right we pass the headquarters of Belzén, the gangster, and the hearse brushes against a fearless man in clogs, who's hastily clattering across the road. I lean forward in my seat. By St Erik Bridge the driver seems to slow down and Elin follows suit. She positions the motor car a comfortable distance of about twenty metres behind, with another three vehicles between ourselves and the Rolls. Elin anxiously runs her hand through her hair: 'What the hell do we do now?'

'We see where they lead us.'

'And then?'

'Then we know.'

'What sort of types do you think they are, these bastards?'

'They're coppers.'

'What makes you think that?'

She sounds astonished.

'There are two kinds of people I can smell at a distance. One of them happens to be coppers.'

'And the other?'

'They're picking up speed. Stay with them!'

We make an abrupt right turn by St Eriksplan. Outside the dairy by a pharmacy known as the Ram stands a young woman with a swaddled infant in her arms. She's telling passers-by that her milk's run dry, and asking them to buy her a bottle of milk for the baby. If some kind soul takes pity on her, she'll sell the bottle back to the dairy at half the retail price. She's been standing there for years. God only knows where she gets the babies from.

'You have to talk more clearly!' Elin raises her voice in the gloom.

'What do you mean?'

'You're mumbling! Speak up!'

'I never said anything.'

Not only is she deaf as a post, she also hears voices.

The playground in Vasa Park lies deserted. The familiar apartment buildings at the bottom of Odengatan's long incline go flying past. Elin's hands clutch the steering wheel. A feeling of unease is growing stronger and stronger in my belly. Once again I visualise Petrus with his throat cut open like a slaughtered animal on a meat hook.

'Damned butchers.'

Outside his bazaar on the crossing of Roslagsgatan, Johnsson is limping about, bringing in the apple boxes filled with cut-price bargains from the pavement. I almost bite off my cigar when the Rolls turns left towards my own home.

'Damn it!'

Now we only have a Volvo between ourselves and the Rolls, and Elin slows down to increase the gap as we continue north along Roslagsgatan. I'm squeezing the criss-cross pattern of the pistol butt so hard that it hurts. I glance at the police station on Surbrunnsgatan.

'Where are they going?'

We're coming up to the next crossing. On the pavement outside the jumble shop, old man Ström and Rickardsson, Ploman's gangster, are caught in the beam of the Rolls's headlights. They both stare at the car.

'Where do you think? Turn left, for Christ's sake!'

'But we don't know where they're going yet! I mean, they're going past your house but how would they know you live there?'

Again I see Doughboy before me, the smell of his unwashed head of hair and the feeling of his slender fingers caressing my chest. I think about his new serge suit hanging in the kitchen.

'I'll tell you later! Turn off!'

Elin swings the car violently left into Frejgatan and immediately stamps down on the accelerator. I put my hand on her shoulder and look at her. The redhead and I are no longer hunters.

We're prey.

Stina's room in the flat on Dalagatan smells distinctly of the sea. The fishwife herself is spending the night with her bloke, the copper.

I lie awake in her bed, although the bells of Matthew's Church have just rung one in the morning. A trace of a chiffon curtain is visible in the dark. A couple of gilded picture frames gleam over a crocheted tablecloth. On the bedside table lies a novel with the title *Matrimonial Cares*. With a sigh I turn over for the hundredth time. The sheets give off a smell of mothballs. I stare at the wall.

'Damn it, Kvisten, this time you've really made a mess of it.'

I pull the blanket up to my nose, coughing slightly. My thoughts keep churning, revisiting the widow's cigar shop, Doughboy, Beda and Petrus, and how the superintendent at the Institute must be mixed up in this whole blasted mess. And those men in black who increasingly seem like hitmen of some kind.

'It won't exactly be child's play taking care of them.'

The sound of cautious steps interrupts my mumbling. The steps stop by the door; the handle is pressed down. A draught of

238

air tells me the door is opening. My muscles tense up under the blanket. I pretend to be asleep.

'Are you awake, Kvist?' whispers Elin, taking a few steps into the room before coming to a stop. I peer at her through slitted eyelids. A flickering paraffin lamp lights up the wall. I have an annoying, tickling need to cough, which makes me even tenser.

'If you're not holding your breath, then you must be dead. Go on! Shift up!'

Cold air sweeps over me when Elin pulls aside the blanket. I'm only wearing my underpants. The bed creaks as she gets inside. The soft cotton of her night slip touches my body. Her matronly bust presses into my back as she makes herself comfortable behind me.

'There's no need to pretend. I know how you are. It doesn't bother me, but can't I lie here with for a bit and warm myself up?'

She puts her hand on my left shoulder. My muscles unwind like vagrants spreading their bundles under a bridge.

'I suppose you can.'

We lie in silence for a while, breathing in unison.

'She was my mother, but to you she was more than a mother. Could one put it that way?'

'Don't know if they're quite the right words.'

'But something like that?'

'Suppose so.'

She slides her hand over my upper arm. I feel a tingling in my stomach and my cock comes to life. The feeling hits me like a sucker punch. The taste of Doughboy flashes across the roof of my mouth.

'Do you really think the police are behind this?'

'They're involved, at least.'

'Are you sure?'

'Absolutely.'

Elin's breasts heave against my back; her warm breath caresses my neck. My pulse picks up. A couple of pipes are sighing in the wall. I turn on my back, and look at her. The light of the paraffin lamp on the bedside table behind her sparkles in her red tresses. About half a minute goes by. Elin inhales: 'There's gossip about you but it's none of my business.'

'Probably not.'

'Was it something you picked up in the navy?'

Outside in the street, the distant sound of a passing motor car can be heard. The muscles in my stomach bunch up, as if in preparation for a body punch.

'Why do you want to know?'

'Just curiosity.'

I quote her mother: 'The heart is not a carthorse that can be shackled any old way you like.'

'What do you mean?'

'It's not a choice. It's cost me dear.'

'Why?'

'That's how the world is.'

Something about the way I put it silences me. I shudder. I used the same words in another situation a couple of days earlier, but I can't remember what I was talking about. It feels important to remember. I clamp my eyes and rub my battered fists against my forehead.

Damned memory, more holes in it than a Swiss cheese.

The bed creaks as I sit up. I climb over Elin and go over to my coat, flung over a chair by the door. The room brightens when Elin turns up the lamp. Keeping my back towards her, I tie an extra-hard knot on the string of my underpants. I get out a cigar and strike a match. My lungs fill with a sense of calm.

I exhale.

'So it's not because of my ear?'

I turn around. Elin hoists her plucked eyebrows and looks at me for an instant, before averting her eyes.

'Your ear? What are you talking about?'

'Nothing.'

I grunt and take a deep drag on my cigar.

Next to the lamp on the bedside table is a pile of letters that Elin has brought in. They're tied with pack-thread, a neat little bundle. Elin follows my eyes.

'They were in that box of clothes from Mum. I mentioned it the other day. Haven't had the energy to look at them yet. Too depressing.'

I go over to the table, put the cigar in my mouth and pick up the bundle, bending it and riffling them with my thumb like a deck of playing cards. I untie the bow and check through the envelopes. Most of the letters seem to be about the running of the laundry: receipts, payment demands and letters from various public bodies; but a long way down the pile, I find an envelope that doesn't look like any of the others. It bears the royal seal, and the sender is the court's overseer at the palace.

'What the hell!'

Elin looks up. With a trembling hand I snatch up the letter and open it; it's typed and dated the thirty-first of August. I remove the cigar from my mouth and read:

> *Concerning your personal letter of the third day of this month. Claims already made, and any future claims concerning the matter of compensation from the Court, including all claims relating to members of the royal household, of whatever nature, are rejected.*

TUESDAY 26 NOVEMBER

Once, in a market in Malaga Harbour, I saw a sailor drunk enough to go head-to-head with a dancing bear. They'd lashed a couple of boxing gloves over the beast's paws, and put a muzzle over its mouth, to even out the terrible odds.

I think I was watching with a lad I was friendly with at the time, by name of Jorge. The spectators cheered, the ragged flags whipped in the wind, and the bear roared furiously when the sailor managed to land a couple of left jabs. Halfway into the first round the bear knocked the sailor through the ropes with a massive swing of his paw, and the match was over. In fact the outcome had been inevitable all along, but you had to give the lad credit for having the stupidity to try.

I think about that sailor as I walk down Dalagatan from Elin's flat. I button up my coat all the way and fold up my collar. Someone has scraped a large swastika in the morning frost on the cobbler's window. In the doorway a dirty stray dog lies rolled up like a dark-brown bagel. It's shivering with cold.

My trainer used to praise my ability to roll and punch back when I was up against the ropes. In the course of the night, I've realised that I have to somehow strike back against my enemy however powerful he is. The gong has sounded, it's the final round, I'm losing, and my only chance is to go for a knockout. For the sake of Beda, Doughboy, Ida and myself. It's too late to give up.

'Those swine don't know who they're dealing with. Harry Kvist in a magnificent comeback.'

An armada of workers are cycling down Odengatan on their way to work. Many of them are wearing earmuffs. Several have wound scarves around their heads. They weave in between garishly coloured newspaper vans, and bakery boys' carts, piled high with their fragrant cargo, rumbling along on iron-shod wheels.

I wait for ten minutes outside 'No. 74', a confectioner and tobacconist opposite the Post Office, until they open. I jog back and forth and glare at the postbox as if it were an opponent waiting in the opposite corner of the ring – just before the referee calls us into the middle.

I get out my envelope from my pocket; the letter to Ida. It's been franked and on the back of it is a rust-red stain. Christ knows when I bled on it. I should really have replaced it.

Clerical workers and nine-to-fivers are gathering at the tram stop on the other side of Odensgatan. I cross Dalagatan. A group of schoolchildren, carrying satchels or just school books roped together with old belts, come running along the pavement. With a tremulous hand I drop the letter into the postbox, which snaps its jaws shut as if trying to bite off my fingertips. Once again I turn towards the tobacconist's, just as the assistant is tossing out a bucketful of mopping water. I hurry back.

'Good morning!'

She looks less than twenty years old. She's wearing a deep-blue dress and looks a little tired, but her make-up's well done. Her soot-black eyebrows arch boldly over her almond-shaped eyes.

'Thanks. Damned cold today.'

I stamp my feet and look around – it's a big shop. On the glass counter is a handwritten sign: 'Excellent cigars in many price ranges'. Under the glass is a selection of tobacco pouches and zip-up leather purses. On the shelf behind are piles of cigarette cartons and round towers of tobacco tins. The girl nods and smiles. For a moment I think about the widow Lind and her cigar shop. Tomorrow morning is my last chance to act on her offer. After that, she'll let it go to someone else.

'How can I help you?'

'Twenty Meteors, and a local telephone call.'

'The telephone's in the cubicle over there.'

She points at a box at the far end of the room, and I touch my hat in thanks. After closing the door, I place my call and ask the operator to put me through to the police headquarters.

As I suspected, Hessler's already at his post. The chief constable seems willing to do anything to avoid his wife and children. I ignore the vinegar-sour tone of his voice and give him the revised registration number. After the call I go back to the counter.

'Was there anything else?'

The shop assistant's shiny morning eyes look me up and down.

'Cigarettes, as well. And another telephone call. Local.'

'What brand would you like?'

'I trust you.'

'Many men have made that mistake. So a pack of Bridge would suit you, then?'

'They're not for me.'

I take my goods and pay for them, then go back to the telephone box. I hold up my pocket watch and check the time. Ten past eight. I'll give Hessler another five minutes. If he runs he'll make it.

I light a fresh cigar and lean back against the wall with a sigh. I missed Dixie's evening walk last night and if I don't ger her out soon the apartment will definitely smell of dog piss.

If someone from the royal family is involved in this bloody story, I might be able to go to the press with it, but so far I don't have much to go on. Just a series of remarkable coincidences, and those four-eyed pen-pushers would probably keep things under wraps for the royals.

I don't have much care for the newspapers.

One time they spelled my name wrong. Harry with one 'r'. I couldn't understand how a thing like that could happen. But when I telephoned the sports editor he claimed it was a printing error. Damned liar! As if a mistake like that would happen in the printing presses.

I stand there smoking for a while. A customer comes in: a slender man wearing creased trousers and a scruffy overcoat. I feel I recognise him but can't quite place his face. He takes off his cap, exposing his bald pate. As he moves towards the counter, he glances in my direction. Just to be on the safe side I acknowledge by touching the brim of my hat.

The little man stops abruptly. His eyes look as if they're about to pop out of his skull. He spins around and leaves. The door slams hard behind him. As he hurries by the shop window, I realise who he is. I can't remember his name but he works as a night porter at Hotel Boden in Klara Norra. I asked him a few questions a couple of years ago and ended up burning his face with my cigar so badly that he pissed himself. I chuckle at the recollection before going back into the telephone box and picking up the receiver. Hessler answers almost right away.

'Why are you so interested in that Rolls?'

'It ran over a dog belonging to a client of mine. She wants compensation.'

'That won't be easy.'

'Why's that?'

245

'I waited for you until a quarter past ten last night.'

'Another time, Hessler. Tell me, will you!'

I hold my breath. A faint echo of women's voices can be heard from the crossed lines. Hessler rustles a piece of paper.

He clears his throat, and lowers his voice: 'The car belongs to a special unit of the city police. Watch out for those blokes. They're not to be trifled with.'

'Black poplin overcoats, eh?'

'You will take care of yourself, won't you, Harry? You know I'm fond of you.'

I spin the lever to break off the call.

Driving Lundin to Brunkeberg Square to fetch the corpse of a foundry-man by name of Verner Wernström, I'm looking in the rear mirror more than I am the road ahead, but I don't see any sign of a Rolls. We turn off by Johannes Church, where Döbelnsgatan merges with Malmskillnadsgatan.

'Aim for the telephone tower,' wheezes Lundin and points dead ahead at one of the strangest constructions in the city.

I peer up. It looks like the pictures of the Eiffel Tower I've seen on postcards, but it's a stockier Swedish version. The square latticework of steel beams sits on top of the Telephone Company offices and stretches up some fifty metres, with a series of gantries inside the construction, connected by ladders. These days, a gigantic revolving clock advertising the NK Department Store sits at the top of the tower.

'I wasn't much older than you when they put that up,' says Lundin, twisting his moustache ends. 'I always thought it was like a medieval castle with those little cages on each corner, like turrets. Can you see the flagpoles on them?'

'You've told me a hundred times before. About your brother and the Motala works and Christ knows what else. What's the address we're headed to?'

'In the olden days there were different flags meaning this or that. A white one with a big "H" on it meant there was plenty of herring in the shops but they had to stop flying that one, because once they saw it the old girls wouldn't stop bloody haggling.'

Lundin gives a croaking laugh and flicks his left hand in the air, while clicking his bony fingers. The shoulder holster rubs against my side as I turn towards him; it'll be the first time I turn up armed at a house in mourning.

'Yeah, you told me before. Beridarebansgatan, isn't it?'

'My brother, bless his soul, was involved in the construction, as you might recall. In those days all the telephone wires in the city stopped here. Looked like a bloody nightmare, a big lace cushion, and when there were so many of 'em that you couldn't see the sky any more, they buried them instead.'

I peer up at the tower as we draw closer, and I shudder. The sky's a dark grey, like the smoke of my cigars. I check the rear-view mirror again. Nothing there except a rubbish truck.

'Apparently his son's a really decent marksman.'

'Who is?'

'Ragnar Lundin, my nephew. Took part in the Olympic Games in target shooting.'

I head for the big water-pump in the middle of the square. I go past it and change down a gear to make a U-turn. More than once I've waited here for some runaway lass who needs to be put back on a train to go home. Towards midnight, flocks of cackling whores gather around the pump, their faces heavily daubed, drunk on fusel and cheap wine.

'Up there, by those damned kids.'

Lundin points me to the right building and I park up. He goes ahead up the front steps and I lug out the clumsy coffin and lean it up against the wall. By a little barred grate to the cellars sits a boy in a sports cap, pumping a fishing line up and down. The City has stopped paying for rat tails, but you can still get a couple of öre from the landlord's agent with a bit of luck.

A couple of curious young lads gather around the hearse as if a dog's been run over. A small one in knee socks and short trousers plucks up the courage to knock on the coffin, then cups his hand to his ear as if to listen for a response, sending the others into peals of laughter.

'Stop that, it's for Kjell's dad,' says a pale, red-nosed lad, wiping his snotty nose with the back of his hand. 'It is for Kjell's dad, isn't it?'

'That's right.'

I light a Meteor and lean against the wall. An emaciated bloke with white stubble hobbles across the street towards me. His trousers are held up by a hay-bale strap tied in a bow across his stomach.

'Will there be ale at the wake?' The old bloke bites his thumb knuckle, then takes his hand out of his mouth. 'Can you get me in?' He holds out a couple of blue relief coupons usable in NORMA restaurants.

Might be all right for a little celebratory lunch tomorrow for me and Doughboy after his release.

'I'll see what I can do.'

I take the food coupons and put them in my trouser pocket at the same time as Lundin opens the door and grabs the head end of the coffin. I take the foot end. We lift.

'This bloke here was wondering if he can take part in the refreshments?'

Lundin shakes his head. I shrug, and then we carry the coffin up the stairs. The skinny bloke's lips start trembling.

The hall smells of ten o'clock coffee. I kick at an escaped chicken that comes running down the stairs. My cigar is wedged in my mouth. Smoke gets in my eye, so I clamp it shut. Lundin balances the coffin with the narrow end facing downward, and rings the doorbell.

'The hard part of the job is bringing this thing down. We'll have the whole team of pall-bearers here for that.'

Lundin lifts his top hat a tad and mops the sweat off his brow with a white handkerchief. I'm supporting the weight of the black coffin, which is leaning against me; it's like propping up an old mother-in-law during a wedding waltz. Lundin adjusts his jacket and opens the door; I angle the coffin down and he takes his end.

Death has released its unsettling sweet smell in the flat, and the bereaved wife has a good deal of grey in her dark hair. Her eyes almost brim over when she catches sight of the coffin, but she closes her eyes and squeezes out the tears into her wrinkles, then wipes them off with a white lace handkerchief. We stand for a while in the hall before she realises she has to let us into the living room.

The curtains are drawn and everything is resting in the gloomy light of loss. In the adjoining room, four lads of mixed ages sit on a yellow and brown rug. Between them they have a shiny red fire engine made of metal. Scant consolation.

Next to a big mirrored cupboard, the foundry-worker Wernström lies in a double bed. He's wearing a long night-shirt. His bloodless lips have already receded, revealing a couple of yellow teeth. He's unshaven, with red blotches on his face, although otherwise damned pale. There's still a bit of caster's soot around his ears. Someone has stopped the wall-mounted clock at a quarter to six. We put the coffin on the cork mat next to the bed and go back down the stairs to pick up the rest of the equipment. I take a deep drag on my cigar.

We carry the things into the flat. The widow watches us in silence. From time to time she makes a movement, as if intending to help us, but every time she draws back, crestfallen. Lundin goes up to the corpse.

'You want us to cut him?' Lundin opens his cut-throat razor.

'That's the same suit he was married in, fifteen years ago.'

The widow points at a black suit hanging over the gable of the bed. 'It's the only one that'll do. He should go into the ground decently.'

There's a sob in her voice. She takes a couple of shaky breaths.

'We'll cut it open on the back, it's not a problem.'

'Kjell will have his watch, but you can put it in that snuff tin on the table.'

She points at a bark tin on a crocheted cloth on the bedside table. Lundin taps her on the shoulder with his free hand.

'You go out to your children and we'll take care of the rest. Should we cut him?'

'He was called unawares, and hadn't decided anything.'

'We'll do it just to be on the safe side.'

The widow nods tersely and leaves us. I slam the zinc bucket down next to the bed. The foundry-man's wiry muscles are stiffened by death; his fingers are knotty, and his nails outlined by soot. We're a few hours early. Lundin sighs, kneads himself a ball of snuff from the tin on the table, then puts it in the coffin.

I force the arm straight like you do with the arm of a jumper frozen on the clothesline. Working together we manage to get the foundry-man's hand into the bucket, and Lundin slashes his wrist with the knife. The blood is thick and grainy, almost like

250

porridge, and it flows slowly. Very slowly the dead man opens his hand.

'I'll take care of the swaddling, and you arrange the room. We don't have much time if I'm to get to my doctor's appointment as well.'

I spit out my cigar stub. It bounces against the foundry-man's fingers and lands with a sizzle in the zinc bucket. Lundin wipes the knife on a towel. There's a rasping sound on the dead man's cheek when Lundin starts shaving him without lather. I unpack the things we brought in the coffin.

I cover all the furnishings, also pictures, mirrors and windows, with white sheets that I tie together with broad black ribbons. Lundin wrestles with the corpse and its clothes, his cough shattering the silence of the flat. I fetch the table and put it at the long end of the room and throw a white sheet over it. In the middle I arrange black runners and piles of plates and cutlery, and set up the paraffin candles at either end. In the kitchen, the widow has burst into tears. She sobs loudly.

One of the sons comes into the room. He's a freckled lad with ginger hair, about seven or eight. He's wearing dark turn-ups and a black silk waistcoat. He stands in a corner and covers his ears with his hands. I line up the glasses on the table.

'Will you give me a hand putting him in?'

Lundin's coarse voice cuts through the silence. On my way through the room I stop in front of the boy. I get out my wallet, put it in my mouth, take hold of his lower arms and force his little cold hands down. He's almost as stiff as his father. I get out a faded cinema ticket.

'Tarzan.' I hold the ticket out. He stares at it; I nod. 'It's yours.' He takes it. I continue: 'Now go and take care of your mother.'

*

251

By the time the black-dressed old girls show up, we've got Wernström tucked into his wooden box. It's up on three kitchen chairs, surrounded by cut sprays of spruce. As you'd expect, they arrange a spread of brawn, herring gratins, cold stuffed cabbage rolls and a fresh cheese decorated with raisins in the form of a crucifix. The widow herself contributes a piece of roast veal.

The blokes from the union knock on the door, and set up their association's bold red banner in a corner. A smell of food fills the room. The pall-bearers are going to miss the toast in honour of the dead man.

The blokes knock back their sixth of a gill and a couple of the old girls have one too. The pall-bearers show up in the doorway, and to their disappointment they have to line up with their bowler hats held in both hands like black beer-guts against their stomachs.

Lundin points at the pall-bearers with his schnapps glass and leans in towards me: 'You go on the front left again.'

I nod. The ginger-haired lad is standing a little apart from the other urchins outside the kitchen, clutching my cinema ticket in his hand.

Heavy with veal and cake, and with awkward feet, we carry the coffin down the stairs. Those of us at the front have to keep our carrying straps short. They dig into our shoulders and necks. In front of us walks the elder of the union blokes, carrying the red silk banner. The rolls of fat on his neck are covered in white hairs. He stumbles, totters and curses. Someone behind me laughs.

'Let's not drop the coffin on top of him, lads.'

Pall-bearer's sense of humour.

Outside it's still drizzling. I and the right-hand number one have to get inside the hearse to get the coffin in. The spruce smells good in here. Gently we put down Wernström on the floor.

The funeral guests line up opposite each other, in two open charabancs. They take cover under umbrellas and blankets. The widow and her sons travel in a carriage with a hard top. The wet black horses give off a sharp smell. I put my hand on the muzzle of one of them. I think it's Loke. He throws his head back, tossing his mane at the rain-heavy sky. Lundin nods at me.

The hearse starts after a bit of coughing. I release the clutch and carefully pull out into Beridarebansgatan. In my rear-view mirror I see the driver of the two-horse carriage at the front smack his long reins over the rumps of his horses, and the cortège is set in motion. The iron-shod wheels rumble against the street. By the ochre-coloured house next door, the chicken lies in a pool of blood. It's been run over. Its white feathers have spread across the wet cobblestones like the foam of a storm swell.

Still unsteady on my feet a couple of hours later, after funeral schnapps and psalms, and with the church bells ringing in my ears, I park outside the undertaker's on Roslagsgatan. I give Lundin a parting nod and wander northwards up the street towards Wallin's place, with his uniform under my arm, until I'm standing outside his house.

On the other side of the road, the Jewel comes walking along, her black dress fluttering in the wind under her unbuttoned coat, a mourning veil over her hat. Her arms hang lifelessly and she stumbles now and then as if she's drunk.

Wallin still has the blinds rolled down on the first floor. Maybe he's worked through the night and is sleeping. I wait until the Jewel has passed, then hurry across the road. I don't have much time to pick up Elin and get to the police station before most of them go home.

The stairwell smells strongly of smoke: there must be a blocked stove or ceramic wood-burner somewhere. It's as dark as the inside of a sack. I stop outside Wallin's door. My cough echoes between the walls, I gob on the floor between my shoes and knock.

I put my cigar in my mouth, try the door handle. The door glides opens with a creak. I step into the hall.

'Wallin? It's Kvist! I've come to give you the uniform.'

There's a crunching under my feet as if some plaster's fallen from the ceiling. I stumble over a pair of shoes and almost land on my face. I fumble for the light switch.

'As dark as a goddamned bat roost. Are you sleeping it off, you bloody drunk?'

Carefully I feel my way along the wall into the flat, but I knock into something that starts to sway back and forth, like a sandbag. I gasp and instinctively put my fists up. The package containing the uniform thuds onto the floor.

'What the hell?'

I take the cigar out of my mouth, blow on the glowing end and hold it up. In the orange light I catch a glimpse of Wallin's swollen, unshaven face. His lips have formed themselves into a distended purple ring, and his eyes stare blankly although they're nearly popping out their sockets. His body turns slowly on the end of a clothesline hanging from a hook in the ceiling. I squeeze his arm.

He's been dangling there for a good while.

The hearse rattles in the powerful wind as Elin and I sit in the front seat, on Bergsgatan, keeping a lookout. It's about an hour since I found Wallin. I think about him and that damned Rolls we were following up Roslagsgatan yesterday. We turned off before we saw where it stopped. I lost my nerve. I'll be damned if I haven't become lily-livered, now that Doughboy is almost within reach.

I look over at Elin. Maybe I should try to sort this out on my own. Do what I do best without having to worry about her safety. Outside, six constables are ushering a group of dirty tatterde-malions along the pavement towards one of the back entrances to the police station. A florid-faced bloke, wearing trousers with braces and a laddered thick jumper, limps along at the front. His trouser legs have frayed and he leans on a knotty branch as he walks. Behind him is a tart in a soiled dress. Her colourful shawl flaps behind her in the wind. Men, women and children drift half-heartedly along the pavement like flotsam on a grey sea. The coppers try to hurry the gathering along by slapping at them with the sides of their sabres and their black batons. They've probably just raided one of the slums or gone around the harbour lifting tarpaulins.

'How long are we supposed to sit here?' Elin puts her NORMA food box on the dashboard and carefully wipes her lips.

'It takes as long as it takes. It's part of the job.'

'Private detective.' Elin snorts. 'I can't understand how you put up with it.'

'Strong bladder, strong fists, the rest takes care of itself.'

On the other side of the street the tart turns round towards one of the coppers and yells something, her mouth wide, stab-bing her finger in the air. With a savage grin the copper grabs her wrist and hurls her forwards; she stumbles, struggling to hold her skirts down, and falls to the pavement.

Elin drums her fingers on the instrument panel: 'What do you think about that letter from the palace?'

'I've already said, three or four times.'

'Mum's letter, with some sort of demand in it, was sent on the 3rd, but it took more than three weeks for her to get a reply.'

'They must have a lot to get on with. Polishing the crown jewels and arranging balls.'

'And then it takes another three weeks before she's murdered.'

'It might not be connected.'

'A coincidence?'

'I don't know. Your mother had a lively imagination. She talked about the King, his family and other important people as if they were neighbours. It wouldn't surprise me if she wrote them letters too.'

'I have a headache. There's a thunderstorm coming, mark my words.'

An imposing black car comes up the little hill from the police headquarters. Elin holds her breath, but it's not the right make.

I look away from the building and across at her: 'What difference does it make to you?'

Elin takes her black clutch bag from between the seats. She opens it with a clicking sound.

'What do you mean?' she says, irritably.

'A month ago you didn't even know she existed.'

There's a jingling of keys, coins and hatpins as Elin roots about in the bag. She lowers her voice: 'I want justice.'

She finds a lipstick and adjusts the rear mirror.

'Justice?'

'If you had a family of your own, you might understand.'

Elin paints her lower lip first, then her top lip, and presses them together. I look out of the side window and bite back a curse. I wonder just how long it takes for a letter to cross the Atlantic these days. I find a half-smoked cigar in my pocket.

'We should have hired a different motor car. Following them again in the hearse is suicide, pure and simple.'

Evening has come and darkness has fallen over the rain-drenched city. Schoolchildren with satchels on their shoulders pass by, as do women holding baskets of groceries for supper. As the working day comes to a close, secretaries in dresses, draughtsmen, caretakers and clerical staff in suits follow. A little later, the dispatch companies spew out their delivery boys, and the factories and construction sites their workers: squat blokes with blue overalls stained by bricks and mortar. When I was put away in Långholmen, during the Depression, construction seemed to have stopped altogether. Everywhere one saw concrete skeletons of buildings, as if there had been a war; but now it all seems to have started up again. Last of all you see the street musicians emerging from buildings and hurrying to their pitches; these are their most lucrative hours.

Light after light goes out in the police headquarters, and before long there's only a handful still burning.

Elin has dozed off, her mouth agape. Her light snoring fills the interior of the car; I keep my eyes on the police station. The wind is blowing so hard that I can hear its windows rattling. I check my pocket watch for the hundredth time. It's now only fourteen hours until Doughboy is released. If something's going to happen, it better happen soon. I should have given this case up long ago, but now it's too late. Damned women and their obstinacy.

Briefly I entertain the thought that the Rolls is parked on Roslagsgatan, and that the men in black have my house under surveillance. The easiest thing might be to go and have a look. But I've hardly finished the thought before I see a black car in my side mirror. Elin protests sleepily as I push her head down into my lap and duck down over it.

The hearse trembles in the draught of air as the big Rolls swishes by. I stick my nose up above the dashboard and bring the motor stuttering to life.

Dark, ragged clouds blow across the moon. We drive behind the Rolls at a safe distance, travelling up Hantverkargatan.

The sentries around Belzén's headquarters give us curious looks, but apart from that the city lies deserted. Up in Fridhemsplan, the car makes a detour around a couple of apartment buildings before it heads south. For a second I get the idea that we are on our way to Konradsberg, the asylum, to kill another lunatic or two, but the Rolls continues towards Väster Bridge.

The darkness of Rålambshov Park surrounds us, and for the second time in recent days we follow the Rolls towards the apex of the bridge. The wind-tormented city lies exposed down below, like a knocked-out whore surrounded by symbols of authority: the church steeples, the City Hall and the telephone tower all seem to loom over her menacingly. In the black waters of Mälaren, about thirty metres below, reflected lights glitter like pearls scattered from a broken string.

I look over the water at the stone walls of Långholmen: 'That's the way the world is.'

'What are you muttering about?'

'I was just reminded of the world's injustice.'

'How do you mean?'

I point: 'I said the same thing on that rock there a week ago. I stood there gawping at the inauguration ceremony for the bridge.'

'You're raving.'

'The King was speaking. His party included those four blokes in poplin overcoats.'

'Damn! And you only mention it now?'

'My memory's not what it used to be.'

A powerful gust of wind rocks the car, Elin gasps. My grip on the steering wheel tightens. A couple of splashes of rain hit the windshield.

'The same blokes that the Rymans saw outside my mother's?'

'The same.'

'Are you sure?'

I nod.

'What does that mean?'

'Bad things.'

On the downward slope I glance at the island to the right. The grey prison walls can be glimpsed in the darkness; a light shines in one of the guard towers. Somewhere in the midst of all that, Doughboy has just gone to bed, his last night of captivity. Maybe he'll dream of his new suit. Involuntarily I press my right shoe down on the accelerator.

When the car in front of us turns into Hornsgatan, I can see there are three people inside it, two in the front seat and one in the back. Elin steadies herself with a hand against the dashboard when I make a sharp left.

'Why on earth would the superintendent of the Asplunden Institute socialise with those types?'

'Bridge evenings?'

'Very funny, Harry.'

'Do you know who Ploman is? The gangster?'

'I've heard of him.'

'He keeps a mute street girl he won in a game of cards.'

'Bloody lovely gentleman.'

259

'Mute girls don't gossip. Some say she was like that from the start, others say Rickardsson cut off her tongue with a cut-throat razor.'

Elin flinches: 'Rickardsson?'

'He lives on Roslagsgatan. We saw him yesterday outside Ström's. There's nothing especially wrong with him apart from that.'

'And what does that have to do with the Asplunden Institute?'

'That's what we have to find out.'

By New Slussen the car in front of us suddenly accelerates. I peer up at the Tyska Church; it's almost a quarter past eleven. I pick up speed. In the distance, the sound of thunder falls in with the growling of the motor. Thirteen hours until Doughboy.

We roll down towards Old Town and Skepps Bridge at high speed, windscreen wipers squeaking. All the noise of the quays in the daytime – rattling winches, rolling wheelbarrows, steam whistles and swearing – stopped several hours ago. Now everything is calm apart from the flapping of the flags in the wind. The long-necked cranes have stopped their pecking at the innards of the ships. Only a handful of nocturnal swingers are out and about on this night, which seems to be gearing up for a proper autumn storm.

The road loops around the oldest district of the city. The narrow alleys hide the sailors' bars and whorehouses in their gloom. In front of us, the red tail-lights of the Rolls fade in the night. Before long, the car has disappeared round a bend in the road.

'Don't lose them now, for Christ's sake!'

I change up and stamp angrily at the accelerator. The corpse-crate protests and slowly picks up speed. I chew the end of my cigar. In front of us the road straightens and we pull up towards Logård Quay where the Norrland steamers are waiting to go into their winter berths.

'They must have swung left on the hill in front of the Royal Palace.'

The massive palace soon comes into view, its wings on either side jutting out like the paws of a lion lying in wait.

As I turn the wheel, I hear the distant rumbling of thunder once again.

The headlights of our motor car reflect off the golden trimmings on the uniforms of the castle guards, standing along the walls of the palace. Guard duty won't be very pleasant tonight.

The cobbles make the entire vehicle shake as I accelerate up the hill. I scan the open area in front of Storkyrkan. Nothing.

'Damn it!'

I turn around the corner and take the car along the edges of the outer courtyard. There are no vehicles in it. I swear again and thump the steering wheel with the palm of my hand.

'Where did they get to?'

'Christ knows.'

I put my arm across the back of Elin's seat and reverse out, then turn around. After driving across Palace Hill I stop and carefully reverse the car in behind the Royal Telegraph Office. We are screened off by the low wall running down the hill. I turn off the engine.

'What now?'

'More waiting. We've hardly done much else.'

'Can't we be seen?'

I open the door. Keeping one hand on my hat, to stop it being whisked off, I circle the hearse to make sure it doesn't stick out of the shadows. It doesn't.

The shop signs are banging like pistol shots. The wind roars in cellar window alcoves. I'm just about go back into the warmth when I hear the faint sound of an engine through all the noise.

A flash of lightning lights up the obelisk up on the hill. I throw my cigar on the ground and put my boot heel on it, then slide onto the driver's seat of the hearse and hunch down.

My heart beats hard; a clap of thunder rattles the windows overhead. Even though it's dark and the Rolls passes at a distance of ten metres, I'm quite sure of what I see: there's a fourth man in the back seat. A tall, gangly type, his oval spectacles glittering in the gloom of the passenger compartment.

TUESDAY 26 NOVEMBER

A few drops of rain fall against the windshield as we drive across Norr Bridge and the foaming waves of Strömmen. The black Rolls goes around Gustav Adolf's Square and bolts up Malmskillnadsgatan through the light rain. I follow at a distance, with my headlights turned off. Somewhere beyond Brunkebergsåsen there's a lightning strike. The massive, sooty steel skeleton of the telephone mast is lit up for a moment. We reach the large triangular plaza and pass the house of mourning where Lundin and I picked up the foundry-man Wernström earlier today. The Rolls slows down and turns right, I follow suit.

I bring the hearse to a halt. The Rolls turns right again and parks on the north-eastern corner of the plaza, with its nose pointing at the palace a few hundred metres to the south. The hearse is partially hidden from their view by the hundreds of bicycles parked between us.

For a few seconds everything is quiet; all I can hear is the rain, which drums against the bodywork of the car with increasing strength. A wet dog runs across the road with its tail between its legs and takes cover under a pushcart a few metres in front of us. The tarts have fled the plaza, but I see one of them standing in a doorway further down the street, her shawl draped over her head. She peers up at the dark skies.

Even though we're about twenty metres away, I can clearly hear the door of the Rolls slamming. The raindrops on the windscreen blur the outline of the black-clad heavyweight, but I'm fairly sure that he's the skin-headed bloke, the one who looks like a bull. As he hurries around the car, he's opening an umbrella. He holds it out when he opens the back door. Elin puts her hand on top of mine, which is still gripping the steering wheel. She squeezes it hard.

The passenger is so tall that the other bloke has to reach up with the umbrella, but even so his head is obscured by it when he gets out. His overcoat is trimmed with an oversize fur collar.

Flanked by the man with the umbrella, the passenger crosses the road and disappears into the house next to the offices of the Telephone Company. The street number is written in yellow on a grubby black glass plate over the door: 24. Elin gasps for air. The interior of the Rolls lights up for an instant when someone inside lights a cigarette.

'Did you see him?'

Elin's voice is shaking.

'Hardly. You?'

'Not quite, but… it's him all right. But why? With those thugs.'

'You've heard the gossip, haven't you?'

'Was it really him?'

'I think so. You saw him yourself.'

'What are we going to do?'

'I haven't the foggiest.'

I stare at the ground floor of number 24. Several of the windows are lit up, white, but a couple of the rooms lie in darkness, so the line of windows is as gappy as a six-year-old's teeth. The rain grows heavier. The droplets on the windows are eaten up by rivulets running vertically down the glass. Under the pushcart, I see the stray still lying there with its tail between its legs, trembling with fear. I take the Husqvarna out of my shoulder holster, open the magazine and slot it back into position.

'Ellinor.'

Elin's voice is so faint that I can hardly make it out. I look over at her. Her hands have wilted in her lap. Her jaws are churning as if she's chewing on an old bit of bread.

'What's that?'

'She turns twelve this spring.'

There's a stabbing feeling in my heart, my heart moves up one level, my temples are thumping. Elin looks out of the side window before going on: 'I was no better myself. No better than Mum.'

'I see.'

'I think she's having a good life. She's living with a family on Lidingö. In a green house with white-painted corner posts. Sometimes in the summers I take the bicycle and pass by. Once I think I saw her… on her way to the garden bower.'

Elin's voice cracks. I squeeze my pistol hard.

'She looked quite well, maybe a little pale. I wonder if they give her enough food to eat, but I suppose they do – I mean, they have a house and everything?'

'I'm sure they do.'

The plaza is lit up by a bolt of lightning; the clap of thunder follows almost at once. The rain picks up even more. In the Rolls, the cigarette has gone out.

I put my hand in my left pocket and get out the pack of Bridge and the box of matches I bought earlier at the tobacconist's. I put these in Elin's lap. Her mouth trembles slightly.

'There's still time. Tomorrow you'll go to find your daughter.'

Elin nods, and swallows, smiling cautiously.

'And you, Harry?'

'Did I ever tell you about the sailor who boxed a circus bear?'

'Don't think so.'

265

Elin leans her head back against the seat and stares up at the ceiling. Her hair falls back, and for the first time I notice she's missing her right ear. A dark hole, surrounded by flaming red skin, goes right into her skull. No wonder her hearing's worse than an artillery soldier's. I refocus on the Rolls.

'Another time. Leave the car outside Lundin's. I'll make it home under my own steam.'

'What are you doing?'

'I don't bloody know. But I won't pull my punches.'

Carefully I open the door. Elin puts her hand on mine and squeezes it.

'Will I see you again?'

'Maybe as early as tomorrow. But swing by Lundin's and remind him to walk Dixie if you don't.'

I tip my hat in farewell and slip out into the driving rain.

Hidden behind the bicycles, staying hunched down, I run across to the vaulted entrance of the Telephone Company. I dart into the shadows and press myself against the wall, before cautiously peering around the corner. The rainwater is gurgling in the gutters.

The stuttering engine of the hearse, once it starts, can hardly be heard over the sound of the storm. A match is struck in the driver's compartment, but it goes out almost at once. A hand cups itself around the glow of the cigarette. Elin reverses carefully into Beridarebansgatan. Half a second later she's headed off northwards.

The passenger door of the Rolls opens. A little skinny bloke jumps out and quickly scans the area. I draw my head back into the shadows. Carefully I cock my pistol. By the time I dare stick my hat back out into the rain he's gone. From my angle diagonally behind the car, I can't tell whether he's gone back into the vehicle or the house.

I leave the shadow and follow the wall towards the car until I can take cover behind one of the bare trees a short distance from the corner. From here I can see both the car and the door of number 24 where the other two went in. If I look up I see the red-and-green neon NK clock rotating hazily through the rain, about fifty metres above the telephone tower, a slap in the face for Klara district and its poverty and misery. The rain sings its gloomy song in the corner drainpipe.

I put an unlit cigar in my mouth to assuage my need to smoke. No more than ten, fifteen minutes have gone by when the door of number 24 opens again.

The sturdy bloke holds up the umbrella to screen the tall passenger. The lanky figure supports himself against the other's shoulder as they take a couple of unbalanced steps on the slippery paving stones. In his other hand he's got a cigarette holder with a glowing cigarette in it. I crane my neck.

According to the signs, number 24 is situated in a block known as the Thunderclap, and by now the thunder is simultaneous with the lightning. The bolts of lightning hound each other across the dark sky. Even the ground under my feet is shaking.

The storm booms like an anchor chain on its way into the locker. The rain hammers against my hat brim. For a moment the lanky bloke in front of me looks up at the sky. There's another crash. The lightning gives a milk-white sheen to his oval spectacles. The tips of his curled moustache point directly upward. Just like on the inauguration podium on Väster Bridge a week ago, his large horse-like teeth show when he smiles.

I'm still shaking when the rear lights of the Rolls disappear down the hill, back towards the castle. I take a couple of tremulous

267

breaths and try to get my limbs under control, standing there with my head lowered, under the tree branches. It feels like the rain is cutting me into fine pieces.

Yet another peal of thunder wakes me up. I look around and quickly shuffle across Malmskillnadsgatan. I cock my pistol with my thumb, open the door of number 24 and slip inside.

My eyes quickly grow accustomed to the darkness. The stairwell smells of decaying wood, cigarette smoke and turpentine. The floor is covered in cracked flagstones. A well-used flight of stairs with a banister polished from years of use leads up. Somewhere on the first floor there's a weak light shining. I throw away the drenched cigar, shake the water off my hat and light a fresh Meteor to calm my nerves.

Quietly I start up the stairs. On the second floor there's a lone bulb burning on the ceiling. From higher up in the house, I hear a faint noise. It's intermittent, a sort of guttural weeping. It hardly sounds human even. The windowpanes rattle whenever a crack of thunder is heard. I peer down into the street: no people, no motor cars.

I follow the eerie noise up the next flight of stairs. I hesitate for a moment on the third floor, and grip my pistol. I am not quite sure if it's a sound of crying I'm hearing. Far below, a door opens and closes. I take a couple more drags on my cigar and then wedge it in my mouth. Holding the pistol in front of me, I stalk up another flight of stairs to the top floor of the building. Again, there's a single light bulb spreading a jaded yellow sheen over the dirty corridor. Rat droppings are scattered along the skirting boards. Four of the doors are shut, with surnames on the doors, but the fifth is unmarked. The sound is coming from behind a peeling stairwell wall. I realise that someone is sitting on the attic stairs, blubbering.

I recognise a secret vagabond's mark scraped with a knife by the frame of the fifth door, meaning that no one is going to open it when you knock. I raise my Husqvarna and shoot the door open, then peer into the dark single-room flat. The cigar falls out of my mouth in amazement.

Heavy drapes hang over the windows, and a floor lamp with a tasselled shade gives off a faint glow. Nonetheless I can make out a couch placed in the middle of the room, with a white blanket of some kind on it, and a pair of silk cushions gleaming slightly.

The floor is graced by a Persian rug, the walls with pictures of naked youths posing in all sorts of provocative positions: a twisted temple of Eros.

Closest to the door are a pair of men's shoes. The leather has cracked in several places, but someone has filled it with shoe polish and soot.

In the space of a second, the memories of my own meeting places come flooding back: public lavatories, dirty third-class bathhouses, mouldering berths and crappy back lanes in dingy harbour towns, always ducking and diving to avoid insults and the watchful eyes of the police, those guardians of public morality.

The guttural sobs behind the stair wall bring me back to reality. I tread on my cigar and turn around. I cross the corridor, press myself to the wall and follow it to the corner, and peer up. There, curled up by the attic door, ten steps up, sits a young lad, rocking back and forth with his face in his hands. His hair is standing on end. He's wearing a light-green shirt with the buttons done up wrong, and a pair of sturdy trousers. One of his socks has a hole over his big toe. On a step below him lies a coin.

I clear my throat but don't get a reaction.

'Are you all right?'

Nothing.

'Are you from the Asplunden Institute?'

I climb a few steps. The coin is a two-krona piece.

I raise my voice: 'Can you hear me? Can you hear what I'm saying?'

My shadow falls over the lad when I take another step. He looks up with a hunted expression, and a few awkward sounds press themselves out. He's about twenty years old; his eyes are close together, greyish blue. He presses himself against the door. His green shirt breast is soiled with a thick goo.

Royal blood may be blue, but royal seed is as white as any other.

I put my Husqvarna back in the holster and slowly offer him my hand. I pick up the coin and sit on the step below. For half a second I stare at the engraved portrait of the King.

'With the People for the Fatherland,' I read, and hand him the coin. He snatches it from me.

'The Asplunden Institute?'

I move my lips as much as I can, and shape my hands into the angle of a roof. I point at him, feeling like a proper idiot.

'Asplunden?'

'He can't hear you.'

A voice with a strong Gotland accent makes me flinch. I quickly get to my feet. Seven steps below stands one of the thugs in his poplin overcoat – the big bloke with the weak chin and the waxed moustache. His eyes glitter with malevolence in his wedge-shaped face. He's attached one of those cylindrical silencers to his pistol, the kind that Hessler mentioned. It's pointing at the lad.

'You can't get away. The others are waiting below. You followed us in that hearse. We're starting to recognise it.'

'This deaf whippersnapper here isn't doing you any harm.'

The youth makes some pathetic sounds, grasping for my coat-tails. The Husqvarna is calling for me in its holster.

'He's practically dead already. You too. The only difference is that he hasn't realised it yet.'

'Damned rat!'

'Where is she?'

'Who?'

'Your female companion.'

'You're off your head.'

Hessler was quite right, the shot doesn't make much more noise than a champagne cork. The lad's head is thrown backwards into the attic door, in a spray of blood. He bounces forward hard and slides down the steps on his stomach.

The thug changes position; I draw my Husqvarna with a sound of steel rasping against leather. Without taking aim I let off three or four quick shots from my hip. The sound of the shots reverberates in the narrow stairwell, making my eardrums throb with pain. Despite the close range I miss. Shooting has never been one of my strengths. The copper ducks back around the corner, letting off another shot as he does; the bullet strikes the door behind me.

My eyes fill with tears from the acrid cordite. My ears are screaming. I fumble behind me with my left hand, and find the blood-spattered door handle.

I throw myself through the attic door and slam it behind me. My steps ring out as I back down a narrow passage between walls of wooden planks. I fire a few more times at the door. The bullets go right through the wood. I turn around and run into the dark labyrinth of the attic, holding my left hand in front of me.

There's a smell of old dry timber. The rain is hammering down on the roof overhead and my heart beats wildly. Fumbling, I go around one corner and then another. I hear the attic door being opened, and I press myself against a dividing wall of planks by a storage unit, my pulse strong against the butt of my pistol. I have two bullets in the magazine, one in the barrel and none in reserve.

A clap of thunder shakes the attic. Dust falls from the roof beams. I gasp for air. There's a click somewhere, and the lights come on, dazzling me.

A floorboard groans on the other side of the wall, to the right. I hiccup with tension. As quietly as I can I move away from the sound, turning into a gloomy passage where the ceiling lights have gone. The tenants have made short shrift of the walls here, stripping them for firewood. My coat sleeve catches on a nail sticking out of a joist. I rip it free and move on.

I sneak past a brick chimney stack where a tramp has made himself a nest to take advantage of the warmth. I can make out a blanket, a couple of empty green bottles and some old newspapers to sleep on. I come to a junction. Somewhere behind me I hear another floorboard creak.

I peer first to the right and then left. At the far end of the corridor, I catch a glimpse of a ladder leaning against the wall. There's a hatch in the sloping ceiling. I withdraw into the dark passage again.

'You're surrounded! You have nowhere else to go!'

The voice echoes through the narrow space. These coppers will never leave me alone. Tiptoeing back into the darkness, I fetch two empty bottles from the tramp's nest by the chimney stack. I place them across the passage about thirty centimetres apart by the junction.

Carefully I place the ladder against the wall next to the trap-door and climb up. The hatch is locked with two sturdy bolts. The first of them I can open without any trouble, but the second one seems to have caught. I thump it a couple of times with my left hand to try and loosen the dust and dirt.

'There's no point trying to get away. We know you now, Kvist. We know where you live, how you work, we know your whole smutty background.'

The voice is closer now. I hit the bolt with the pistol butt and at last it moves. The hatch whines as it opens. The last thing I hear as I heave myself onto the slippery-as-ice copper-covered roof is a man coming at full speed across the floorboards.

I slide down the green-scarred wet copper but quickly grab onto the edge of the hatch with my left hand; then, pulling myself back up, on my stomach. I point my pistol into the opening, taking aim at the dark junction a few metres away.

The rain is everywhere. It freezes my hands, makes my fingers cramp up. It runs down my neck, and my spine like ice water. It even finds its way into my boots.

My heart hammers against the cold, wet copper.

The rain is falling so hard against the roof that it's difficult to tell whether the clattering of shoes in there has stopped. I give the ladder a shove with the pistol, it bounces against the wooden wall, then slams into the floor.

The metal edge of the hatch cuts into my left hand; my fingers have already grown numb. Water drips into my face from the brim of my hat, making me blink. Inside, the man kicks one of the bottles and I see a shadow. The Husqvarna recoils in my hand as I squeeze the trigger. My slippery hand loses its grip on the edge but I catch hold of it again.

The man returns fire. I hear two muted shots, and see a puff of smoke. The bullets whizz over my head. I fire my last-but-one bullet before my wet, aching left hand slips and loses its hold on the metal edge.

Helplessly I slide down the copper roof.

*

273

Although the roof is not especially steep, its wetness makes it as slippery as glass. Water sprays all around me and I tense every muscle in my body as I slide down between two bevelled ridges about two centimetres high, and try to get some purchase by wedging my boots against them. I glance over my shoulder and see the drop approaching at a terrifying speed. Six floors down I see the ground; any fall here would mean certain death.

I pinch onto one of the ridges with my left hand and jam my right foot into the gutter. It groans under my weight but holds up. I refuse to look down, there's a fluttering feeling in my stomach. Instead, I rise to my feet. Just as my pursuer sticks his head out of the roof hatch, I start to run across the roof towards the Telephone Company some twenty metres away. I don't know how many times I slip and almost fall into the courtyard below, but I reach the black roof of the next building, and keep moving. My steps are almost silent, drowned out by both the driving rain and the thunder and the thumping boots of the goon on my heels. He yells something at me but I can't hear what he says. Above me, the enormous telephone tower rises up, with its abundance of criss-crossing steel beams. Again, a flash of lightning illuminates the skeleton of the tower like an X-ray. I stuff the Husqvarna in my pocket and run across the roof until I reach its far corner.

I jump up and start to clamber over the steel beams like a spider. Suddenly my right hand slips off the wet metal, and my boot steps into thin air, leaving me dangling by my left hand. It feels like my arm is being wrenched from its socket. I shout into the darkness as the stitches in my side split and the wound opens.

A bullet hits the metal above my head and showers me with sparks. I don't hear the shot, but I feel a burning sensation on my scalp. Warm blood begins to pool above the sweatband inside my hat, and mixes with the cold rain dripping onto my face. A steel splinter must have gone through the fabric.

With a stinging pain in my side, I swing my body and manage to get hold of the metal frame with my right hand, then find a foothold for my boot. I make my way crab-like around the corner of the tower, and start climbing up the outside. I'm gasping with exertion, and my sopping wet clothes hardly make it easier. Vertigo rips through my stomach.

Through the girders I see a network of platforms and ladders on the inside of the steel construction. I slowly climb closer until I can throw myself forward onto a platform.

I climb ladder after ladder, aiming for the illuminated NK clock at the top of the tower, my wet hands gleaming alternately red and green as it turns. All around me, church towers boom ominously, striking midnight over the waterlogged city. Twelve hours to go until Doughboy. Nearly there, if I can just come through this still alive. A coughing fit forces me down on my knees.

I spit out a lump of phlegm, compose myself and look down. My head starts spinning at once. The black-dressed heavyweight is crawling up after me through the framework of the tower, and soon he reaches the ledge below mine. He's gained on me, but is moving more slowly now. I take aim at his back with my pistol, then I change my mind. The angle is awkward, a mass of steel girders makes the shot difficult, and I am trembling with adrenaline, excessive sobriety and cold. One bullet left.

I shove the Husqvarna back into my pocket and keep going, breathing heavily. The sound of steps behind me spurs me on to keep climbing until I reach the eighth and final ledge. From here, there's a ladder leading up to the system of narrow walkways that forms the roof, on which the massive clock sits slowly spinning.

The shifting colours of the neon light glide slowly across the steel girders. I glance over my shoulder and then climb the ladder.

I step onto a walkway around the square top of the tower. I run anticlockwise to the north-eastern of the four turrets, cylindrical cages clinging on to the massive construction like babies to a sturdy farmer's wife. The clock, as tall and wide as four men, slowly turns sweeping its green beam of light towards me, but it can't reach me as I hurry on to the next turret, and then the next. There's nowhere to take cover up here. I reach the north-western corner just as I hear the sound of approaching steps.

One damned bullet. Shivering, I stop by the steel balustrade. Maybe I could climb over and get down on the outside of the girders? I put my pistol in my pocket and grip the railing with both hands. The wind is so strong that it sends my soaking wet coat flapping behind me like a cloak.

There's a sucking feeling in my belly. The grey city below is swimming in black water.

The palace hardly looks much bigger than a sandbox. The intersecting streets of Vasagatan and Kungsgatan look like communicating trenches on a battlefield; you can still see one or two undaunted soldiers on night patrol. The night-time trams, like glow-worms, slowly make their way through the storm. A flash of lightning illuminates Kungsholmen, turns dark windowless gables white and lights up the golden top of City Hall, with its three crowns. My head is reeling from the height, my stomach turning, I can't move from here.

I take the Husqvarna out of my pocket. I move forward a couple of metres, then lie flat on my stomach. Through a fine mesh of metal I see my pursuer place his foot on the first rung of the last ladder. The neon light colours his face blood-red. He struggles up with his pistol in his hand.

'Come on then, you bastard. Come to Kvisten.'

I take aim at the top of the ladder some ten metres away. As he climbs through, the side of the clock is towards him so that he ends up in shadow while I'm bathed in green light. I blink blood and sweat out of my eyes. The man in black looks around for me and finds me at once, where I'm lying in wait for him. He raises his pistol and fires two shots in quick succession. Blue smoke whirls up in the wind. The quiet, dry thuds sound like when Lundin knocks together a couple of sections of a coffin with his swaddled wooden club, back home in the workshop. One of the bullets whizzes off in the night; the other hits the steel in front of me and ricochets away, throwing up sparks. I feel the vibrations through the metal and open my eyes. Infinitely slowly, sweeping like the unhurried movement of a scythe, the red beam lights the man up from behind. He drops to his knees, grasping his pistol in both hands and taking aim. I think I have him in my sights now. The recoil rips through my painful shoulder when I fire my last bullet.

They haven't got me beat yet.

The man's face grimaces in the red light and the pistol drops out of his hand. It bounces and disappears. He falls backwards onto the walkway, his legs moving as if he's trying to get some purchase against the steel.

I stand up. My body is shaking with cold and adrenaline.

Holding my hat on my head, hunched over in the wind, I creep along the walkway towards the man from Gotland. He's breathing in fits and starts. He looks me straight in the eyes, his hand clamped against a point between his right shoulder and pectoral.

'Where are the other two, you bastard?'

He clamps his jaws together, hard. I lean over him, grab his collar and pull him up close to my face.

'What are their names?'

He closes his eyes, coughing blood, and tries to smile.

'Answer me, you swine!'

I pull him along by the collar, and haul his upper body into the opening above the ladder like a sack of potatoes. He groans loudly. I'm panting from the effort.

Grabbing his legs, I send him down towards the ledge, three or four metres below. The steel vibrates as he slides down the rungs of the ladder like bale of hay on a ramp. With a dull thud he hits the platform below head first, then lies there, writhing among some old porcelain fuses that have been left there. I climb down after him.

Dirt has mingled with his blood, covering his whole face in a brownish-black, coarse-grained muck. His nose is flattened, and in the green light sweeping over the platform, I see a couple of his teeth glinting. I take him by his collar again and drag him to the next ladder.

'Where are the others?'

His body catches on something, maybe the rusty head of a rivet or similar, and I have to tug at him to get him free of it. I push his body halfway into the opening over the next ladder.

'Another seven floors to go but I could do this all night.'

I give his arse a shove and he falls headlong down the ladder. He hits the ledge below with his shoulder first, but then he bounces, slips under the side railing and plummets soundlessly to his death.

'God damn it, Kvisten.'

I sit down in the opening, my feet on one of the ladder rungs, peering down into the darkness until vertigo squeezes my innards.

I get out a snuff handkerchief from my pocket and wipe my face. Then I fold it into a small square, take off my hat and press it against my scalp. There's a small hole with blackened edges, just above the grey silk band, but the wound can hardly be very deep. I lean my head back and hold the handkerchief in place against it by pressing down my hat.

I want to check the corpse for identity papers and ammunition, so I climb back down the ladders, feeling increasingly relieved the closer I get to the ground. The thunderstorm is slackening off now, and the rain too. Every movement I make causes me pain.

On trembling legs I reach the final platform, the Husqvarna jolting my hipbone every time I take a step. I peer down and can just about make out the black body lying on its side on the roof below. As I hurry down the last ladder, a pistol is stuck through the rungs in front of my face before I reach the bottom. The small, bird-like man comes out of the shadows: 'Did you forget about us?'

Us? I hear a scuffing sound behind me. My head collapses; the whole world shrinks into a red-glowing drop of molten glass. The pain shoots from the back of my head down my spine, and a feeling of weightlessness comes over me.

The last thing I see before the darkness sweeps over me is Doughboy standing on his own in his shirtsleeves outside the gates of Långholmen. He scratches his flea-bitten neck and wonders where I've gone.

279

WEDNESDAY 27 NOVEMBER

'What's the time?'

My voice echoes in my head. I have a nagging feeling I'm repeating myself. This probably isn't the first time I've regained consciousness.

'The time is good morning.'

The sharp voice is followed by a swift left and a right to my body. I wince with pain, the wound in my side thumps like a steam hammer, and at least two of my ribs have gone to hell. There's a rattling sound; my whole body sways like a punchbag. I wiggle my toes to try to get a foothold. The metal of the manacles cuts into my wrists. I am hanging naked by a chain suspended from the ceiling. It's cold, but I'm covered in sweat.

Finding the floor with the tips of my toes, I breathe again. Slowly I open my eyes and look around the blurry room.

Gradually my vision recovers some of its sharpness. I am in some kind of dusty warehouse or barn. The only furniture consists of a dining table with four chairs. In a corner lie an old broom and a couple of vegetable crates. The hemp sacks nailed over the windows filter the daylight of all its gold, leaving only the dust. It's morning.

The skinny little weasel with the hooked nose sits at the table. In front of him he has a cup of coffee and a couple of shot glasses. His poplin coat hangs over the back of a chair.

'He can't take much more. He's finished. Time for the ending. Or should we call it "the final reckoning"?' The little man has a strong Söder dialect. He laughs drily.

'Like hell he is. I know what he's about. Pour me another shot of vodka.'

The sharp voice rings out behind me. There's a soft thudding as he goes for my kidneys, like when you pound beef between two flat stones. I roar with pain and the chain rattles.

The bloke behind me grabs my hips and spins me half a turn anticlockwise. He follows through with a straight right, directly into my knife wound. I pull up my knees towards my belly but straighten them again when I feel the agony in my wrists.

The big bloke, the one who looks like a bull, grins in my face. Somewhere nearby a boat sounds its steam whistle. I'm not far from the water.

'The asylum worker Wallin helped you get into Konradsberg. Andersson called and said he was followed from there by man and a woman... in a damned hearse, of all vehicles. Which is registered to Lundin's, a funeral parlour. Ten minutes later he let us know he was going to sort out the problem on his own, and told us where he was leaving the car. We only have two questions: what happened to Andersson and who is the woman?'

'I don't know what you're talking about.'

'Damned stubborn, aren't you? Four times you've woken up and four times you've denied all knowledge.'

He whacks me hard on the head a couple of times. It feels as if the thunderstorm from earlier is erupting again inside my skull.

'Leave his bloody head alone. He'll only pass out again.'

'I know what I'm doing! Well? Who is the woman? Don't you think we saw you last night? If we weren't shepherding the old man, we would have nabbed you right off.'

'There's no woman.'

'Oh sure. Actually that would make sense, what with you being a fucking homophile, Kvist. Worse than the old man, even.'

Again he raps me on the head with his knuckles. Harder, this time. Without any prior warning I throw up. There's a splashing sound when some of the brownish-yellow gastric juices hit the bloke on his arm, and over his leg. For a moment the big brute stands there, his mouth agape, his teeth full of black fillings.

'Crafty fucker!'

Little droplets of saliva hit my face when the bloke screams with anger. I retch and spit in his face. The punch comes in from the left, I can't guard myself. Again my head collapses and at last I can get some sleep.

'Did she see him?'

The voice sounds tinny, like he's talking to me through a long pipe. I'm gasping with pain. I think about Ida and my letter. I think about Doughboy. I think about Elin and her Ellinor. But mostly I think about Ida. I force myself to open my eyes.

'Answer me! Did she see who he was?'

'I don't know… don't know…'

The bull-necked man sticks his thumb in the wound in my side and wiggles it about. He might as well have stuck a white-hot iron bar into me. I scream, my jaws clamped together. Tears run down my cheeks. My legs are kicking, as if I'm treading water.

'Don't you think we'll find her anyway?'

Sweat covers my body like a sticky shell, making every cut sting. All my muscles vibrate. I am fighting to climb out of the deep well I'm trapped in.

'What… what's the time?'

'At that fucking deaf school she introduced herself as Elin. Is that her real name?'

'A tart. I hired a cunt for five kronor.'

I'm slurring my words.

'Damned nonsense!'

In the corner of my eye, I see the slap coming but I can't do anything to avoid it. I try to brace against it with my neck muscles, but I don't have the power. My head is snapped to one side, then the other. My field of vision shrinks. It feels as if my hands are about to be torn off whenever the chain sways.

'He's had enough.'

'Like hell he has!'

'We'll find her soon enough. Take him down and bring the car, I'll sort it out in the usual way.'

A short silence: a chair scrapes the floor. Someone sighs deeply. The chain rattles, my wrists burn, and then I collapse onto the floor like a rag doll. The acrid smell of sweat and spew enters my nose. I lie curled up, shaking like the dog I saw yesterday in the rain. The floorboards flex slightly as someone walks over them. The dust on the floor rises and sinks as if the wood was breathing.

A door slams.

'You should have a last drink, shouldn't you?'

I look up and try to focus. I see the dim outline of the table legs and the chairs. With a moan, I sit up on my arse.

'Come on! Crawl if you must.'

Although I still have both hands manacled in front of my body, I press them against the floor, push and get onto my feet. I'm swaying. My stomach wants to chuck up, but I fight the urge.

The table where the small man is sitting is only two metres away, but I still manage to head off in the wrong direction a couple of times before I get there at last. I grip the side of the table and stand there, swaying.

The bloke is wearing a double-breasted pinstripe suit that fits snugly around his slender body. He pushes out the chair in front of him with his foot. I sit down with a sigh.

'Kvist, you look like a crock of shit. Luckily I'm used to handling shit.'

I meet his eyes, as dark as a dog's, with long eyelashes. On one cheek sits a large birthmark, like a rust-coloured bluebottle. A smile hovers at the corners of his mouth.

'Well, you shouldn't take it personally, Kvist. It's a question of national security. Not much to argue about there.' He shakes his head. 'You'll have to excuse us.'

I make a wheezing sound, then clear my throat: 'So the tittle-tattle is true, then?'

'And the old man's in good vigour. We do our best.'

'And when he gets tired of someone, or ends up in trouble, he orders you to take care of the problem?'

The Little Shit makes a croaking sound:

'Oh, Mr G has no idea. Just like he doesn't ask himself who puts out his slippers in the morning, or why there's always food on the table, or who cleans his damned toilet. Some of these deaf-mute lads just disappear. The arrangement has by and large worked excellently until that cunt in the laundry started sending letters.'

'Beda.'

'What's that?'

'Her name was Beda.'

There's a soft sound of pouring liquid as the man beside me fills two three-sided fluted glasses. Carefully he pushes one of them over to me. A spilled drop runs into the scratches in the tabletop.

'Condemned men have always had the right to a last drink in this country.'

He doesn't look me in the eye but he does smile. He raises his glass. With my fettered hand I do the same. I shiver and clear my throat: 'Ever hear the story of the bloke who drank half his last drink and promised to come back to finish it?'

'Except he didn't, did he?'

'I guess not. What's the time?'

We look into each other's eyes. I cough and, at the same time, break off the thin flute of the glass in my hand. There's a snapping sound but the man in front of me seems not to hear. The sharp tip of the flute cuts into my palm, which burns when the schnapps runs down my hand.

'Stop talking about the fucking time, will you? For King and country?'

The man on the other side of the table winks at me. He smiles and moves the glass to his lips.

'And for Petrus and Beda!'

The foot of the glass clunks as I let it fall to the tabletop. I let the three-sided bowl drop slightly in my hand, exposing the broken stem. Quickly I lean across the table and stab it into his eye.

His eyeball gives way to the shard of glass like a boiled egg. The stem sinks halfway into the socket. A viscous liquid gushes out around the glass and over my hand. He falls backwards in his chair, with a cry like a seagull's squawk, and crashes to the ground. A plume of blood seems to hang suspended in the air, before the drops cascade down to the floor as if competing to see which of them can get there first.

His roar bounces between the walls as he thrashes about on the floor, his hands clamped to his face as a clear liquid pours out between his fingers. I crawl over the table with my arse up in the air, throw myself down on top of him, sit astride his chest and

285

press down with all my weight on the glass. Red gunge spatters all around us as I push the stem in as far as it'll go.

There's a popping sound inside his skull.

He sighs, and I do the same. Basically, what I'm doing here is waste management, nothing more than that. He wriggles under me; I keep both hands on the glass and pin his arms with my knees. He stops moving before too long. I slide off, slump onto my side and groan with pain. Wrong bloody side.

I lie naked on my back next to him, my face beside his. For an instant he seems to raise his forearms; they hover just above the floor before falling back.

My lungs rattle like a leaky pair of bellows. I get up, grimace and bury my face in my hands, trying to get my thoughts together. It's like my brain's stuffed with wood shavings. I almost keel over, but I manage to grip hold of the table to steady myself.

The bloke on the floor trembles all of a sudden. I take the bottle of vodka off the table and knock back a mouthful before stepping over him. I put a foot on each side of his face.

I lean over him and empty the bottle over him. The vodka pours over his face; he recoils like a snake, makes a couple of stifled moans and then lies absolutely still.

I slowly rattle my thoughts into place by gently shaking my head. I look around the room. I don't know how much time I have before that damned heavyweight comes back.

I bend over the corpse and dig out his pocket watch from his waistcoat. The lid snaps open with a crisp sound: the long hand is on two.

Ten past eleven. My dream of the cigar shop has gone to hell but my hopes of Doughboy are still alive: fifty minutes to go.

That's plenty of time for Kvisten.

'Never even taken a count.'

I find the keys to the manacles and manage to get them off. I search the bloke on the floor for his service weapon but don't find one. God only knows how he was planning to deal with me.

I look around. I catch sight of the broom in the corner and move towards it, but soon drop to the floor, with all the pain I'm in, and I have to crawl the last few metres.

A spider has woven its web between the broomstick and the plank wall. I lean the broom against the wall and stamp through the wood, snapping it in the middle. The vibrations shoot through my chest. I wince with pain.

I pick up the metre-long upper part of the broomstick and pick it clean of splinters. I'm left with a sort of short spear, like a matador's banderilla – no colourful strips of fabric on it perhaps, but perfectly serviceable for a bull's neck. I try the tip against my thumb.

Just then I hear a car reversing up outside. I stagger over to the closed door and place myself behind it.

The corner I'm standing in stinks of cat's piss. I raise the broomstick over my head and wait. The effort of holding my arms in the air makes them tremble.

I hear steps coming towards the door, then the handle is pressed down. A streak of daylight falls over the floor, and the door almost hits me in the face as it opens. The big bloke takes a single step into the room.

The sight of his downy hairs sticking out from under his collar makes my dry mouth fill with saliva.

'What the fuck?'

Two steps.

Three.

I rush him from behind and stab down. He lets out a long scream as the spike goes into his right shoulder. I press it as far into his body as I can, then let go. For a few seconds he spins around in a macabre dance, trying to get hold of the broomstick. His fat round face turns red. He looks at me and opens his mouth but can't get any words out. He fumbles to get at his shoulder holster.

I shove him hard in the chest, throwing him back against the wooden wall, and pressing the broomstick home even further, making him scream again, his spittle flying over my head. I grab his chin with my left hand, push his head back, then release a straight right-handed punch at his throat. His Adam's apple crunches under my fist, and gives way like a rotten fruit.

The man falls on his side, with one hand around his throat. He's making gurgling sounds, and his face turns even redder. Naked as I am, I lean over him and check his pockets while he's kicking his legs and hissing. His lips have turned purple; the nails of his other hand scrabble frantically against the floorboards. I remove his service weapon from its holster. For a few seconds I consider whether to put him out of his misery. The pistol clatters against the floor when I throw it out of reach instead.

I find my ragged clothes in one of the fruit boxes. As I'm getting dressed, still shivering, the body on the floor stops thrashing.

The bullfight is over. I take a look at the watch. I have forty-three minutes to get to Långholmen and meet Doughboy. I grimace as I stretch my arms to put on my shoulder holster.

I pick up my hat from the floor: 'Kvisten doesn't doff his cap to anyone. Especially not with this damned hairstyle.'

I tear down one of the jute sacks and blink as the daylight comes flooding in. Using the sack as a rag, I start wiping down all the things I may have touched. The blood around the smaller man's eye socket has already started congealing. I try to get a grip on the edges of the glass, but I only manage to pull out a couple of curved shards. I roll him onto his stomach and turn his jacket collar inside out to check his size. The suit is by Bracco, an Italian brand, and it has fashionable broad lapels. The thick wool material feels expensive. With a few adjustments by my tailor, Herzog, it should fit.

I think about it for a moment, asking myself if I have time for this, and then I strip the smaller man of both jacket and trousers. His pale legs are covered in black hairs. On his knee are signs of scar tissue from an operation. I tuck the garments under one arm.

When I get to the door, I look around one last time. I dig out a Meteor from my coat pocket. My ribs crackle as much as the cigar when I puff at it. I step out into the daylight and check my pocket watch.

Thirty-six minutes.

There's a light rain falling from a thick grey sky. I look around the gravelled courtyard, surrounded by a number of single-storey buildings and warehouses with roofs of cracked tiles or corrugated iron. Right ahead of me, there seems to be an abandoned blacksmith's shed, with the stalls empty.

Behind the buildings I see the towering chimney of the München Brewery, and I can smell the malt and the fumes from Wicander's cork factory.

The Rolls is parked with its back end towards the door.

I'm not far from the slums around Tavastgatan, where I moved with Emma soon after Ida was born. I had slaved to get the deposit together, working eighteen-hour days, seven days a week, for fifty öre an hour, even though the Dockworkers' Union had stipulated a minimum of one krona. I'm not proud of that, but necessity knows no law, and I had more or less promised Emma a fairy-tale castle. She had to spend the first evening sweeping out the cockroaches that covered the floor. Not that she held it against me; she wasn't the type for that.

I blink into the hazy daylight and have another puff. The cough that follows almost brings me to my knees; my chest is rattling like a desert snake. If I walk across Skinnarviksberget, I should be able to make it to Långholmen within half an hour without running into too many people.

It's very quiet. I hang Doughboy's schnapps-smelling suit over my shoulder and totter out of the courtyard along a winding gravel track filled with puddles from the night's bad weather. The rain has gouged deep trenches in the gravel, and here and there the base rock emerges. On either side, the narrow lane is flanked by run-down wooden shacks painted yellow and red, but I see no signs of any people. Every step, every breath, hurts me and a thin trickle of blood runs down the side of my face from that damned cut on my head. I wipe it with my handkerchief.

The sweat is pouring off my body, smarting in the wound on my side. On the next right-hand bend, I stop and rest for a while with my hand on an old grey plank. I breathe as shallowly as I can, then clench my jaw and press on to the next hill. A few times I groan with pain as my foot slips in the gravel.

I met Emma on the other side of a rock I can see just ahead of me now, at a dance held on Walpurgis Night by the Social Democratic Youth Association. I think it was in 1920. I was a bit worse for wear, but sober enough to take her for a couple of proper turns on the dance floor.

She was wearing a long dove-grey dress, with a floral-pattern scarf over her shoulders. She screamed with pleasure when I picked her up and spun her round. Her dress billowed from her waist while the tones of the accordions spun their webs around us.

I had been on more than friendly terms with other lads long before that, and by and large I had never taken much interest in women. But something about Emma was different. I suppose it was a kind of love. She became pregnant, and we had to hurry up about getting married.

Once we'd got ourselves set up in the draughty one-room flat, and I was being referred to as the country's best middleweight talent, I used to run up this hellish hill every day, training for the big fight that would be my last on Swedish soil before I turned professional. Emma and Ida had set sail for America a couple of months earlier, and I was left behind on my own. Too lonely for my own good.

Before that, I had always viewed the ropes of the ring as a clear demarcation between two worlds. Inside the ring it didn't matter who you were, if you were rich or poor, white or black; it was just two blokes in there competing on equal terms. I was counting on those damned ropes keeping out my other life, but instead they gave way. I lost my family, my good name and my career. All the people I had trusted turned their backs on me.

I clench my jaw and turn left around the next bend. The tears are falling down my cheeks, making their way through my three-day stubble. Every joint in my body is shaking.

Doughboy's Italian suit weighs me down like a fifty-kilo yoke on my shoulder. I step in a puddle and press on up the hill.

Ever since that time I have wandered alone, branded, and I've never thought there could be anyone out there for a bad apple like me. I reach the pinnacle of the grey granite rock. I stand there swaying slightly in the wind. The water extends in all directions below. Two white steamboats seem to be racing each other towards the quays of Kungsholmen. Overhead, a couple of seagulls whirl about, screeching. I let my gaze stray to the left over the Mälaren shipyard and the Väster Bridge. There she lies. The green isle.

Långholmen.

WEDNESDAY 27 NOVEMBER

The bell above the door of the confectioner's on Bergsundsgatan jingles like a cowbell as I walk in. The sales assistant is a young woman, lost in the dream of some weekly ladies' magazine and hardly even visible behind a counter piled high with jars of colourful pastilles, burnt almonds, sugar goodies and candied apples. There's a pleasant smell of cinnamon and Seville oranges.

I clear my throat: 'Telephone?'

'Twenty-five öre.'

She points at the wall-mounted telephone in the corner and holds out her hand, but scarcely looks in my direction. Maybe the close proximity of the shop to the prison has hardened her to the presence of brutes like me.

I notice she's wearing an engagement ring as I put the coin in her hand, then I go over to the telephone. I lift the receiver and ask for Standards. Elin answers at the other end. She's quiet for a second, then speaks: 'Thank God, it's you, Harry. How are you?'

'Bearing up.'

'I'm afraid.'

'Not bloody surprised.'

'My nerves are in a state. Didn't get a wink all night.'

'I caught the odd nap now and then.'

'Are we in danger?'

'Don't think so, but I'm not sure.'

'What should we do?'

293

'Nothing. But if you run into me in our neighbourhood, act like I'm invisible.'

'Is that really necessary?'

'I don't know.'

We stay silent for a moment. My mind is still is in a daze from all the violence. I get out my pocket watch.

'Elin?'

'Yeah?'

'I read that in America they're not wearing waistcoats any more.'

'I doubt that.'

'It's not fashionable any more.'

'If that's right, it's more than I know anyway.'

'Okay.'

Again there's a silence. From the crossed lines comes the echo of many voices, almost like ghosts speaking, and then, loud and clear: 'Take care of yourself, Harry.'

I nod to myself: 'Tonight you can sleep well.'

I break off the call, make a farewell gesture at the shop assistant and step back out into the street. A hundred metres away, I can see the dirty yellow walls through the bare trees. The screws patrolling the walls aren't visible from here.

At the Bridge of Sighs I hang Doughboy's new Italian suit over the red railings and go down to the reed-covered water's edge at Pålsundet. The willow trees bend over the little canal. Bream used to spawn here not long ago, before the motorboats took over the waters.

I wash my hands in the ice-cold water; then wet my dirty handkerchief, rub it against my face and wipe the sweatband inside my hat.

Judging by the water's surface it's raining a little heavier now, but the weather will hardly make much difference tonight, when Doughboy and I lie tucked up in my big bed at home on Roslagsgatan. I pick up the suit from the railing and wipe the collar with the handkerchief. Again I check the manufacturer's label, smiling to myself. It should be good enough and more. I hurry across the arched bridge.

I hobble up to the door of the prison reception with a few minutes to spare. After tucking my watch into my waistcoat pocket, I light another cigar from the embers of the old one. I flex my feet. It feels easier to breathe now. Maybe the broken bones have settled into place in my chest; or it's just that the excitement of my expectation is stronger than the pain. I managed to get revenge for Beda and Petrus, as well as making it back here in time with the suit and all. My bottom lip trembles. I'm good at waiting, but a week never felt so long to me.

I take out my pocket watch again. It's stopped, maybe some damp got inside the mechanism. Just as I'm checking it the clock strikes midday in the prison courtyard. The last strike ebbs away, and is followed by a silence. From the shipyard on the other side of the island comes the sound of the odd hammer-stroke. From the bridge, a distant drone of traffic. I stare fixedly at the door of the guard room.

I step over a puddle and bang on the wooden door.

Steps come closer. I close my coat collar and straighten my shoulders. An observation hatch is opened, and I stare into a large beard and a pair of evil eyes, belonging to Jönsson, the same screw who let me out seven days ago.

'Kvist? What a bloody mess you look!'

'I'm here to meet Doughboy. Gusten Lindwall.'

'Lindwall, you say? One moment.'

The hatch closes firmly. I cough and grimace, running my hand over my stubble and looking around. A little further off, a small girl comes walking down the road. She's wearing a corn-flower blue dress and has tied a white pinafore apron around her waist. Her coat with its rounded collar is unbuttoned all the way down. As she gets closer I realise she's the same girl I met here a week ago when I was released. Maybe her parents work at the prison.

With a scraping sound, Jönsson's face reappears in the open-ing. He grins broadly at me, the gaps between his teeth blackened with snuff.

'Kvist is running a bit late. Lindwall was released five days ago. Last Friday, in fact.'

My heart staggers to the corner of the ring, and slumps onto the waiting stool. All the pain shooting round my body hits me at once. My brain spins in circles like a raffle wheel, the rigged type, which never lets you win.

'That's not right. The given day was Wednesday.'

'What's that? Speak up!'

'It was supposed to be Wednesday.'

'Don't you think we know where our prisoners are? Lindwall was released last Friday. Go to hell, will you.'

The hatch bangs shut once again. I flinch at the sound, stagger and lose my balance. I sit down on my arse in the puddle behind me. I drop Doughboy's suit. My cigar is extinguished with a hiss in the dirty water.

The water splashes over my hands and quickly seeps through my layers of clothes. I shiver, and bend double: 'Lies… all lies…'

An overwhelming tiredness streams through all the aching limbs of my body. I try to lift my arms but they stay limply in my lap. The rain makes little dimples in the water between my parted legs.

'You're sitting in a puddle.'

I look at the boots and woollen socks of the lass, standing half a metre away at my side. She's carrying the same one-eyed rag doll as last time. I frown with the effort and raise my eyes. She's bareheaded. The gentle rain is clinging to her brown locks.

'Must have got the day mixed up. I was planning on a Saturday bath.'

The girl laughs. With a shaking hand, I take a cigar from the cigar case in my inside pocket and put it in my mouth. A wave of pain runs through me when I turn and spit out the end.

'When you're finished with that puddle, you can feel my tooth.'

The girl sticks out her chin and shows me her lower jaw. One of her front teeth is wonky.

'I can do that. Do you know how to count to ten yet?'

'Course I know. Want to hear?'

'Take it slow.'

While the girl starts counting, I strike a match and puff some life into the cigar. The rainwater runs all over me when I haul myself onto all fours. My head's spinning. I groan with pain.

When she gets to five, I get up on one knee. A wave of nausea passes through my body; everything is spinning. I blink and breathe in.

I gather strength and put my hand on the girl's shoulder. Her little hands grab my arm and try to help.

Six.

Seven.

Eight.

I get up on the ninth count. The ground is swaying, like when your feet first feel solid land after months at sea. My legs are trembling and I almost lose my balance, but I stay on my feet. I look down at the girl, who keeps counting. Her hair is unbelievably soft under my scarred hand.

'Fifteen, sixteen…'

I gaze up for a while at the iron-grey sky and let the raindrops fall over my face. Then I pat the lass on her head. She's reached twenty-fourteen now.

'Harry Kvist in a magnificent comeback,' I mumble, taking a pull on the cigar that makes my ribs shake.

'What did you say, uncle?'

'That things don't always work out the way you planned them.'

'If it was Saturday we could have some fudge.'

I make a croaking sound, put my hand on my chest and grimace.

I get out my wallet, pull off the elasticated strap and find a twenty-five-öre coin: 'Do you know another name for Wednesday?'

The girl's eyes are glittering. She stands on her tiptoes to get closer to my ear, and with great effort I bend down. She cups her hand around her mouth and whispers: 'The maid's Saturday.'

I straighten my back, put my left hand in my trouser pocket and smile at her.

'And you must be your mother's best maid, I suppose?'

The lass nods eagerly. I point with my cigar towards the bridge: 'I think there's a sweet shop there, just up Bergsundsgatan.'

'Mother says I'm not to leave the island.'

'I know exactly how that feels.'

'But maybe if you go there with me, and then I come straight back?'

'I don't see why not.'

I give her the twenty-five-öre coin and she curtsies neatly. I put my hand on her shoulder again. The gravel crunches under our feet as we start walking.

Leaning on the little one I leave Långholmen behind.

———

NEXT IN THE
STOCKHOLM
TRILOGY

SLUGGER

PUSHKIN VERTIGO

AVAILABLE AND COMING SOON
FROM PUSHKIN VERTIGO

Jonathan Ames
You Were Never Really Here

Augusto De Angelis
The Murdered Banker
The Mystery of the Three Orchids
The Hotel of the Three Roses

María Angélica Bosco
Death Going Down

Piero Chiara
The Disappearance of Signora Giulia

Frédéric Dard
Bird in a Cage
The Wicked Go to Hell
Crush
The Executioner Weeps
The King of Fools
The Gravediggers' Bread

Friedrich Dürrenmatt
The Pledge
The Execution of Justice
Suspicion
The Judge and His Hangman

Martin Holmén
Clinch
Down for the Count

Alexander Lernet-Holenia
I Was Jack Mortimer

Boileau-Narcejac
Vertigo
She Who Was No More

Leo Perutz
Master of the Day of Judgment
Little Apple
St Peter's Snow

Soji Shimada
The Tokyo Zodiac Murders
Murder in the Crooked Mansion

Masako Togawa
The Master Key
The Lady Killer

Emma Viskic
Resurrection Bay

Seishi Yokomizo
The Inugami Clan